JOHN MANUEL

A BRIEF MOMENT OF SUNSHINE

First published in English worldwide by
Lulu Press, www.lulu.com

Typeset in 12pt Garamond by the author.

All characters in this book are fictitious and any resemblance to real persons, living or dead, is purely coincidental.

Front & back cover design by the author.

Photography front cover: ***Gallery Photography***, Rhodes, Greece.
http://www.gallery-photography.net/
E-Mail: info@gallery-photography.net
Tel: +30-22410-36275

Photography back cover courtesy of Allison Wiffen, ***http://www.awceramics.co.uk***

ISBN 978-1-291-71859-1

Also by John Manuel

The "Ramblings from Rhodes" series
of Grecian travel memoirs:

Feta Compli!

Moussaka To My Ears

Tzatziki For You To Say

A Plethora Of Posts

A Novel:

The View From Kleoboulos

All of the above available from Amazon worldwide
in paperback or Kindle format
and from the publisher, www.lulu.com

More information about the above titles can be found on
John Manuel's blog:
http://ramblingsfromrhodes.blogspot.com
and from his website:
http://johnphilipmanuel.wix.com/works

I have seen something else under the sun:
The race is not to the swift,
or the battle to the strong,
nor does food come to the wise
or wealth to the brilliant
or favor to the learned;
but time and chance happen to them all.

- Ecclesiastes 9:11

A BRIEF MOMENT
OF SUNSHINE

1. A Bridge Too Far

June 15th 1990 was a cool night in Bristol. It had promised to be a fairly acceptable summer by British standards as May had been exceptionally warm and dry. Everyone in the UK was talking up a heatwave and shoppers in the supermarkets plus people supping pints in pub gardens were all sporting strappy tops and cut-offs. Every year is like that in the UK. Those who live here will it to be a long hot summer and look for any encouraging sign. Are the crow's nests higher in the stands of trees where they sway? Have the swallows arrived early? Did some crackpot from Norfolk get on the BBC saying how his pet hamster always did thus and so if the weather was going to be good? The fact is, no one really knows. The capriciousness of the British climate may be very frustrating to many, but it's also responsible for one of the most beautiful landscapes on the planet. It has created lush green rolling hills with woodland hollows that turn fiery red and orange in Autumn. Breathtaking sweeping downs and mountains where hares box in spring time and lapwings swoop over ploughed fields in the Autumn months. The UK has an embarrassment of riches, all to be enjoyed ...weather permitting.

June 15th was a Friday and the day had been overcast and drizzly.

Not much fun for the campers, or people hiking along Offa's Dyke, but no problem for innumerable ducks on rural ponds all across the isles. It hadn't been the kind of day to linger out of doors, as it had been rather cool for June. As darkness fell across the city of Bristol, the Avon Gorge faded from view and was replaced by patterns of amber streetlights through the deep, damp, black murk.

At something approaching midnight, a man waits near the eastern Pier of the famous Isambard Kingdom Brunel engineering marvel that is the Clifton Suspension Bridge. He is staring down into the darkness at the nearly invisible muddy Avon river a frightening 245 feet below. He wears a long dark coat and has his collar turned up against the night-time chill. His attention is drawn to the lights of a small vessel, making its way far beneath him toward the Bristol Docks a little to the South. The man would be hard to describe, since the night is damp, the air slightly misty and the coat he is wearing is very dark. His hair too appears to be dark and not particularly long. His trousers, what can be seen of them, are probably black, as are his shoes. Were the Police to ask someone who'd seen this fellow if they could describe him, they'd probably be at a loss for much to say. Perhaps the orange glow of a cigarette being lifted occasionally from the fold of his coat up to his lips by a black-leather-gloved hand, then returned below once again as a curl of smoke escaped his mouth, would enable the observer to testify that the man was a smoker. That would narrow it down to about ten million in the UK then.

A few minutes after midnight, a tall handsome man with a good head of swept-back blond hair approaches. He wears only a smart, dark suit, white shirt and silk tie. No overcoat. His top pocket sports a pocket square, also silk. It matches his tie. This man would give the voyeur a lot more to go on. Unfortunately, no one was within easy viewing distance of either man at this hour. They were quite alone in the chilly night's inky gloom. Whatever moon may have lurked above the clouds was irrelevant to the light situation. The cloud cover was far too dense for any budding astronomer to make any observations about what phase earth's satellite was currently in.

A conversation ensues, the man in the long coat asking,

"Well, have you got them?"

The other man replies, "Of course. I shall be only too pleased to see the back of this whole affair. Nothing is written down you understand. As per the instructions I received."

The other man nods and asks for 'the numbers'. The tall man in the suit recites a series of them. Several times he does this, because the other man needs to commit them to memory. They are offshore account numbers where some rather huge sums of money are sleeping. The be-suited man has been sitting on the cash for several years as a favour for someone he'd rather not be involved with. He likes to do things by the book. He's never been in any trouble. But when an old school 'friend' had approached him some time ago and made it pretty plain that he was the man for the job of minding this money for a while until some kind of 'heat' had died down, he reluctantly agreed. When a couple of minders exuding the air of "we don't mind if you'd prefer your kneecaps broken" accompany your visitor, it tends to throw a different complexion on things.

The tall, elegant man well remembers the day when the 'old school chum' had come calling. During their days at Grammar school the unexpected guest had been a short boy, always looking for a reason to pick a fight. How often short pupils display this characteristic. It seems that they're perpetually complexed about their height and so compensate by trying to prove how tough they are. Barely a week would pass without this particular classmate going home with a grass-stained blazer, a torn shirt, or scuffed shoes, after he'd scrapped like a wild thing with another poor unfortunate in his year. His was always the loudest voice in class during breaks. He was always swaggering around the quadrangle, looking for a glance that meant he could accuse some defenseless boy of looking at him the wrong way.

"You lookin' at, ay? You wanna fight then, eh? EH?" he'd say, before beginning to shove his victim hard in the chest, hoping to add another notch to his wooden slide rule, further proof of his superiority. Least, that was how he saw it. No one else did, of course.

Several decades after the man in the suit who'd arrived on the bridge at around midnight on Friday 15th June 1990 had thought he'd truly seen the back of this unpleasant boy, he goes and turns up at the front door one Saturday afternoon while the suited man's wife is out, probably doing some shopping. The 'old friend' is accompanied, as previously mentioned, by two delightful companions who could have passed for shaven gorillas trussed up in suits. He'd made it very clear as he'd strode into the house, heavy shoes leaving grass and mud on the cream Axminster pile beneath his soles, that, having heard about the kind of business his "dear old friend" was now in, and making a very good fist of it too, he'd decided to entrust him with a little windfall that had come his way. It would probably only be for a few months, plus there would be a reward in it at the end, but his old friend wouldn't mind now would he?

Now, following a telephone call a couple of days earlier, coming after several years of silence, the obnoxious and now middle aged short-house bully, decidedly suspect in all things financial, had arranged for our debonair, be-suited and entirely respectable businessman to give back the cash. He'd have to be discreet. He'd also be best advised to do as instructed, if he wanted to keep both kneecaps intact that was. So, he found himself telephoning his wife to tell her that he had a little business to conclude at a rather unusual hour and that he'd be home late. He'd omitted to tell her that it may be some time in the early hours of the next morning. Feeling anything but comfortable, yet hoping that this would put an end to the affair, he'd followed instructions and left his car some distance away, not far from home in fact, and walked the twenty minutes or so to the Suspension Bridge, where he was told he'd be met by a "representative".

Overcoat man kept one hand gripped firmly on the forearm of suit man, while he once again went over the numbers.

Having eventually satisfied himself that he could remember these numbers, the man in the coat assaults his 'companion'. He takes the other man entirely by surprise, lending him a great advantage. There is a struggle, but be-suited man isn't the fighting type. Plus he's been taken entirely off guard by this whole thing. He loses his balance and feels himself being bodily lifted. Overcoat man is an inch or two taller, and that makes him about six foot six. The man in the overcoat finally lands a blow to the other man's head, knocking him momentarily senseless, time enough for him to finish what he'd set out to do. After some moments of heaving, which bring him out in a cold sweat under the armpits, during which he's continually glanced this way and that for fear of anyone approaching, the tall man in the suit is falling 245 feet to his death on the mud banks below.

The man in the coat straightens himself, then walks calmly away, flicking into life a cigarette lighter, which he then raises to the cigarette that he's just slipped between his lips with hands still shaking from his moment of exertion.

2. Claire on an Aeroplane. June 2007

I so enjoyed the wedding. Not only did I feel it a privilege to be there, but the location was just perfect too. How could there be anywhere more beautiful than that for such an occasion? I often reflect on how different my life would have turned out had I not approached that poor nervous young slip of a girl at Kefallonia airport. When was it now? Yes, the summer of 1998, the month of June. I'd taken a last-minute package to stave off yet another of my maudlin moods. I would have been forty-seven and Alyson, ooh, I think she was barely twenty.

Here I am now, sitting on an Airbus A3-something or other, on my way back home to Bristol after probably my most enjoyable few days since young Alyson and I toured Greece together. I can't believe that it's already June of 2007, almost seventeen years to the day from my beloved Charles' death. Seventeen years. Where have they all gone? And here I am none the wiser as to what actually happened that night. Funny how everything in my life seems to happen in June. Well, to be accurate, everything since Charles died. He died in

June of 1990, I met Alyson in June of 1998 and now here I am returning home from seeing my young friend finally wed her true love Dean in June of 2007, in St. Paul's Bay Lindos.

Those three years during which Alyson and I roamed all over the land of the gods were probably my happiest ever; well, not counting my oh so brief a time with Charles, of course. That poor girl, torturing herself as she did, took my mind off of my own reasons for self pity and made me concentrate on being the shoulder that she so obviously needed for all of that time. Even when we wound up in Lindos, ooh it must have been 2001, we remained close for four or five years until her beloved Dean turned up, against all the odds, and so began the slow extraction from her life of worrisome old me. It was how it had to be, of course. She always knew that some day she'd be back with him and - despite a couple of monumental hiccups, they were wed a few days ago and I was there to see it.

If I am brutally honest, I'd have to say that Alyson Wright, now Alyson Waters, is the nearest anyone's ever come to feeling like my own child. I know I didn't raise her, but from that moment in 1998 when we encountered one another she just embedded herself further and further under my skin, in a good way. She so needed protecting. She so needed a mature shoulder. She got me of course, so she could have done better. But then, we don't deal the hands, we just play them.

Thinking back on it, I really didn't want or expect to complicate my life in the way in which it was complicated by my meeting up with Alyson but, in hindsight, I couldn't have wished for a better distraction. I still haven't the faintest idea what it's all about really, this life thing I mean. I still don't hold with all that grandiose atheism of Mr. Dawkins, who simply makes my flesh creep every time I hear him speak in that superior manner of his. Doesn't he realize that in robbing his disciples of any purpose or meaning whatsoever he impoverishes them all desperately? It doesn't work to say, "there probably isn't a god, so just get on and enjoy life." How in hell can one enjoy something that's entirely futile? If I allowed myself to go down his route I'd just be a hamster in a wheel.

Here I go again, tiring my brain out with all this stuff. Must think about something else.

Julia. Yes, Julia, dear Julia. How's that for a result then? If I hadn't run into Alyson then I wouldn't now have the best business partner one could wish for. Look at her, sitting beside me on this plane, earphones in and Radiohead or something of that ilk helping her drift through the four-hour flight, eyes closed and at peace with herself. At least, that's how she comes across to me. But then, I always assume that everyone except me is like that.

I'm probably way off the mark.

What a miracle it was, though, Dean coming back from the dead like that. That must account for a huge sum in Julia's 'credit'column, under 'peace of mind'.

Claire and Julia, Clifton, Bristol, April 2007:

"You know what?" said Julia, mug of freshly brewed filter coffee from the machine in the gallery that was used for making browsers among Claire's pictures feel at home, "We've actually made some money this past month."

Claire, having just come down the stairs to the back of the gallery from her studio up in the attic, grinned in a way that she hadn't done in a very long time. "You're kidding me Jools," she replied.

"Nope. I kid you not. It's all there in black and white. My

spreadsheets never lie."

Claire, at fifty six, still drew whistles from white van men as they drove past when she walked around Clifton. She had the look of a sixties Bohemian about her still, but it had been ever so slightly tempered in recent months by her business partner Julia's influence. Julia was hatched from a different fashion mould. A little younger than Claire, having been born in 1954, she was now fifty-three. She too, though, was still in pretty good shape and both women had lost count of the number of times they'd been chatted up in local wine bars by suited men decades younger, something which had given them endless hours of laughter.

They'd been thrown together by circumstance in the summer of the previous year. In July 2006, when Claire had been sitting at a table on the waterfront at Haraki, Rhodes, Greece, along with five other women, one of whom had been Alyson, the bride whose wedding had given occasion to this rather low-key hen night; the groom's mother had turned up rather unexpectedly and introduced herself as Mrs. Julia Waters. Claire and Julia had hit it off from the start and after Dean, the groom, had disappeared over a disastrous misunderstanding which had left him believing that his bride-to-be of the following day was his half-sister, Claire and Julia had kept in touch. Julia had left Dean's father that very week anyway and so was looking for some way to reconstruct her life. Claire was alone with her recently re-established art studio in Clifton and so very soon the idea was hatched that Julia become Claire's business partner and manage the gallery.

Julia's statement about their having gone into the black made Claire feel extremely happy that they'd struck up their deal. No longer was it a business partnership anyway, both had become very fond of the other and they were now close friends.

The Gallery telephone rang, its electronic beep of urgency making both women start momentarily. Julia picked it up from its charging cradle and tapped the little button with the green icon. She only had time to say one word…

"Hello…"

"Mum? It is you isn't it?"

Julia was taken aback. She was struck both numb and dumb. Her son had been missing since the previous July, when that terrible misunderstanding had led to him disappearing on a hot Lindian night on the island of Rhodes just hours before he and Alyson Wright were to be married. He'd now be thirty years old, but no one knew, no one had any clue as to his whereabouts. The Greek police thought that he may perhaps have killed himself by jumping from the cliff at the Tomb of Kleoboulos out on the headland near Lindos Bay. No body had ever been found and thus all concerned had to believe that Dean could still be alive. But as the months had passed Dean's loved ones had to begin to fear the worst. Julia and Claire hadn't spoken of Dean for a couple of weeks, though he was always just under the surface. He was always an unspoken agony that they both shared. Now here was this disembodied voice on the telephone, asking Julia if she were his mum.

"Dean? This can't… I mean, is it…" she found all further words stuck in her throat and she welled up, tears flooding her eyes instantly. The voice continued,

"Mum, it is me. It's Dean. I'm still on Rhodes, in Lindos. Alyson is sitting next to me. I've come back mum, I've come back."

What a story to have been a part of. I can't begin to imagine what she went through during all those months when Dean was missing, feared dead. Now here we are flying home after the loveliest wedding

I've ever attended. That includes my own to Charles I have to admit. Not that ours wasn't a marvellous day, but the setting for Dean and Alyson was St. Paul's Bay, Lindos, Greece. How fabulous the photographs are going to look. The photographers, Chris and Karen I think their names were, pulled a stroke of genius by having the happy couple paddling in their wedding gear, with Dean splashing Alyson from the sea's surface with his hands and she screaming with delight as he scooped her into his arms and held her as if she were a mermaid he'd just caught out in the bay.

And the light; so crisp, vibrant, luminous. The blue of the sky is something we just never see in the UK.

Alyson. Of course, she already has a mother. I'm not stupid enough to believe I could ever muscle in on Christine's place in Alyson's life. But if there were ever a child needing an extra mum for a while, it would have been Alyson in 1998.

Something I never told Alyson, not during all that time we spent together, was that back in 1985 (was it really that long ago?) Charles and I almost became parents. For the merest fleeting moment, there was a little sunshine in our lives.

3. Marianna

June 1985.

Charles and Claire have been married for almost four years. Since they were both in their fourth decade at the time of their marriage - granted Claire by only a gnat's whisker as she was thirty, while Charles was thirty-two - they'd decided to start a family right away.

Decisions are one thing; seeing them come to fruition quite another. They live in a fashionable Victorian property in Pembroke Road, Clifton and to the casual observer are sublimely happy. Claire in particular would like to conceive. To have the raising of another human being as a project for the better part of two decades would give her life some badly needed purpose and keep her mind off those deepest, darkest corners of her enquiring brain. Her husband Charles is all she'd dreamed he would be. She had married him whilst fully expecting that he'd be a different person after a few years of marriage. Thus far, she is happy to have been proven quite wrong.

Charles actively encourages her to paint, even decorating and kitting out her studio on the first floor in what would have been described as bedroom number three by an estate agent. The light from the tall Victorian windows is just perfect and she can create her works in there quite undisturbed. They'd made a pact that if she ever closed the door whilst working then Charles would leave her be. So far, with the occasional exception when he's knocked the door to tell her that a tray of tea and biscuits was outside, he'd kept to his part of the bargain. Charles is an international business property developer and has an uncanny knack for making money. Occasionally he'll go away, quite often abroad, for a few days but never longer, and always comes home with a huge kiss, an embrace and words of solace for his wife about just how much he'd missed her, not to mention an expensive gift.

All that they need to complete their lives is the patter of tiny feet. Sadly however, so far, there's been no sign of them. Both Charles and Claire have been for tests and been told that apparently there's nothing amiss. Occasionally, one consultant had told them, it just doesn't happen and so the anxiety becomes a vicious circle. Being too anxious can affect the body's systems and therefore the best they could do was to try and relax, not think too deeply about it and surely something would happen when it's good and ready.

Still no joy. The relationship between the two of them, though, could hardly be better. Claire sometimes stares at her husband whilst they're flopped out on their huge Chesterfield watching TV, she'll run her fingers through his magnificent mane of strawberry blond hair and whisper to herself that she still can't believe her luck. She'd had a quiet, modest upbringing in a rural area and still remembers the first time she took Charles home to meet her parents.

Claire's parents had a comfortable home, set back from the road, which was little more than a country lane, near the village of Alveston. Entering the driveway through a five-bar gate, you drove along fifty metres or so of gravel drive to arrive at the ample turning area in front of the bungalow, which enjoyed views of open countryside to the rear. Miniature conifers in terra cotta pots stood sentry either side of the front door. An old cast iron foot scraper, which bore evidence of recent use, revealed the residents' penchant for country walking. Caked mud decorated the top of the horizontal iron shoe-scraper and dollops of the same were scattered on the patio tiles beneath it.

It was only during the drive to the house that Claire had told Charles that her father was in the early stages of dementia. He was still relatively young to have been diagnosed as such, but nevertheless it was a confirmed case. Charles had replied that he'd wished that she'd told him before, since it only increased his anxiety about meeting Claire's parents for the first time.

Having arrived at the front of the house and Charles having also pulled a couple of compact suitcases out of the back of his Jensen FF, Claire had squeezed his hand as she'd tapped the door knocker and told him not to worry unduly. It would all be fine, he'd see. It was a Sunday morning at about 11.45am as the door had opened and Claire's mother and father had stepped outside to greet their daughter and her 'boyfriend'.

Claire's mother was of average height, slightly portly and bore a head of permed, auburn-dyed hair. She had a comely smile, which cracked lines around her eyes that revealed the fact that smiling was something she did with great regularity. Her glasses sported one of those cords around her neck which bespoke of the fact that she rarely went anywhere without them, such was her need to wear them whenever she needed to read something. She wore those kind of slacks that women in the nineteen-fifties all seemed to wear, made of some sort of synthetic brownish-taupe-coloured material that never lost its sharp crease all down the front of the leg. The apron tied about her showed that she'd just emerged from the kitchen and, since the smell of roasting chicken and potatoes wafted out around both her and her husband from further down the hallway, Charles instantly felt pangs of hunger.

Mr. Barrett, Claire's father, was five feet nine and white-haired, although still in his early sixties. His glasses were a permanent fixture across the bridge of his nose, which was what one would have described as of the 'Roman' variety. Due to the overall shape of his somewhat distinguished face the nose actually added to the impression one would have of him that he'd been quite a looker a couple of decades ago. His cardigan, with those 'old brown leather football' type buttons, revealed his conservative nature. The Sunday Telegraph was still suspended from his left hand as he extended the other to Charles in invitation to shake it.

Having exchanged polite kisses with Claire's mum and witnessed Claire giving both parents a genuinely warm hug, Charles followed the other three into the hallway and - after depositing their cases there - immediately to the right through the door into the "front room" as Claire's mum and dad still preferred to call it. There was a pipe rack on the top of a Bureau against one wall, in which were suspended a half a dozen or so pipes, all of the straight-stemmed and full-bowled variety. The furniture, whilst in good condition, was evidently several decades old and there was one of those gas fires with a beaten copper hood gracing a 1950's style tiled fireplace and hearth, on which stood one of those old companion sets. Claire's mum, addressing Charles with one of her disarming smiles and telling him not to be formal and to call her Marje, pulled one out from her nest of tables and then told no one in particular that she was off out into the kitchen to make some tea.

After a few moments conversation, during which Gordon,

Claire's dad, had exchanged a few thoughts with Charles about sport, the government and gardening, Charles had begun to think that surely Claire had been joking when she'd told him that her father had dementia. A more normal bloke he'd yet to meet, so he found himself thinking.

It was then that Claire stood up and said that she was going to see if her mum wanted any help, and so she exited the room, closely followed by her father too, thus leaving Charles alone in the room, with time to peruse his surroundings and again wonder why Claire would have said what she had about her father.

After an interlude of probably only three or four minutes, Charles looked up to see his hopefully future father-in-law re-enter the room, glance his way and adopt an expression which could best be described as a mixture of indignation and shock. Just as Charles was going to re-start their rather relaxed conversation, his words never quite reached his lips as Gordon Barrett exclaimed:

"What the BLAZES are you doing in my house? Who the DEVIL do you think you are, coming in here uninvited!?"

Charles was thunderstruck. Before he could even begin to respond with, "But, we've just arrived, I'm Claire's partner, we..." his girlfriend's father was angrily tugging at his rather expensive woollen jumper and he found himself rising and being shoved rather roughly towards the door. Any attempt he could muster at resistance was futile as his assailant was getting redder in the face by the second and in no mood to listen, or even hear anything that Charles might have said. Gordon Barrett was shouting about calling the police when he finally wrested open his front door, shoved Charles out on to the drive and slammed it in his face, along with a few final words like "bloody cheek, who the hell did he think he was, cool as a cucumber..?"

Now Charles had a dilemma. Here he was standing out on the front driveway, his girlfriend the other side of that front door, as were their cases, and he'd just been thrown out as though he were a total stranger. Could he risk Mr. Barrett possibly calling the police if he were to knock again at the front door? He gave himself a few moments to calm and compose his mood and decided to knock again. After all, there was no other choice.

Not without some degree of trepidation, he lifted the lion's-head knocker and tapped it loudly twice. Almost a minute passed and the door was opened once again, this time by Claire, thus bringing Charles a huge wave of relief.

"What are you doing out here, darling?" She asked.

Hadn't she heard? Thought Charles, surely she must have heard what was going on.

"Your father, he… he… Claire, he threw me out. Said something about calling the police. He acted like he'd never seen me before. What do we do now?"

"Oh, dear, I'm so sorry love. I should have thought more. I oughtn't to have left you alone like that. I did tell you about Daddy's condition, didn't I. He often can't remember things that happened only minutes before. His long-term memory is marvelous, but ask him what you'd just been talking about and he wouldn't have a clue. Well, to be honest, it comes and goes. Anyway, don't worry, just let me handle it."

No sooner had Claire said this than her parents once again arrived at the front door, whereupon Claire looked at her father and said, "Daddy, meet Charles, he's my boyfriend and he's been dying to meet you." There followed a virtual carbon copy of the conversation that had occurred not a quarter of an hour earlier. It was evident that Marje knew how to deal with such things, living with Gordon's problem as she had been for some time already. As they re-entered the house, Charles trying very hard not to show his nerves, Claire whispered,

"Don't worry, I won't let you out of my sight now. That way daddy will always associate you with me."

It had been much later that evening that Charles had asked why Claire and her mother hadn't heard the commotion. Claire had told him that it was because she and her mother had gone out of the back door and some way out into the back garden to pick some herbs to go into the Sunday lunch.

On the sofa, Claire bursts into a fit of the giggles whilst ruffling her husband's hair.

"I know what you're thinking about and it wasn't funny, my girl!!"

"It was from where I was standing," she replied and collapsed into laughter.

Charles, acting the hurt one, reaches for the TV remote and says, "Shove a video in and we'll watch a movie. Let's get off this subject!"

One month later, July 1985.

Charles Mason is walking the Bristol streets during a sunny lunchtime. It's a mixed month weather-wise, but today is sunny and in the lower seventies Fahrenheit and Charles wants to do some thinking about a contract he's working on. He finds himself in Upper Maudlin Street and above him rises the huge and quite ugly, in his view, building that is the Bristol Royal Infirmary.

Sitting on the pavement, her feet in the gutter, is a young woman. She looks like she can't be much more than twenty years of age, but Charles can't see her face because it's buried in her hands.

Judging by the way her shoulders are convulsing, she's crying, no, sobbing would be a more accurate description. She wears a pair of well-worn denim jeans and a short-sleeved t-shirt with some bold logo emblazoned across the chest. Charles can't see what it is as the girl is hunched over, her head almost touching her knees. Her dark hair looks as though it could be quite beautiful, falling to probably halfway down her back, but it's in straggles at the moment, probably something to do with the girl's current situation. Her trainers have seen better days.

Finding it impossible to walk on by, Charles stops just behind the girl and wonders what he should do. Perhaps it's none of his business, or perhaps she wouldn't thank him for getting involved. But then, what if there is something he can do and yet doesn't make some offer of help? Almost against his better judgment, he speaks.

"Are you..?" he is going to say "OK" but stops. It is patently obvious that she is not OK. Disregarding the potential consequences to the seat of his expensive trousers and the tails of his suit jacket, he sits down on the pavement beside her. Tugging the silk handkerchief from his top pocket, he rests it gently against the back of her hand and says, "here." At first she ignores him, but then, ever so slightly glancing toward this Samaritan, she takes the handkerchief and dabs vigorously at her eyes before blowing her nose into it. Charles makes a mental note not to ask for its return.

"Thank you," she mutters. Then again "thank you. I'm alright. You don't need to stay there. You can't do anything anyway. No one can."

"No one can." repeats Charles, "That sounds like you're in a pickle alright. Why don't you at least tell me about it? I still have half an hour before I have to be back at my desk.

"Tell you what. Why don't we begin with introductions? My

name is Charley Mason, and yours?"

"You don't look like a 'Charley' I must say," the girl responds. Charles is instantly annoyed with himself for thinking that 'Charley' would sound less formal, even less upper-middle class than 'Charles'. He replies:

"OK, call me Charles if you think it suits me better. Do you drink coffee? Tea perhaps? I mean just around the block there's a small coffee bar, all Formica tabletops and stuff, but a cheaper, more cheerful cuppa would be hard to come by. Um, by 'cheaper' I don't mean…|"

"It's alright," says the girl, "Marianna by the way. My name's Marianna."

Now he can see her eyes and, surrounded though they are by acres of smudged makeup, he decides that she's really quite pretty. What can be so bad that a pretty young thing like this needs to sit in the gutter and sob in full public view?

"So," Charles ventures, "You going to talk about it? I mean, if no one can do anything, then at the very least it may help to unburden yourself. Look, I'm happily married and a great many years your elder. You need not fear that I'm a threat you know. I'm afraid that you've aroused my curiosity and I just can't pass by without trying to be of some assistance." He can see that her mind is weighing him up. He feels the armour beginning to crack. Taking her elbow, he assists her as she rises to her feet.

"I haven't got any cash." She declares. Resisting the temptation to say "I'd rather guessed that," Charles replies that it's OK. He could do with a cup of coffee anyway and perhaps he'll buy her a pastry before seeing her on her way.

Sitting in the window of a small workers' café, she waits while Charles returns from the counter with a tray on which are two white, steaming mugs and a Danish pastry on a small plate with a tissue and a knife, which he places before his young charge.

"All right. Now, young lady, try me. Tell me what brings a pretty little thing like you, who can't be much more than twenty years of age, down to the point of sitting in a public street crying yourself silly. I'm not going to move from here until I at least decide that you're going to be OK, or least feeling a little more hopeful."

Marianna looks Charles directly in the eyes; it's as if she's gauging him. She decides that she may as well tell him the problem, and so begins.

"I'm nineteen years old and two months pregnant. It's been confirmed." Seeing in Charles' eyes that this puzzles him, that oughtn't this to be good news, she goes on, "It has ruined my life. The father has abandoned me; I don't have any idea where he is. Haven't seen him for over a week and he hasn't been in contact. I'm on my own. There's no way I'm going to keep my job and I can't afford the rent on the flat, now he's gone.

"I don't have much family. You can tell from my accent that I'm not from Bristol. I've been down here only a year. I only have a couple of cousins and a stepfather up in Worksop who's so gross and never stops leching over me since my mum died. He's the reason I came down here. I'd met the baby's father when he was working for a couple of weeks up near me and he asked me to come to Bristol. Anything was better than staying with that man I could never call 'dad'. Oh yea, I took a risk coming all the way down here, but staying there I'd have ended up on the streets even sooner, just to escape that monster. Still, makes no difference now does it? Give me another month and I'll be living in bus shelters, begging for money. I have no one, nothing and a second mouth to feed in seven months from now. I'm afraid that, even though it's probably the best thing to do, I can't kill my baby. I can't abort it. I can't do it.

"So you see, Charley, things aren't exactly great for me right now."

She stops talking, takes a sip from the hot tea in her mug and stares out of the window at a passing bus, as if expecting that this charming smart gentleman would now politely excuse himself and leave her to her fate. Charles leaves it a moment before responding.

"Look, Marianna, I'm sure I could help in some way. My wife and I could surely come up with a plan, or some money or something."

"I don't want your money! Where would that get me? A couple of weeks on and I'd be back where I started. Like I said, NO ONE can do ANYTHING." She speaks these words so loudly that a couple of dusty workmen a few tables away glance in their direction, before returning to their doorstep bacon sandwiches.

Charles admits inside himself that he does feel somewhat impotent to help this poor waif. Almost automatically, like he's just paying a cold call on a potential client, he reaches into his inside pocket, draws out his wallet, to a look of alarm on Marianna's face, but extracts simply a business card. He slides it across the table toward the girl,

"Take this," he says, "take it and keep it safe. Do keep it safe my girl. I want you to have a think and if there's anything, ANYTHING that you think I can do for you, you give me a call. You understand? I'm not taking no for an answer. I shall wait for you to call me. Don't disappoint me." With that he rises and adds, "Well, I really must be back at my desk. People to meet I'm afraid.

"It's been …nice meeting you Marianna. Now do please try and remember that you're a lovely young girl with a lot of life ahead of her. This may look bleak, but I'm sure there's a way out of this. Keep your pecker up."

Charles reluctantly leaves Marianna to her Danish pastry. Once he's gone she takes a bite and, to catch some crumbs that may fall into her lap, she picks up the tissue. A Twenty Pound note falls out of it on to the well-worn Formica. She stares at the money and begins to cry again.

Charles arrives home at around 6.30pm. Claire greets him with a kiss on the cheek and the aroma from the kitchen draws him towards that room before he has even put down his keys and executive case. His wife following behind, delighted at his enthusiastic response to the smell of her cooking, he lifts the lid from a saucepan that's simmering on the hob and asks if it's smoked salmon pasta that Claire's preparing.

She nods and he places his executive case on the antique pine kitchen table, throws his keys on the top of it and draws his wife into his arms.

"You certainly know how to keep your man happy," he says and kisses her on the lips. "I had a rather unusual encounter today. Is there some red wine open, by any chance?"

As Claire pours her husband a glass of Cabernet Sauvignon, she asks, "So, you going to tell me about it?"

"Yes, of course, darling. It's just, where to start. I was out for a bit of a constitutional around lunch time, I had some time before I needed to meet Trevor about a new contract in Belgium, so, since the sun was shining and it seemed too nice out to stay indoors, I thought I'd pound the pavements of Bristol for half an hour or so. As I was passing the Infirmary, there was this young woman balling her eyes out on the floor."

"On the floor? What, you mean the pavement? Was she a beggar or something?"

"No, not at all. But she was sitting on the kerb with her feet in the gutter sobbing for England. I couldn't just walk past so I asked her if I could help." And so Charles continues on to relate the whole episode with Marianna to Claire.

No sooner has Charles finished the story, than an electronic ringing sound emanates from his executive case. He opens it and retrieves one of those brand new Motorola 8000x "Brick" mobile phones from its interior. About the size of a house brick and sporting a substantial rubber-coated antenna at the top, it's Charles' new toy and he's quite delighted that someone is calling him on it.

"Hello, Charles Mason." He says. Claire watches him, assuming that it's a business call for the first moment or so, before her husband's facial expression suggests that perhaps it's the young girl he'd encountered earlier that day.

"Yes, OK. Look Marianna, I'm glad you called; it's really no bother. Where are you?" Again silence while Marianna tells Charles where she's calling from. "OK, OK." replies Charles, "Look, stay there and don't move from that spot. My wife and I will be along in ten minutes. We'll bring you back here for a good meal and we can talk, all right? Trust me Marianna, we really do want to help you." Another slight pause, then, "NO, we DO, OK? Just stay put and we'll be there directly." He presses the "End" button and places the phone back in his open case.

Looking at his wife, Charles says, "Looks like we have us a project my sweet. Can that saucepan hold on for half an hour?"

"I'll turn it off and get it going again when we get back. Where is she anyway?"

"Call box just off Park Street. We can be there and back in twenty minutes. You OK with this?"

Claire's expression gives Charles all the assurance he requires and soon they're in the car and driving down to find the girl.

As Charles approaches the call box, sure enough, there is Marianna, still in the came clothes he'd seen her wearing earlier today. He draws up on the double yellow lines alongside her and Claire hops out of her side of the vintage 1970 Jensen FF, invites the apprehensive young girl to sit in the front, before first slipping into the back. After a split second of doubt, Marianna slides into the passenger seat and closes her door.

"Hello again, meet my wife Claire," says Charles, patting the anxious young Marianna on her knee. Pulling out once again into the flow of traffic, Charles continues, "I'm glad you called. Please don't worry Marianna. We are only interested in your welfare. I've explained what you told me earlier today to Claire, so she's well aware of your predicament. Let's get us home and we'll talk over a nice cozy dining table. I hope you like pasta? Smoked salmon in the sauce. It's one of Claire's specialities."

Marianna is having trouble taking in what's happening to her. She's on the verge of tears and doesn't know how to react or what to say. She stares out of the window, conscious of the soft leather upholstery that is supporting her small body. She feels out of her depth. During the short drive back up to the Masons' house, she more than once contemplates whether to throw open the door and bolt on the couple of occasions where Charles has to stop the car. How did she come to be here, sitting in this obviously very posh car, with two well-off people whom she doesn't know from Adam? What's going to become of her? Will this all turn out well, or will she disappear, never to be heard of again? But then, why would these people do such a thing? There's nothing to be gained. She has no money, hardly any family and no contacts worthy of a ransom being demanded for her safe return. No, she concludes, the chances are more likely that they're genuine folk who want to help someone in distress. Before she can agonize much more about things, the car sweeps into a driveway in front of a respectable Victorian house with bay windows and she realizes that it's too late now. She's in this and had better hope that it will turn out right.

Once in the kitchen Marianna begins to feel better. The delicious smell of Claire's cooking makes her feel very hungry and, once she's declined a glass of wine and accepted sparkling mineral water, she even finds that she can crack a slight smile. Charles has left the women for a few moments while he freshens up and puts his case in his office upstairs. He re-enters the kitchen a few minutes later in tracksuit bottoms and a black t-shirt with the word Yale plastered across the front in big American-type capital letters.

Claire asks her husband to lay the table and she places a huge glass dish of tossed salad in the centre of it. A couple of wooden salad servers are lying across the dish. After she's placed a ceramic bowl of her delicious pasta concoction on each of the three place mats, she flops into her chair opposite the nervous Marianna. Charles is sitting at the end of the table to the young girl's right and gestures her to tuck in.

"Do please help yourself to salad" he says, whilst proffering the handles of the salad servers.

Once they've all had at least a couple of mouthfuls, Charles resumes,

"Now then, Marianna. Let me first say that you are in safe hands with us here. So before you think about cutting and running, please do relax, OK? Are you quite sure that there's no one we can call to let them know where you are, or what your situation is?"

Marianna shakes her head, "No, there's no one. No one who'd be bothered anyway."

Claire interjects, "Charles, could we have a quiet word?" then turning her face to Marianna, "It's OK, Marianna, I have something I want to run past my husband. Just give us a mo and do please eat all you want to. There's more sauce in the pan on the hob."

Claire and Charles withdraw to the hallway, where Marianna can hear a vigorous, whispered conversation ensuing. The young girl tries to listen, but cannot make out what is being said. All kinds of things go through her head. Ought she to try and leave? But then, that would mean pushing past this couple, since they are now between her and their front door. How did she get herself into this? Earlier today, when she'd finally been overcome by the apparent hopelessness of her situation, this kind man in a business suit had plonked himself down on the pavement next to her and given her his silk handkerchief. Yet, he didn't seem to be coming on to her. Not that she wasn't used to slightly older men having a go, especially the married ones.

Eric. Her thoughts strayed now to the father of her child, this tiny human that she now knew for certain was growing within her. She'd so thought that he was a good sort; that he would stand by her. How can he have just gone like that? OK, so she knows that he didn't have much money and even less prospects. But that wasn't Eric's fault. How was he to know that the firm he'd worked for was in trouble? When they laid him off it was totally unexpected. He was a good mechanic, but no matter how good you are, if you can't find an opening, you may as well be a brain surgeon, for all the difference it makes. But where had he gone? She'd come home from buying a few things at the local supermarket to find the flat empty, his side of the wardrobe cleared of his things. Well, so he'd left a couple of trainers that were clearly so beyond their usefulness that they were only fit for the bin, which was where Marianna had consigned them with some degree of fury.

She so thought that she knew Eric. Surely he knew what a hole he was leaving her in. Surely he'd come back. But then, over a week had gone by and she'd drawn blanks from his friends in the pub. From his old workplace she'd only received shakes of the head and words like, "Look love, once he finished here we had no idea where he'd gone. Haven't heard a dickie bird."

Friends in the pub. Yea, what friends? She'd made the cardinal mistake of thinking that they'd become her friends too. Yet it's funny how you suddenly revert to being the outsider when one of the group is threatened. He'd obviously told them what he was going to do; told them that if Marianna were to come asking they were to not tell her anything. Act ignorant, which they did.

I dunno, she thinks, as she loses her appetite for what she has to admit is very good pasta, maybe Andy, Mark and Phil really didn't know where Eric was. Perhaps she's being too hard on them. Smoked salmon, she's never tasted it before. It's really lovely, yet somehow the knots in her stomach are preventing her from lifting her fork to her mouth again.

Still this couple whisper in the hall. Yet, a calmness does come over Marianna. 'I have nothing', she thinks, 'so how on earth could they have any other motives than to help me?' She comforts herself and decides to sit it out. She sips some of the mineral water that Charles had placed in an elegant glass before her. At least she finds that she can now drink a little. She's never tasted water like this, but the sparkling aspect seems to appeal to her palate and so she sips, albeit very small amounts, to pass the time.

After what seems like an age, but was probably only six or seven minutes, Claire and Charles return to the table, their lips hinting at the beginnings of a couple of smiles. Marianna looks from one to the other. Starts to speak:

"Look, I don't know why I phoned you, Charley. I know you told me that I should, but maybe I ought to go now. I…"

"Marianna," begins Claire, "calm down, I think we may have a solution to your problem. It's perhaps a little radical, but we're going to run it past you anyway." She glances in the direction of her husband. Swilling the wine gently around in the bowl of his long-stemmed glass, which he clutches between the thumb and index finger of his right hand, left arm thrown back over the back of the solid beech kitchen chair, he begins. Staring directly into Marianna's eyes, he says:

"You have a baby on the way that you can't see how you'll be able to look after. Admirably, you don't want to get rid of it, yet you can't see how your life will proceed if and when you have it. Does that about sum it up for you?" The girl nods, cautiously. Charles goes on, "Well, I'll tell you something about us. We are madly in love and have been since the day we met. We've now been married for a few years and would very much like to start a family. The thing is, Marianna, nothing happens. Claire just can't seem to fall pregnant. Do you perhaps see where I'm going with this?"

Once again, the girl nods and her body language indicates that she's getting the idea, but that she doesn't think it'll work. Charles senses this and carries on.

"Marianna, you're shortly to become homeless, we understand." Pausing, he looks at her again, seeking affirmation, she gives it with a slight nod, "Well," he continues, "we may need to establish a few ground rules, perhaps talk about a 'trial period', but what if you were to move in here and, for as long as you're able, you could work as our housekeeper, that is until you need to start resting as you approach full-term? That way we could pay you, which would give you a degree of self-respect. When you go into hospital to give birth, Claire and I could adopt the child as our own. We've even talked a little about adopting but have been quite shy of approaching the relevant people owing to, well, our fears I suppose. We do have a stable and fairly over-adequate income. I have my business, which earns well and Claire is an artist who works from home. Most of her work is commissions, but how good it would be for the baby to always have a mother on hand.

"Of course," Charles reads the look of apprehension that's now flowing across the girl's face, "we'd be only too happy to make it possible for you to watch the child grow up. Yes, you may need to adjust to how huge a sacrifice it was that you'd have made, but think what kind of life your baby would have rather than the absolute uncertainty of staying with a mother who stands to be homeless and penniless, as well as without family to whom she could turn for support.

"Marianna, am I making some kind of sense to you? Do you understand what I'm saying, what we're asking you? In a way, you'd be giving us something of inestimable value in return for the kindness and protection that we're offering you. Once the baby is born and we've brought it home, you'd be free to rebuild your life and, who knows, there might come a time in the future when we could all three of us explain to the child what the circumstances were under which it came into the world."

Claire, also looking intently at Marianna's eyes, interjects, "Marianna. All we ask right at this moment is that you think about this. Why not stay in our guest room tonight and perhaps over breakfast tomorrow we'll see if you have come to a decision? The fact is, we really want a child to bring up and you have one that you aren't in a position to care for. I'm sorry, I don't mean to express it in such cold terms, but that is about the bones of the situation isn't it? Oughtn't the child's interests to be paramount here?"

The young girl at their kitchen table seems to have shrunk in size. She hunches over the table, tears freely flowing and seems unable to express herself. She looks from one to the other and her eyes tell both Claire and Charles that they perhaps oughtn't to pressurize her further now.

Claire and Charles eat their meal whilst Marianna picks at the food before her. Claire asks, "Aren't you going to eat some more Marianna? You really need to eat, you know. But then, I understand. No, let me rephrase that, I don't completely understand, but I sense that you're in such a tizz that you've lost your appetite. Look, why don't you go and sit in the lounge, put your feet up and watch some TV for a while. Just let what we've said sink in while Charles and I clear up. Then I'll make us a hot drink and I'll show you the guest room. How's that?"

Marianna nods her assent.

Next morning, as Claire is busy scrambling eggs and the delicious smell of coffee grounds fills the kitchen, Marianna, in a borrowed dressing gown, appears at the kitchen door. It's 9.30am and it's Saturday. Charles has taken a stroll down the road for some newspapers.

As Claire gestures for her to sit at the dining table, Marianna speaks:

"I think I shall take you up on your offer."

4. Charles, Claire and Marianna

August 1985.

"Lewis' store is huge. Have you ever been in there Marianna?" Asks Claire. She and the young Marianna are sitting at the kitchen table on a weekday, their hands wrapped around mugs of filtered coffee. Charles is in Germany for a few days seeing some potential developers about some property over there.

It's almost a month since Marianna accepted Charles and Claire Mason's offer of taking on her child, which will be born around March 1st or 2nd, 1986, if it makes its entrance on schedule. The Masons had helped Marianna to pack up her meagre belongings at the flat she'd shared with the baby's father, who abandoned her not long before she encountered Charles on the street outside Bristol Royal Infirmary. Marianna has been sick this morning, but is feeling a little better now. She has a plate, on which sits a slice of wholemeal toast smothered in marmalade, in front of her on the table.

"No, I haven't. But I've walked past it a couple of times. I know near enough where it is."

"Well, how about we go down to Broadmead today and we'll attack Lewis' and a few other places. See what we can do to give you a slightly better wardrobe, plus get some things for you to wear a little later on, agreed?"

Marianna has already quit her job at the petrol station, so she now has a flexible schedule as housekeeper for Charles and Claire. In the few short weeks since she moved in, she seems to be proving the Mason's faith in her to be well-founded. She's a well-mannered young woman who also demonstrates a high degree of intelligence. Granted, she is still very awed by what's happening to her and still feels rather insecure about the whole thing. But initial signs are that she will be an asset around the house as long as she's able and hence she will be well looked after right up until she has to go into hospital to have the baby. She is ace at ironing and has already re-arranged Claire's kitchen cupboards in a way which Claire approves of heartily. She can now find things that she used to take ages looking for. Marianna has taken to housework with great enthusiasm, even to the point where the Masons are telling her not to overdo it. She is pregnant after all. Yet the girl can barely be restrained from attacking every aspect of homecare with an almost vicious fervour. It's as if she feels the need to prove something.

She's already confided to Claire that, had she not been compelled by circumstances to flee the home she'd been sharing with her mother's second husband, a man she'd felt very uncomfortable with after the death of her mother from lung cancer, she'd entertained ideas of becoming a nurse, but had abandoned all attempts at a career after moving to Bristol to be with the young dashing Eric, who'd found her the job in the petrol station ('It's only temporary, babes' he'd said) through a mutual friend of the person she was to replace there.

Now, here she is living in this huge house with these two quite well-off people who seem to her to be kindness itself. Surely this can't last. She doesn't know how to show her gratitude, it's all rather overwhelming. Had she not fallen pregnant, what would she be doing now? Probably still selling petrol to reps in Ford Sierras who sported Filofaxes and wore dark suits and ate takeaways in the car park nearby. She'd be waiting in on Saturday afternoons while Eric went to Bristol City home games and sometimes came home later than he ought to and rather the worse for beer.

St. Paul's wasn't really her idea of residential heaven. The flat was OK, but the area, well, it frightened her to walk some of it alone at certain times of the day. Of course, had she been after obtaining a supply of soft or hard drugs she'd have felt right at home. Eric is, was, a good man, though. He had ideas about what he wanted to do, where he wanted to go. He had qualified as a mechanic and was one day going to open his own garage, or at least workshop. Trouble is, you need to save up quite a lot of cash before you can do that and he'd recently been laid off and not been able to secure another job. The chances of finding another flat with him out of work and Marianna selling petrol part-time were virtually nil. What a time to fall pregnant. But at least she'd thought that he was going to stay with her; stand by her. Had she been too naïve in thinking that they might even marry? As it turned out, the answer was an unequivocal 'yes'.

Yet, for all the fact that she's now in this position that will result in giving up her baby next year, she at least stands to get her life on to an even keel, thanks to the Masons. She really doesn't know how she ought to feel about this child. It's all a new experience for her anyway. She only knows that her upbringing has instilled in her a deep-held belief that to abort would amount to murder.

Why, her benefactors have even promised that she can continue to stay with them for an indefinite period after the birth, so she can be a useful help to Claire and go with them to the relevant people and places to get the adoption organized on a legal basis. "When you're good and ready," Claire had told her, "then you can make your way in the world. We'll be sure to give you a good start, maybe even help you enroll on a training course so that you can become qualified in whatever field you then decide you'd like to pursue." How can all this be happening to her now? Yet, she has to admit that Charles and Claire do seem to be to just as appreciative of her as she feels she ought to be of them. They so look forward to bonding with the baby and bringing it up as their own. Can that be wrong? Marianna doesn't think so. She for a certainty couldn't make that child any promises on her own part. That's for sure.

"Mari? Are you in there? The lights are on, but..." Says Claire. She's been talking to Marianna but the girl has been in a reverie. She comes to and apologizes.

"Sorry, Claire, what did you say? I did get a little lost in thought there for a while. I just can't seem to convince myself that this is all happening. I'm sure I'm going to wake up on the pavement outside the hospital again any moment now."

The women are soon in the city centre, several large shopping bags at their feet as they chat excitedly across the table of the wine bar to which they've now retired. Marianna orders a Perrier, since she's now off alcohol for the duration. Claire orders a chilled white wine. They decide to eat a light lunch before going home, before taking a walk on Clifton Downs during the afternoon. It's not a good summer this year, but today is warm and dry, if somewhat cloudy.

A couple more months drift by. Now, in October, with the bump becoming more apparent on Marianna's compact body, the three of them are at Clevedon on a Sunday afternoon. They watch the boats from Portbury pass along the Severn Estuary and gaze across the brown waters at the Welsh hills behind Newport. They've just taken a pub lunch and are now sitting together on a bench with a view of the Estuary.

"Claire and I," begins Charles, "have decided to make the back bedroom upstairs into the nursery; the room next to yours Mari. Do you agree?"

"It's not really for me to agree or disagree is it?" Replies Marianna, before she realizes that her comment didn't come out sounding all that agreeable. She quickly adds, "Sorry, Charley. I didn't mean to sound offish or uncaring. What I mean is that whatever you two want to do is something I oughtn't to interfere with. I'm sure that room will be just perfect."

"Well, even though we're going to become Charley junior's mum and dad, it's no reason to not consult you. After all, like we've said, there's no way we're going to want to shut you out from his upbringing. He'll benefit from knowing you as he grows up, even though he may see you as his aunt. It would be too cruel to bar you from his life anyway. I'm sure we'll be able to work out the fine details as time progresses."

For a few moments the three of them sit in comfortable silence. Marianna makes as if to speak, but then stops herself. It's apparent to the other two that she has something on her mind. Claire asks:

"What is it Mari? There's nothing you can't talk to us about. You know that."

"I, well, I don't know what to say, how to express myself anyway. I'm all confused. Don't get me wrong. I'm not backing out or anything. It's just that I don't know where I am. Not like, where I am, as in here with you two in Clevedon. I mean, where I am in life. I don't know how to deal with all the emotions that I'm struggling with. Do you follow?"

Claire opens her lips to comment, but Marianna continues, "I'm just turned twenty years old and already my life looks like it's on the rocks. I've screwed up. I know it's water under the bridge, but what if Charley hadn't come by when I was really down that day? What if I'd still been going it alone? I can't bear to think about it, but I can't bear to think how much I depend on you two now either. It can't be right, can it? It can't be right that you two have had your lives completely thrown upside down too because of me. What kind of person must I be to have ended up screwing up my life and complicating yours? Why did my mum have to go and die like that, so young? What did I do? Perhaps I deserved a leery stepfather, maybe it wasn't his fault."

The girl's eyes fill up and she fights back the urge to cry as a wet line runs down both sides of her nose. This time Claire has the opportunity to speak.

"Marianna, love, you're all wrong about a lot of things. No one deserves anything and no one gets what they deserve, if that makes any sense. Life's one huge lottery. We're all victims. We're victims of our genes, victims of our upbringing, of how our parents or guardians acted, how they treated us, the kinds of values they brainwashed us with when we were growing up. Attitudes and morals, yes we can deduce our own as we get older, but it's always going to be a fight against what's been pumped into us as children.

"It's one of the reasons why I can't get religion. If, for example you'd been born in Iran, you'd be a Moslem; in Italy, a Catholic; in Albania an atheist. The same goes often for politics. Everyone is brainwashed and none of us should think otherwise. Now I'm going off the subject I think. But what I'm trying to say is, Marianna, when we're born we haven't done anything. The slate is clean so to speak. By the time we start school we're already set in some of the beliefs that may well stay with us for life, rightly or wrongly. What says, ...who says, that because you're born, say - Greek Orthodox, that this makes it the right religion? And if any religion will do, then there can't really be a God, because they all teach different things about him, her or it, don't they? Me personally, I prefer to believe that there is a God, but that he doesn't approve of all his self-styled 'reps'.

"I'm not making a very good job of this Mari, but what I'm trying to say is that the hand that life has dealt you is not your fault. Well, I'll qualify that, not necessarily your fault. You have made some choices, perhaps not particularly wise ones, but then they were born of necessity and if I had a Pound for every time I'd made a wrong decision thinking it was the right one I'd be a rich woman. Marianna, don't beat yourself up about all this.

"Plus, love, you haven't turned our lives upside down. You've enriched them. Charles and I want to be parents. We'd probably have ended up adopting anyway because I'm not so much concerned with going through a pregnancy myself as I am with bringing up a child that I can love, cherish and give a good start in life. It's a bonus to actually know the mother of the child we're hopefully going to bring up as our own.

"I'm not pretending that this is easy for you, of course. But you're so very young and you still ought to have the chance to make some decisions that aren't born of circumstances that have been thrust upon you. You're not thick. You're a bright girl. Set your mind to something and I'm sure you can do it." She may wish to carry on, but Charles feels the need to add a word or two. He interjects:

"Marianna, in view of what you are giving to Claire and I, it's really nothing for us to do what we can to help you make something of your life. We're in the position to be able to do so, so why shouldn't we?"

Marianna now gives in to her urge to cry and Claire slips an arm around the girl's shoulder.

"You know Mari, I can see us becoming so fond of you that you're almost like a daughter to us anyway. I know we're not old enough, at least not quite, to be your parents, but we both feel that we can love you like you were our own flesh and blood. Don't fight what life has now offered you. Accept it. Why should we punish ourselves when things go pear-shaped, yet also do the same when something good turns up?"

Marianna rests her head on Claire's shoulder and tries to shake off a feeling of dread that she finds she's dealing with continually. No real reason for it. It's just that she's convinced that life's just never going to deal her a winning hand. She doesn't deserve to be happy, despite all the reassurances from Claire.

Something is bound to happen to spoil everything.

5. Claire in Kefallonia

August 1998.

"She's a sweet girl and I know something's bothering her deeply. No doubt she'll tell me in her own time. I don't think, though, that I can face up to telling her my story, at least not the full details. Why? I suppose if the truth be told it's because I can hardly bear to face up to what happened myself.

"June 15th 1990. It was a Friday. A telephone call and then next morning a visit from the Police; could I ever have imagined that I'd live to experience such a night, such a soaring high, but then a terrible, bitter low, all within a few hours of eachother? Eight years gone already. Eight years that could have been so different, so much more filled with happiness.

"If it weren't for Greece, this heavenly place of light and smiles, of legend and a laid-back vibe that infuses me with calm, what would have become of me? What happened to you Charles? Was it my fault? Did I drive you to it? I probably did. I don't know why I have to be so preoccupied in the way that I am with existence, being, purpose - or lack of it. I just can't shake off this thing, this gnawing absence in everything. Perhaps if things had been different back then I would have, but then again, how will I ever know?

"You know one thing my girl, meeting Alyson at the airport has made you focus on something else for a change, for probably the first time in all these years. Talking to myself in the bathroom mirror while I apply a subtle amount of eye shadow, does that qualify me as mad? Probably. Anyway, it's gone 8.15 and we've agreed to meet on the bench across the road beside the water's edge for our first joint foray into Argostoli at 8.30, so you'd better get a move on my girl.

"I chose Kefallonia this time. I even took a package, something rare for me. Is this what people mean when they say 'fate'? No, can't be. Too many people are starving in the third world for us here in the first one to be so smug. Let's just say it's likely to be good for me to have this young fragile waif to look out for."

As Claire Mason sits on the bench across the road from their rooms, waiting for this new young friend to join her, she begins softly to cry. Not in a melodramatic way, no, but the tears roll silently down both cheeks as she once again castigates herself for what had happened to her husband Charles. She is saved from sinking further into a depression of self-blame by the arrival of Alyson Wright, the young woman she'd encountered as they were waiting for their luggage at the airport earlier in the day.

Little does she know now, that within a few days she and this girl will embark on a three-year tour of Greece, she to suppress her perceived guilt over the loss of her husband, Alyson to keep from returning to the man she loves and - as she sees it - destroying his life.

6. Claire and Marianna, then Charles.

January 1986. Marianna has about two months to go. The pregnancy is going well and she is beaming with health. She still keeps house for Charles and Claire, although they don't let her do certain things any more.

They opened a bank account for her some time ago and now pay her directly into the account. The last day of every month a generous sum goes in which she can't quite believe is hers. She and Claire have become very close and she knows that Claire feels that she and Charles had been right to trust that she'd be dependable and liable to keep her side of this strange bargain. She hardly spends anything as she eats with the Masons and doesn't pay rent for her room at the house. She doesn't know anyone in Bristol apart from Eric's friends and she hasn't gone near any of their haunts since she questioned them about Eric's disappearance. A virtually non-existent social life suits her anyway. She and Claire do have an outing at least once every week and that suffices.

They've quite taken to having an afternoon in the cinema. They've already been to see *Witness* and *The Colour Purple*. They enjoyed *Out of Africa* so much that they sat through it twice. This week they're queuing to go in at the Bristol Odeon to see *Cocoon*. Claire insists on a huge box of popcorn and a couple of cans of cola. Marianna tries to protest, she says that the fizz gives her terrible wind, but doesn't fight too hard as Claire thrusts the can into her hand as they show their tickets and enter the auditorium to find their seats.

"It seems impossible that I've been with you and Charley for nearly six months. I still can't believe all this you know, Claire."

"Well, I must say Mari, if you'd told me last June that we'd be the two of us sitting here in the first week of January 1986 and with you showing that great bulge too, I'd have been just a tad skeptical." She gave Marianna a warm smile and squeezed her thigh through her lycra trousers with the elasticated waist. "It's really amazing how Charles has taken to this whole thing too. I think he sees it as what I needed to get me on an even emotional keel. I suppose it's still possible that we'll produce a sibling for young Charley in there too." She glances as Marianna's 'bump' as she says this. The doctor has suggested that Marianna may like one of these new ultrasound scans to see if they can determine the baby's sex, but she's refused. It's still not one hundred percent reliable and anyway, neither she nor the Masons care, as long as the baby is born healthy.

Marianna stuffs a generous helping of popcorn into her mouth, and, after chewing and swallowing most of it, says,

"You know Claire. I've been giving this a lot of thought and I'm coming round to thinking that it may be best to limit the amount of contact I have with the baby as it grows up. I don't really know how I'm going to feel later, but logic tells me that it will only complicate things for you and Charley. I was also thinking, what if he or she looks too much like me. Won't others start wondering? I mean, some might even think that Charley and me, …I mean, well, you know. That would be awful for you wouldn't it?"

Claire's expression reveals that this is something she hadn't even thought about. She can, though, only wonder at how cruel it would be to cut Marianna out of the baby's life. She is and always will be its natural birth-mother, after all.

"I hadn't thought about that at all Mari. But, surely we can't just cut you out of the equation. Won't it be hard for you to deal with?"

"But we've made a deal that you will be the parents, Claire. I've often thought, especially in view of my background, that a person's real parents are the ones that bring them up. Now, I know that my step-father is a dirty old man, but if he'd proven to be a really good 'dad' then I'd have been happy to call him that, wouldn't I? There are people with adopted parents who have no inkling that they were adopted, surely. And I have to ask myself: does that really matter? Is blood really thicker than water, when it comes down to it?"

The lights dim and the program begins. Both direct their attention to the screen in front of them, each chewing popcorn and the thoughts that Marianna had just put into words.

Charles has begun making enquiries about how to legally adopt the child. Some things that he's learned he already assumed would be the case. Marianna will have to forfeit all legal ties with the child, who'll become entirely and legally the child of the Masons. Apart from the natural birth process, it will be one hundred percent their child to bring up as their own. A leaflet he's been given states that a couple wishing to adopt must be able to show that they will be able to give the child the care it needs to a reasonable degree. In other words, those wishing to adopt don't need to be rich, but if they have an income or living circumstances that could be described as below the poverty line, then their chances of success in the adoption procedure are virtually nil. Shouldn't be any problems there then.

Some adoption agencies apparently even have an upper age limit of 35 or 40. 'We're just about going to make it', he thinks. Some, Charles has discovered, won't entertain the idea of a couple adopting who can't prove that they are unable to produce a child of their own by natural means. The couple has to have been married for at least three years say most agencies. 'I presume' thinks Charles, 'that this gives them some hope that the marriage will endure and not cause the child undue distress were it to founder.' There's religious persuasion, racial origin and cultural and linguistic background to be considered. What about if the would-be parents smoke? At least that's not an issue here. Charles' mind is going around in circles thinking about all the possible pitfalls, yet, on the whole, he's optimistic that all will go according to plan. Something which really frightened and depressed him was the fact that he was told that only about 10% of applicants actually end up being adoptive parents.

'Yet, taking all the circumstances into account, especially the fact that the birth mother lives with us and is willingly giving the child up for adoption, I can't see why this shouldn't succeed', he tells himself, more to bolster his hopes of success than because he has any absolute assurances.

He talked recently to someone at an adoption agency who told him that their pre-approval checks can take months. He resolves to get the process going immediately. He must talk to the women tonight and see what they can start by doing.

He wonders whether he ought to tell Claire about the rather substantial amounts of cash he's 'looking after' for the 'old school friend'. Ever since that afternoon when Alan Evans had turned up with his two 'friends', Charles had been freaked by the whole thing. Thinking back, he hadn't really been given any choice in the matter. Perhaps he had been a little too acquiescent, but then, since he had no experience of the kind of world this ex-school 'friend' now inhabited, he'd decided that he ought to do as he was being asked. When all said and done, it seemed that it would not inconvenience him to too great a degree and he had been assured that some of the interest accrued would come his way by way of payment for his cooperation in the matter. Quite where all this money had originated he wasn't about to ask. Ignorance is bliss he decided. All he knew was that Evans wasn't working as a PAYE employee anywhere and hadn't been for some years.

He curses his knowledge of the financial world; the fact that he knows about how to place significant sums of money in certain countries without too much interest in where it came from being shown by the bankers concerned. It's only because of the vast sums that move when commercial properties change hands, or new projects are commissioned, that Charles has had to involve himself in such things.

'How in hell did Evans get wind of my "expertise" or experience?' he asks himself. He's asked himself this same question many times. It's almost as if by asking it again and again he'll come up with some answer or other that'll make the situation feel more comfortable. He lifts a china cup of Twinings Rose Pouchong tea to his lips, his favourite tea that his secretary Joan takes great pains to procure and prepare for Charles whenever he's in the office during the afternoon hours; no milk or sugar and a slice of fresh lemon. It's patently obvious that Evans got someone to do a bit of research into what some of his old school chums were up to these days and, as a result, selected Charles as his man. They were never close at school. They'd gone from the first form to the fifth, when Evans had left to start work in a tyre depot, whilst Charles continued on to complete his sixth form years, without having much more to do with eachother than perhaps having played football in a group on the school playing field during breaktime. He only remembers a few occasions when he'd conversed one to one with Evans when the irritating fellow had behaved threateningly toward him in the quadrangle; but then, Evans had behaved threateningly towards every boy in the class by the time the first term of their first form year was completed.

Anyway, Charles sips his tea and tries once again to contemplate the portfolio he has on his desk before him. It's a huge new development up near the M4-M5 interchange which could net a tidy profit. Several years' construction lay before him if his company decide to take it on.

He can't concentrate. He looks at his watch and sees that it's approaching 4.30pm. 'Stuff it,' he thinks to himself. Shoving the portfolio with the proposal into his case, he finishes his tea and rises to leave for home. Before he comes around his desk he also picks up the folder containing all the information he's gathered from several adoption agencies and walks into the outer office, where he grabs his raincoat from the coat stand and tells Joan he'll be at home if she wants him.

'When am I going to be able to get shot of this infernal money and Evans into the bargain?' he thinks to himself.

7. Father and Mother.

Monday March 3rd, 1986. 'It all happened so fast.' Thinks Claire. She's sitting in the waiting area of the maternity ward at Southmead Hospital. Marianna has been in labour for several hours. Claire had held her hand for much of the time but, since she hadn't slept a wink all night and almost fell asleep on her feet at the bedside, the midwife told her to go and try and snatch forty winks outside.

Last night at about 11 o'clock Marianna's waters broke. They were at the hospital for around midnight and now it's dawn. Claire bites her nails and reflects. Is she really about to become the legal mother of a newborn baby? Will Marianna think differently about this whole thing when that infant is placed in her arms? So much is riding on the next few hours that Claire can't sleep, even though her eyes sting and she feels bone weary. Perhaps life is about to take a turn for the better for her and Charles. Perhaps they will be able to bring up a child and give it a good start in life. 'Will I', thinks Claire 'cuddle it while it cries over the first of its teeth coming through? Will I bathe a grazed knee and buy his or her first school uniform and satchel? Will Charles and I really sit and watch our child in the school play? Will our child be good at some aspect of athletics and make us proud on school sports day? Will he or she drive us bonkers by staying out beyond curfew time? What kinds of friends will he or she bring home? What kind of partner will he or she end up with? Will I sit at parent-teacher evenings with Charles and be told good things, or perhaps that our child isn't behaving properly?'

So many questions and potential scenarios of the coming years roll around in Claire's head. 'Will I be a good mother? Will I find it makes a difference that I wasn't the child's natural birth-mother?' She even wonders if she can cope with it all emotionally now that it's actually happening.

The sound of a tiny infant's cries brings her back to the present. She looks along the corridor to see a member of staff emerging from the delivery room and beckoning to her.

Claire hurries along the corridor and through the swing doors into the delivery room. Marianna looks totally done in, her hair matted against her glistening forehead, her face red from the exertion of the past few hours. But across her lips there is a broad, bright smile of achievement, of satisfaction. In her arms, swaddled in whiteness, is a tiny human being, moving just enough within its wrapping to tell Claire that all is well.

Marianna looks up at Claire, tears now evident on her cheeks. She smiles at her benefactor and says:

"Say hello to your new daughter."

The following day, Claire and Charles sit across from eachother at the breakfast table. Charles chews on some wholemeal toast and sips fresh coffee from a bone china mug. Claire is eating muesli topped with yogurt and chopped banana. It's about 8.30am and there is bright, spring sunshine invading the room from outside the sash window over the kitchen sink. Shafts of yellow light like beams from a spotlight illuminate the room with an optimistic glow.

Both are still in their silk gowns, Charles' bearing a deep blue Paisley pattern and Claires a wine-red one of similar design. After a few moments quiet while both swallow the contents of their mouths, Charles says:

"You're quite sure that she's OK with this? I mean really sure?"

"Darling, I've told you half a dozen times. She said before I left the hospital yesterday that all was fine. Yes, she is fighting her heartstrings, which she says are tugging at her really hard to keep the child. But she told me that she wasn't going to change things now after all we've done for her. She told me that she'd see this through and that she understands that it's for the good of the baby, our baby daughter, Charles."

"I know, I know. It's just that I've read so many things about how once the birth mother has held the newborn child she can't go through with it. I read about a really messy legal case in America. These things take ages to resolve and I just can't deal with the prospect after all these months of Marianna and us two becoming enemies over this whole affair. How many times have I played over in my mind that day when I came across her in the street like that, crying her heart out on the floor. So much seems to have happened in just a few months. Are we really being just a little too hopeful Claire, are we?"

"The sooner you and I get over to the hospital the better, darling. Once you're driving home with both Marianna and the baby you'll feel better, more settled. Don't you think? Anyway, I know that case you're on about and it's to do with surrogacy, it's not the same."

"You're right, of course. But there are lots of parallels with our case aren't there?"

"Chas, love, trust me. I spent hours at the bedside yesterday. We've already got the paperwork. We just need to get the girl home here, ...the girls home here, I should say, and then we can start the legal ball rolling. Now relax, finish your breakfast and we'll get going. I'm jumping into the shower."

With that Claire rises, walks around the table and kisses her husband's forehead as he lifts a hand to touch his wife's as she breezes out of the room.

Charles picks up the newspaper from the table in front of him. He looks at the front page, yet is unable to see any words. How long he and Claire have wanted to start a family. Not that Charles is hugely broody about the idea, but he knows, or rather believes that he knows, that this will make Claire more complete. It will give her a project to get stuck into and hopefully keep her from those dark moments when she can't shake off the melancholy, the malaise that so often afflicts her. She can't deal with mortality, she can't grasp the prospect that someday this world will carry on and she won't be part of it any longer. How often they've sat at this table, or sprawled on their sofa with the TV on, sound muted, while Claire tries to explain what churns in her mind. How often has Claire said, "Charles, I sometimes think that this whole existence thing is purely within my mind. If I cease to exist, will the whole world be no more too? Will everything just vanish the moment that my mind stops functioning? How come we have such a complicated mind and yet don't put it to use in such a short human lifespan? I've read somewhere that in seven or eight decades, the human brain is only put to something like 0.1 of a percent of its actual capacity? *"The Enchanted Loom"* someone had called the brain. I read that it in a book, written as long ago as the 1940's I think, called something like 'Man On His Nature'. The brain is the most complicated thing known to man in the universe. Where is my consciousness, Charles? Why is there this sophisticated, elaborate, convoluted, or whatever else you want to call it, 3 pound mass between our ears?"

Charles has so many times listened patiently while his wife expounded her theories and fears, but it all comes down to - in Charles' mind - the fact that there are some things that we'll never fathom. But his wife finds it impossible to go for too long without returning to her broodings. So, when she talked enthusiastically about starting a family when they married, Charles thought it was the very best thing for her. It would give her focus. It would give her purpose. It would be the anaesthetic she needed to dull the pain. Now, here we are in 1986, he muses, and we've been married for four and a half years. If there is someone up there, maybe, just maybe, he's sent us Marianna to solve this particular dilemma. "Not the way I usually think, but I may be wrong," he says to himself.

It's time for Charles too to take a shower and get dressed for their trip to the hospital. Claire calls out to her husband from the shower upstairs that it's now free. He responds by placing some crockery in the sink, taking the final piece of toast from his plate and popping it into his mouth as he breezes out of the kitchen, into the hallway and climbs the stairs.

Half an hour later they're sitting in the car on the way to the hospital.

"What say I stop and pick up some flowers and chocolates or something? Be nice to give Marianna a little gift after all she's just been through, eh?" Says Charles.

"Why not?" Answers Claire, "But I'd keep it in the boot until we get her out to the car for the trip home. I'm not sure they approve of flowers in hospitals any more."

They're soon on Westbury Road heading up toward Henleaze. Charles drums the steering wheel and Claire decides not to bother to try and placate him further. Once they're on the way home she hopes that he'll begin to relax a little more. She's really quite touched at how edgy he is about all this. It's not like her husband to be so nervy, he's usually so controlled, so cool-headed. Once past Henleaze Charles keeps right onto the B4056 Southmead Road. Each time he has to slow down or stop for traffic lights or other vehicles his drumming becomes more vigorous. In his mind he's like this because of his concern for Claire. She sees it differently. She is excited, yes, but is pleased to see that all this means so much to Charles.

They pass the junction with Kingsholm Road and there's a newsagent on the left where Charles says he can grab some chocolates. He stops on double yellow lines and sprints into the shop. Luckily, there are no customers in front of him. Grabbing the largest box of chocolates he can see, he pays for it and is soon trotting back across the road, where he throws open the door, tosses the chocolates into Claire's lap and slams his door shut. Southmead Road is now all semi-detached and link houses on both sides. The traffic's mainly small vehicles, residents and delivery vans, stuff like that. The occasional bus slows things down a little and Charles resumes his drumming. After what seems to him to have been an age, Charles indicates and swings right into the hospital grounds.

"We're going to be parents," he declares enthusiastically, lifting his left hand from the wheel and squeezing Claire's, which rests in her lap. He turns to her and gives that smile she's seen innumerable times, the smile that says, 'It's you and me against the world Claire. We're going to be OK. I'll never leave you. You're the love of my life.'

It takes Charles far too long to eventually squeeze the FF into a parking space and they're soon half-walking and half-running toward the hospital's main entrance, Charles almost pulling Claire along by the hand. Once inside they patrol the corridors, making their way toward the maternity ward, eager to see their two charges, keen to get them home.

Entering the ward, they are surprised to see a young man sitting beside the bed, leaning toward Marianna, who's holding the newborn close to her chest and toying with a tiny hand with one of her own. Marianna looks up as soon as the ward doors swing closed behind the Masons. Her face adopts an expression of dismay, of horror, of shame, all at once.

She opens her mouth, but nothing comes out. Her face reddens and she begins to cry. She looks away.

The young man, perceiving that Charles and Claire have arrived, rises, scraping back the chair's plastic-footed legs on the ward floor. He turns and a forced smile creeps across his face. He's about thirty, maybe younger, has a neatly trimmed beard and collar-length dark hair. He wears a smart leather jacket and designer jeans. On his feet a pair of brogues gleam under the ward's mixture of fluorescent and natural daylight. A button-down Ben Sherman shirt glows white between the open sides of the jacket. He speaks.

"Hi. You must be Charles and Claire. Pleased to meet you both."

"And you would be?" Asks Charles, a sickening dread that he already knows the answer to the question creeping across his mind.

"I'm Eric. I'm the baby's father."

8. Claire Implodes.

Sitting on the sofa, on the same evening that Charles and Claire had encountered Eric, the baby's father, things are not going too well in the Mason household. At first there had been stunned silence on the part of Charles and Claire. Then anger, coupled with incredulity about how the baby's father could have known when Marianna would be giving birth.

Following an almost ugly scene at the bedside, Charles had taken control of himself and suggested that he and Eric go outside and talk. Charles was annoyed at first over the fact that this young man was frustratingly likeable. With some considerable degree of contrition he begged that Charles hear him out before things got out of hand. Charles, ever the man for even-handedness, was compelled to acquiesce.

"Mr. Mason," begins Eric, "I can fully understand that you

probably want to punch my lights out. I can't blame you if you do. I deserve it. I know I do. And first and above all I must tell you; Marianna had absolutely no idea that I was keeping tabs on the maternity ward. I have a friend who's a porter in the hospital and he'd promised me months ago to keep an eye out for her as and when she came in. I was pretty confident that it would be Southmead. It's the main maternity hospital for the North Bristol area. I obviously knew near enough the date when she'd be in.

"Marianna knew nothing about my whereabouts for all these months. She's not involved in some cynical plot to use the two of you and then scarper. It's down to me, this that's happened today. It's down to me and me only and I need to explain myself to you."

Charles replies, tight lipped, "I'm listening."

"I ran. Mr. Mason, I ran because I was scared. I wasn't ready to be a dad anyway, but at least when Marianna first told me she was expecting, I had a job. I was going to stick with her, whatever. I'm a good mechanic Mr. Mason, but the firm wasn't doing all that well and they had to let some people go. It wasn't a question of me not being good at the job. It was purely based on seniority and, since I was the last one in the door, I was the first one out again. I wasn't thinking straight and I didn't really treat Marianna right. I…"

"That's putting it mildly." Interjects Charles.

"Sorry, I know. There aren't adequate words to describe how I abandoned her and I throw my hands up and admit that. I can't go back and change things or else I would. But it is what I did. I have a cousin in London who said I could stay with him for a while. Maybe find some kind of job up there, but he had room for me and we were always close so I just packed a few things and hitchhiked up the M4. It was a spur of the moment decision and I regret it bitterly now, you have to believe that.

"Anyway, I did get a job portering in Billingsgate. It opens at four o'clock in the morning Mr. Mason. I had to get up a lot earlier than that. I didn't last long, but that's because I'd already started looking for something in the motor trade. I am qualified as a mechanic. I did my apprenticeship. I just needed to find the right job again. In September I finally got an interview and I got the job. I'm working for a Volvo dealership and they've sent me for further training. They like me Mr. Mason. They like me, as I've already had a modest raise and it looks like I have a chance of getting somewhere there.

"I didn't stop loving Mari and I never stopped thinking about her. I had no idea that things would get so bad for her, I really didn't. I s'pose I didn't think anything through well enough and what's life about if it's not for learning? Well, I have learned. I hope you can believe that, I have. When I went back to the flat, which I did after I'd got the job, there was someone else living there. I got the train and came down from London. The flat never had a phone so I couldn't call her. You know, I stood on the pavement outside that flat for hours. I suppose I thought that she'd walk by or something. I wanted to make things right. I had had time to think about it all and really thought that, now I'd got a half-decent job, I could face up to becoming a father and bring Marianna with me up to London. We could make a new start and I'd be a good, responsible adult, husband, father.

"But there was the problem of not knowing where she'd gone. Mr. Mason, I could have bolted back to the smoke and left it at that. I had nothing to lose, except the fact that I'd have lived the rest of my life wondering what had happened to a child I'd fathered, to Marianna too."

"What about your parents? Don't they live locally. Didn't Marianna know them?"

"They live in Taunton. She'd spoken to them on the phone a few times, but doesn't know them very well. She told me earlier that she didn't try and contact them because it would have only have brought her more problems. You know, girl pregnant, claiming it's their son who's the father. A hanger-on probably, wants to ensnare their boy. Probably slept with any number of blokes, you get the picture. She really didn't think that she'd have got a very good reception, even if she'd succeeded in getting to talk to them. I know she asked Andy, Mark and Phil, who we used to hang around with at the pub, go to gigs, that sort of thing. But I told them not to give anything away when I left. That was when I was still running scared. My mind was on another planet back then."

Charles is staring intently at this young man and fighting the urge to like him. There seems little doubt that he is being truthful, that he does want to set things right. After all said and done, he is the baby's natural father, however much Charles doesn't want this to be so. They are standing in a parking area near one of the hospital's many 'side' entrances, the nearest one to the ward. Hospital staff are scurrying with a sense of purpose to and fro around them. The sun pokes through and Charles feels a warmth on his back. He feels a fire in his heart too. He's struggling to find something to say that might salvage the situation. But he can't find any words. Perhaps sounding churlish, he says:

"Have you *any* idea quite how much time, energy, money, not to mention feelings and emotion we've put into helping that girl these past months, how many times we've sat in offices being questioned by someone across a desk about whether we'd be fit parents if we adopted the child? I presume she's told you about our arrangement, how we'd promised to take the child on and give it a good upbringing as our own. Hell, man, we were going to adopt this baby.

Do you think we can let all of this go now; that we can just watch Marianna walk off with you without so much as a 'by your leave'?

"How many other people would have done what we have, I don't know. Not many I think. We've taken that girl to our hearts and begun to feel like she's a daughter to us. Claire is going to be destroyed by this. What am I going to tell her that can make it right now? God knows what Marianna's telling her even as we stand out here."

"She'll be telling her, Mr. Mason, that should you insist on continuing with the adoption, then you must do it. However much she now wants to keep the child and make a start again with me - and she gave me a pretty hard time when I first turned up this morning I can tell you, but she came round in the end, thankfully - however much she's forgiven me and would like us to reunite with our little girl, she told me that she really can't stand in your way if you want to see it through as arranged. When I walked in there this morning, I had no idea about all this. You can see that, can't you Mr. Mason?"

"Charles, please." He even reproaches himself for this slight move toward friendship.

"Mr. Mason, Charles, all I heard from Tim, my porter friend, was that Marianna was in here giving birth to my daughter, to our daughter, I had no other information. I high-tailed it down here from London last night and only had one thing on my mind, to get to the bedside and beg forgiveness. That's what I did. When Mari started telling me about all you'd done for her and the whole way you'd taken her into your home and all that stuff, what ...I mean, how was I supposed to feel? There IS no 'supposed' to feel in a situation like this, is there? There's no precedent for a situation like this, can you see that Mr. Mas... Charles?"

Charles knows that he's been defeated. He lets out a long sigh, stares for a moment at his shoes, then up at the eyes of the young man before him. 'This young man,' he thinks, 'who doesn't know his ass from his elbow; am I, or rather - are we - going to steal away his new family? Looks like he and Marianna want to do the honorable thing except, they don't really, do they. They actually want to take their baby and go off into the sunset, full of hope, and live a life together, maybe in time bring a little sibling along for their daughter. If we insist on keeping the child now, how often will they be in touch, asking how she's doing, what's she learning, can they see her? It's impossible isn't it. We can't do it.

'With every fibre of my body, especially for Claire's sake, I want to take the baby home. I want to complete the adoption and have a nice little nuclear family. But wouldn't it, when all said and done, amount to theft? Wouldn't we have stolen their child just as if we'd taken her from a pram outside a high street shop? We knew we were taking a risk with this whole project. What a word to describe something like this, "project". I've been in property development too long. Huh, but we knew anyway that there would be an element of risk. We chose to take that risk, we've gambled and lost.'

Eric is standing, watching. He knows that Charles is ruminating the whole thing in his mind. He knows that he must give this man time to do so.

"No. You're right Eric. There is no precedent. The fact is, however, you and Marianna are the child's rightful parents. Let's go back inside."

Charles leans forward from the leather Chesterfield and pours more from a bottle of white Verdejo into his glass. He hovers the bottle over his wife's glass, but it's still almost full. She shakes her head and then rams her left hand, clenched into a fist, back into her mouth. Her hair is a mess and she has mascara running down both cheeks. She has her legs tucked up beneath her and the other hand restrains one of her ankles from dropping to the stripped pine floor. She wears grey fleece tracksuit bottoms and a white t-shirt.

"We will get over this, love, you know that, don't you." Says Charles.

His wife doesn't reply. She just takes the hand out of her mouth and looks away. She stares at the huge canvas on the wall to her left. It's one of hers, daubs of paint representing people in a rural landscape, modern impressionism. She shakes her head for the umpteenth time this evening and lets out a long sigh, punctuated with spasms brought on by too much crying.

Charles says, "Come on darling. Chin up. We always knew that there could be risks. Nothing's for sure until the papers are signed and sealed after all. We have to believe that Mari didn't know that the father would re-materialize out of nowhere, hmm?"

Still she doesn't reply. The light is fading and a gloom to match Claire's state of mind creeps across the room. The dust motes are no longer visible as the sodium streetlamp on the pavement beyond the front garden outside blinks into life, casting a yellowish hue in the half-light. Charles rises and goes to the table lamp in the corner of the room and switches it on.

"Turn that off!" Shouts his wife. "I don't want light, don't give me light! My life is dark and I want darkness. Don't give me any light. I don't want to see."

Charles obeys, but struggles with what to say to help his wife deal with the situation. He knows that they still have to face letting Marianna back into the house to collect her belongings before she goes to London with Eric. They hadn't discussed the fine details with the young couple at the hospital, only the fact that it was for the best if Eric took Marianna and the baby back to his friend's house that evening. Claire couldn't face having them in the house now, not after this.

Charles paces the floor. He stares at his modest collection of CDs, still a new phenomenon in recorded music. He has one of the brand new Pioneer 6-CD players and still needs one more CD to enable him to fill it. He has *Brothers in Arms* by Dire Straits, and a couple of Deutsche Grammophon recordings of Herbert Von Karajan, plus one or two more. He can well afford to purchase them, he just doesn't get much time to go shopping. The thought crosses his mind of playing Verdi's *Requiem*, but he thinks better of it. To play any music at all would probably be interpreted by Claire as insensitive right now. He aches to be able to find some way to make his wife feel better, more positive, but the wound is still open and sore and probably will be for some time to come.

Claire, rather unexpectedly speaks, momentarily causing Charles to jump.

"She planned this whole thing. She took us and we let her. How could we have been so naïve? How could we not have seen it coming? What a moment for that… that conniving excuse for a man to turn up. A boy rather, that's all he is anyway. I can't believe that we were so…"

"Claire, love, that's not how it is. Think about it. For starters, how on earth was Marianna to know that I'd happen by while she cried her eyes out on the side of the road last July?"

"So, you're taking her side now, are you? I should have known that you probably fancied her anyway. She's a pretty little thing after all. What plans might you have had for her once the baby came along? Set me up as a nanny and off the two of you go behind my back."

"Claire, you're saying these things out of frustration, out of your hurt. You know that was never true. I love you and have done since I first set eyes on you. I'm not taking anyone's side. I'm just trying to deal with this as best I can. We both have to deal with this and we're going to need eachother, to pull together, not to pull apart."

"She still set us up. This whole thing was a clever ruse to get her a nice place to stay and someone stupid enough to finance her through the pregnancy. How do you explain Eric Geesin turning up right at the appropriate moment then?"

"Claire, Claire, my love, he explained that. His friend, what was it now? Tim, yes his friend Tim was keeping tabs on the women coming into maternity. It was a simple job for Tim to phone Eric as soon as he knew that Marianna was in the maternity unit. I don't see why we shouldn't believe that. He strikes me as an OK kind of lad. Yes, granted, a bit capricious, a bit prone to knee-jerk reactions, but that's youth for you. If Marianna hadn't ever been admitted to that particular hospital we'd be cradling our daughter right here right now. It's just how things go. There's no other way of looking at it."

"Whose side are you on Charles?!"

"My darling, I've told you. I'm not into taking sides in this. I'm just trying to accept what's happened. It hurts me too, can't you see that?" He stands in the near darkness, hands palm outward, looking at the shadow where his wife is sitting.

"I'm going to bed." With that Claire gets up from the sofa and storms out into the hallway. Charles stays where he is and listens as she stomps up the stairs. He hears the bedroom door slam, almost off its hinges.

Next day, Charles rises from the sofa, walks into the kitchen and puts on a filter of coffee. He's spent the night on the Chesterfield, feeling rightly or wrongly that Claire would have preferred him not to come to her during the night. Apart from one occasion some time during the small hours, when he heard her go to the bathroom, she hasn't emerged from the bedroom and the door is still closed.

Charles knows that her emotions are in a scramble. He knows that she loves him and isn't really directing her anger his way, but he is the only one she has on hand to vent her feelings to, so he gets it both barrels. He takes it too. He thinks that it's probably for the best to let her go through the grieving process, for that is what this amounts to.

At around 9.30, after he's picked the paper up from the doormat and begun flicking through it, over his second mug of coffee, the phone rings. The extension on the kitchen wall is close to hand, so he reaches out a hand, tucks the receiver under his ear and goes back to sight-reading the newspaper.

"Yes? Charles Mason."

"Mr. Mason, Charles, it's me, Eric Geesin. How are things? How is Mrs. Mason?"

"You don't really want to know young man. Have you called to arrange to collect Marianna's things?"

"Well, not exactly. Marianna was almost in hysterics last night over what she feels that she's done to the two of you. She really does feel this deeply; you should know that. In hindsight, I'm more the villain of the piece aren't I Mr. Ma… Charles? I mean, if I'd stayed in London then three people, probably four including the baby, would all have been a lot happier."

"Water under the bridge my dear chap. What's done is done."

"Yes, but, Marianna's almost spent from the birth, then crying almost non stop all night about you. I can't do anything to pacify her. She especially told me how much she loves Claire and was so happy having her as a kind of surrogate mother, or maybe older sister. Before I came back she was looking at kick-starting a career again, maybe in nursing or something. Can you imagine how I'm feeling right now?"

"I probably can if you can do the same for Claire, Eric. But I don't see where this is going. Seems to me the sooner Marianna is out of our lives the quicker we can rebuild them, if Claire ever will be able to do that of course. You know she's a delicate person, my Claire. She feels everything much more deeply than most people. She finds life a constant enigma. This was the first time in years that she'd been consistently happy for months on end. I don't know why I'm telling you this, it's not really your concern and it's not going to help either of us."

"Then why don't you continue with the adoption?"

"Look, Eric, we talked about this yesterday. It would never work now and I'm sure you can appreciate that. What's done is done and we just have to deal with it."

The young man at the other end of the phone sighs audibly and can't find any words. Charles adds, "Just make plans to come here for Marianna's things and we'll put and end to this whole affair." Just before Eric replies by way of signing off, Charles hears the click that tells him that his wife has heard the whole conversation on the extension by the bed upstairs. He even allows himself a very slight curl of the lips, because he knows that what she's heard will help. At least, he hopes it will. She now knows from the horse's mouth just how deeply Marianna feels about this whole mess too. How much she is pained over what it's doing to Claire and Charles.

Charles is still sitting at the kitchen table, staring at the paper, although not seeing anything on the pages. Images of a lost era are tripping across his mind, scenes from the child's upbringing that will now never be. Both elbows on the table, he runs both hands through his hair and sighs deeply. He wishes that Claire could understand that he is hurting too. He looks up and is surprised to see her standing in the kitchen doorway, hair all over the place and a towelling bathrobe wrapped tightly around her, as though it were like her mother's embrace of protection when she was small and was frightened of bogey men in the dark. Both of her arms are wrapped across her body as though in a straight jacket. He looks at her eyes and she meets his gaze.

"Will you forgive me Charley?" She asks. He turns sideways and extends both his arms in invitation for his wife to come and be engulfed in an embrace. She responds by padding in her bare feet across the floor and pressing herself against his chest as he stands up. She thrusts her head into the crook of his neck and he pats the back of her head.

"Forgive you? For what?" he asks.

"You know, for the things I said last night. I was well out of order, but I was desperate. You know that, don't you love. I just had to lash out somehow, just to vent my pain."

"And you don't think I realized that?" He cups her chin and raises her face to his. Just barely an inch separates their faces as he smiles. "Claire, my darling, this is a tragedy for us. We both realize that. But to get through it we will have to work together. You know, don't you, that my entire life is you. There is no other… nothing else in my life that's of greater importance than you. I know you agonize over the deep things a lot. I know you really thought that this was what you needed to get you away from your darkness, that stuff that's in the recesses of your mind that I don't seem to be able to help you with. But after all said and done, I'm here for you. I'm determined to come out of this with something positive."

She stares into her husband's eyes and understands that she can indeed trust and rely on him. What would she do, what would she be without her Charles? They'd manage, somehow. He'd be there the next time she goes into one of her spirals of purposelessness, just like he has been before. 'Is this' she asks herself 'what true love is? Is this what it means? Perhaps.'

She kisses him lightly on his lips, then they kiss passionately, as though trying to pour themselves into eachother in the quest to find the strength they need to carry on.

"You want some coffee, love?" Asks Charles, softly. She nods. As he's fixing a new filter of fresh coffee, he ventures an idea. "You know, after all that paperwork and all those interviews with the adoption agency, there's no reason why we can't consider adopting another child. What do you think?"

"No." She replies, firmly. "I can't Charles. I felt we had a connection with Marianna's child. Having seen her grow over the months, having felt the kicks and talked to it through her tummy, if we can't produce one of our own, then we'll just have to carry on regardless."

As the months pass, then a year or two, Charles once again charges headlong into his work. He receives another visit from his old school "friend" Alan Evans one day in 1988. "Just touching base" says Evans. "I'll soon be letting you know the arrangements for returning my little possession that you've been minding for me." It had been a much longer period than he'd told Charles in the beginning, but the visit gives Charles some hope that the whole matter will soon be closed. Fortunately, Claire is out at the time reconnoitering a property that a client has asked her to paint; 'the family home' and all that stuff. It'll eventually hang, pride of place, over their hearth. "What do you think of the oil-on-canvas of our pile?" the owners would no doubt soon be asking their dinner guests, "we commissioned a local artist to paint it, you know."

As time passes Charles learns to deal with Claire's ups and downs. Sometimes, when she's furiously creating a picture for someone, she's very positive, very conversational and tactile with him too. He'll open the studio door sometimes and watch her, brush in mouth, hair in a tumble, paint all over her face, on which is a look of pure concentration. At these all too brief moments, he feels that she is completely happy, albeit for a short while.

One of the worst moments, though, had been when the young couple had visited and taken with them all of Marianna's things, but left Charles with the task of turning the nursery back into a spare bedroom. 'Even today,' Charles ruminates one day during the spring of 1989, 'Claire won't enter that room.'

On occasion Claire spirals into one of her black periods. She lays curled up on the sofa, head under her arms and won't move for hours. Charles has learned to leave her be. He does stay nearby when he can, of course, always ready to offer an embrace, make a drink, suggest a distraction.

So it is that in September of 1989 he takes Claire to Greece.

9. Charles and Claire, September 1989.

"Don't argue, but I've a surprise for you. It's time we had a complete change of scenery, so I've booked us a holiday. We're taking ourselves off to Greece for a few weeks," declares Charles as he arrives home one evening.

"What brought that on?" Asks Claire, in a manner that tells Charles that she's feeling about 7 on a scale of 0-10, with 0 being really down and 10 meaning she's happy. She walks up to him, throws her arms past each of his ears and plants a kiss full on his lips. She takes the case from his right hand and puts it on the kitchen table, then opens the fridge and extracts a chilled bottle of white. Two glasses sit in expectation on the farmhouse pine kitchen table.

"Well, for a start I've been rather remiss in taking you off anywhere recently, haven't I? So I decided it's time to put that little oversight right."

Charles is relieved that his wife doesn't seem to object to the idea. So he ventures a little further, ever so slightly digging: "You OK with that, then? Greece to your liking sweetheart?"

"Why on earth wouldn't it be, hub? As you so rightly say, you haven't whisked me off anywhere remotely exotic or romantic for an age. I'll fetch out my suitcase henceforth, immediately and without delay. When are we off?"

"Next week. We fly to Athens on Wednesday. Then we're taking a boat to a little island that I've been tempted to try out by a colleague. Alistair at the office has given me the phone number of a woman who keeps village rooms in the thick of the harbour village on Poros, with a view to die for apparently.

"Poros? Never heard of it, but if it's Greece then let's go. It *is* the most evocative country in the Mediterranean after all. The place for artists, eh? Hold on." While Charles opens the wine, she trots over to the small hi-fi in the corner of the kitchen, slips in a CD and the voice of Joni Mitchell begins to warm the room. It's the album *"Blue"* and Claire has selected the track *"California."*.

Verse two soon begins:

Met a redneck on a Grecian isle
Who did the goat dance very well.
He gave me back my smile
But he kept my camera to sell.
Oh the rogue the red, red rogue.
He cooked good omelettes and stews
And I might have stayed on with him there,
But my heart cried out for you
...California

Claire turns it back down a notch and says: "Ever since I first heard that song I've wanted to meet my own Greek 'redneck'. Perhaps this will be my chance!"

"If he steals your camera, don't come crying to me!" replies

Charles, feeling very pleased with himself. Looks like this may be a good trip, a good shot in the arm for Claire's sense of wellbeing. Time will tell, but it's only a few days before he'll be finding out.

They're soon upstairs, suitcases open on the bed, throwing articles of clothing from their respective wardrobes into them. Before long they're sifting through what they've amassed in the cases and Claire, kneeling by the bed, a couple of bikinis on her lap and a strappy top in her hands, speaks.

"Darling Charley. You really are my whole life, my whole reason to carry on. You do know that, don't you?"

"I sort of had an idea," he replies, before leaning over his wife and pulling her shoulders into his legs and smoothing the top of her head. "You and me gal, we're OK, aren't we?" He's on thin ice here, but continues, ever aware of how she can swing into a different mood in the blink of an eye, "Whatever life throws at us Claire, do we really need to understand anything else, other than the fact that I love you and you love me, possible Grecian redneck excepted?"

She looks up at his face from the level of his thighs and smiles. He goes on, "I really do wonder myself too you know, love. I do ask myself: can this be all there is to it? We pop into this world, a few decades go by and, if we're really lucky, we get to seven or eight of them and off we go, just when we're getting the hang of it, this life thing. So many things can go awry on the way, I know. Our brain is sometimes a curse rather than a blessing, because it drives us up alleys and down corridors and cul-de-sacs that we can't fathom. I'm not sure I buy this primeval pea soup stuff to be honest. Too much doesn't add up." He bends his legs and slides down through her arms until he too is kneeling. They're now head to head, forehead resting on forehead, as if attempting one of those mind-melds they talk about in science fiction movies.

"I read somewhere that our eyes perform something like 10,000 calculations every second as they adjust to focus on whatever we're looking at. I also use a computer now at work and I'm a bit sick of hearing people say how clever they are. I always want to say, "Yea, well, unplug it and then see what it can do."

Claire chuckles. They silently agree to continue preparing for their trip.

•

Exiting the aircraft at Athens airport, Claire finds the smell of the air almost intoxicating. She rubs a hand on Charles' shoulder. He's just in front of her, waiting for the passengers in front of him to descend the aircraft stairway to the hot surface of the apron below.

In the middle of September the temperatures in Athens are still remarkably high in comparison to the UK. Charles soon feels himself perspiring in the centre of his back and under his arms. Claire, looking quite radiant in a short-sleeved white cheesecloth top, navy pedal-pushers and floppy canvas bag flung over her left shoulder, has cut her hair to neck-length, but retained a feminine feel to the style. Her hair has a natural wave, which comes out more when her hair is short, making it almost, but not quite a curl. She's thirty-eight and looks ten years younger.

Aircraft noise suspends conversation whilst the travelers board the waiting bus at the foot of the stairs. Everyone exchanges glances with their traveling companions - partners, parents with children, siblings - and each sports a smile; after all, they've just arrived for the start of their vacation. Once through passport control and out of baggage reclaim, Charles guides his wife to the taxi rank, where they are greeted by the first driver in the row of gleaming taxis awaiting their fares, who very quickly stuffs their hold baggage into the boot of the large Mercedes. He's a man of about sixty, stocky, with a broad smile creasing his well lined and tanned face, which sports a huge salt and pepper moustache all across and quite some distance beyond each end of his almost hidden top lip.

Charles asks that they be taken to the port of Piraeus, to the quay where the island boats are tied up. Not long afterwards they're exiting the taxi, Charles ferreting in his small leather cash-purse for some Drachmas to pay the taxi driver, whilst Claire looks expectantly along the row of gleaming white sterns. More boats than she can count are lined up, all displaying large hoardings, many of them canvas, but all painted in bright reds and blues on a white background with the names of the islands to which each boat is heading. All the boats have superstructures bearing shaded sun-decks above cabins behind which are large steel ramps, dropped to the concrete surface of the quayside, thus creating hungry rectangular apertures in the stern of each vessel, each eager to consume its share of trippers.

A short distance from the quay the busy road hums with the constant flow of city traffic, whilst further back still there are large buildings, lined along at pavement level with awnings keeping the furious sun from the heads of café people, some drinking Greek coffee and reading newspapers, while others talk animatedly with their fellow table-sitters. Above and along the roof line of these buildings four or five storeys up there are huge advertising boards telling the reader in Greek about which brand of cigarette they ought to be smoking, or which airline they should fly with - in most cases here in Piraeus that's *Olympic*, of course.

Along the line of sterns there are lots of men in crisp white uniforms consisting of sharply-creased slacks, black belts and stiff white open collared shirts. Their shoulders sport navy epaulets and peaked caps with white tops, black shiny peaks and navy bands shade their faces. Everyone wears sunglasses. Some of these men have whistles perpetually attached to their lower lip, others throw their arms around as they shepherd vehicles onto the larger vessels, or perhaps off of them.

Charles guides his wife over to the ferry that bears the name "Delfini Express" whilst proudly stating across its rear that it's going to Aegina, Methana, Poros and Hydra. It's one of the more modestly sized boats, but evidently does the trip down to Poros a little faster than the larger, vehicle ferries. Purchasing a couple of tickets for the island of Poros from the woman at the little desk at the foot of the ramp, he gently places a hand on his wife's back as they continue aboard, Charles then returning to the quay to rescue their cases. Once upstairs on the sun deck, yet also under the shade of a stretched canvas awning, they settle on to the bench seats and commence absorbing the view around them. As far as the eye can see in one direction there are ships of all shapes and sizes. From here the open sea is still not visible. To the left and right is a seemingly endless line of ferries, some tied up and waiting patiently for their time of departure, others gradually reversing into their berth while crew members throw lines to other men waiting on the quayside to catch them, still others slowly edging away from the quay with their crew members drawing the dripping ropes aboard, hand over hand, then coiling them on the deck in anticipation of the next time they tie up.

Claire feels good. She feels a sense of calm. Nothing else has any importance at this precise moment. Time isn't passing, at least, not in the normal sense. Everything is suspended while she absorbs this new experience. All her past anxieties are put on hold, filed and vaulted for a while. She's not going to allow herself to feel too much. She's not going to think about what her life is going to be when she gets home again almost three weeks from now. Charles is sitting next to her, his face toward her, searching for some sign as to how she is doing. She rewards him with a genuine smile, one that reaches to her eyes, one that says: 'It's OK darling, I'm going to allow this holiday to work its magic, to soothe my soul, to give me rest from my spiritual ailments.'

She tilts her head back, closes her eyes and feels the warm Greek air caressing her skin, whilst drinking in the sounds of a bustling Piraeus harbour.

It's late afternoon and the boat is traveling across the bay toward Poros, having cast off just minutes before from the quayside at Methana. It's passed through the strait between the northern Peloponnese and the furthest western tip of Poros island and now, dead ahead, Charles and Claire can see the white houses of the cone-shaped village which spills down to the harbour front. To their left is the coast of the largely uninhabited larger part of Poros, which is really almost two islands. The smaller part holds the village and waterfront, which doesn't need to be enclosed by a harbour wall, or mole, since it's protected by not simply the bay across which the Delfini Express is now traveling, but also by its proximity to the north coast of the Peloponnese, which is only metres away. Sitting directly across from the Poros harbour-front is the village of Galatas. Poros and Galatas stare at each other across a hundred metres or so of water like two boxers at the weigh-in.

The boat carves a wake through the centre of the deep blue of the bay like scissors half-cutting and half-tearing through crepe paper. It's engines power down and its speed reduces as the front at Poros

Island becomes close enough for Claire to see the expressions on the faces of people awaiting the boat's arrival. Some will come aboard and travel on, some will greet loved ones returning home and some will tout for business for their small pensions nearby. A line of inviting cafés, all with innumerable tables and chairs out front, one group seamlessly merging into the one next-door, sits just across the narrow harbour-side road from the quay. Looking up the side of the hill, Claire's eyes climb until they see the pretty clock tower that sits proudly above it all, holding court over all it surveys. The clock's hands show that it's around 4.45pm. The crewmembers are throwing ropes to the smartly dressed hands waiting on the quayside and they are now tying them securely to the huge iron bollards that are set into the concrete. Down goes the gangway and people begin to hurry ashore. Charles and Claire make their way downstairs, Charles grabbing the handles of their cases with each hand and they disembark among the melee, which is caused partly by those not patient enough to let the number of passengers who're disembarking dry to a trickle before attempting to board themselves.

Charles beckons to Claire, "This way, love. I've got directions. It's about a five minute walk."

Claire falls in behind her husband as they cross the triangular platia and enter the narrow street in the far corner, leaving the noise of the bustle to gradually abate behind them. They pass the Seven Brothers Taverna and the rear of the fish market. Soon the afternoon warmth and the muffled sounds that still reach their ears from the receding harbour induce a near anesthesia in Claire's mind. She's already entranced by the surroundings as they turn a sharp corner into an even narrower lane and then, after a few metres, turn right up some white steps. Having reached the top of the steps and once more begun walking almost on the level, Claire sees a small sign hanging from the wall of a house to her right. It's in Greek so she can't read it, but the two words painted on it are both very long. The street it so narrow at this point that she can touch both walls with her outstretched arms. A cat dozes on a nearby windowsill and she hears a dog bark from somewhere nearby. There's a small courtyard that they turn into beneath the sign and there, right on queue, since she'd been given warning by Charles of their approximate arrival time, sits Kyria Ioannou, on a small folding metal chair beside a table spread with a yellow flowery oilcloth. There is a tiny white china cup on the table beside her. It contains the dregs of an *Elliniko.*

Kyria Ioannou is in her late thirties and has black hair. She wears black, since she'd been cruelly widowed at a very young age, her husband having died in a freak accident whilst harvesting olives a few years previously. She has a young son and has turned the upstairs of her house into five 'village rooms' in order to make ends meet.

She rises, smiles and says, "*Kalos irthete* Mr. Charles. We meet at last. This [she looks from Charles to Claire] is your beautiful wife, Mrs. Claire, no?"

Charles nods in assent while Kyria Ioannou throws her arms around Claire in a genuine embrace and plants a kiss on both cheeks. She steps back, still holding Claire by the upper arms, looks her up and down and repeats: "Very beautiful. You are lucky man Mr. Charles."

Before they can be shown their accommodation upstairs, they have no choice but to sit in the shady courtyard with their host and take some refreshments after their journey. Kyria Ioannou disappears inside the house through a wooden door and soon re-emerges with a tray bearing a large glass jug, inside of which is a generous measure of her homemade lemonade. Just across the way, on the Peloponnesian mainland, just along the coast a while from the village of Galatas, is the locally renowned *lemonodassos*, the lemon forest, or lemon groves. No one around here is short of lemons. In fact, in most of Greece a home is not complete without at least one lemon tree anyway. Beside the jug on the tray are two glass tumblers containing several large ice cubes. There is also a plate of sliced lemon cake and some paper napkins.

Eventually, after having satisfied etiquette to the required degree, Charles asks that they be taken upstairs so that they can freshen up and settle in. Kyria Ioannou leads them up some narrow, tiled stairs to the first floor, where there are five plain wood-laminated doors, three to the left and two to the right. The central door on the left is apparently theirs and Claire spots a key hanging from the keyhole, with a small coloured plastic key-tag attached to the ring. Their host opens the door, enters the room and immediately beckons them to follow her inside. While Charles heaves one of the cases on to the shelf provided for precisely that purpose, Kyria Ioannou thrusts wide open the two narrow pale-blue-painted, louvred shutters that have been keeping most of the light (and hence the heat as well) out of the room, whilst also remaining open by a couple of inches on the latch designed for such a purpose, now securing them against the outside wall on either side.

Brilliant light floods the modestly sized room and Claire is drawn like a magnet to the French windows and hence the view they afford the occupants. Outside there is a narrow balcony, on which reside two plastic patio chairs and a round marble-topped table. There's just enough room for two people to sit out there with a drink and a book to enjoy the breathtaking view that spreads out before them. Immediately below are the terracotta tiles of the roofs of the buildings just down the hill a short way. Between those are the bougainvillea and vines that cling to the modest porticos that each house is blessed with. Under these can be seen a few tables, chairs, basil plants in olive oil tin plant-pots and other paraphernalia of people's balconies and courtyards. The view drops away to the waterfront, where one can glimpse between the buildings the passing pedestrians and vehicles making their way back and forth along the waterside. Evidence of the presence of some taverna tables right at the water's edge is also visible. Above this there is the narrow seaway that runs between the island and the Peloponnese, drawing the eyes further into the southern distance to the hillsides where the darker green betrays the location of the lemon groves. Looking to the right, one is impressed by the rising hills to the west and the "sleeping lady" mountain towering over the houses of Galatas. All in all, the view is enchanting and Claire is beguiled.

Once their genial host has left them to settle in, Charles speaks.

"I hope it's not too basic for you, sweetheart. It's not a five star hotel. It's just a village room. But I wanted us to be far away from the hordes. Alistair had warned me that it was basic, but I rather hoped you'd approve. And anyway, it seems a crime to come to a place like this and not to eat out each evening."

Claire was smiling as she looked back into the small room, at the plastic-covered metal-framed makeshift "wardrobe", at the two beds (both laid with crisp, clean white cotton sheets), between which was a small wooden bedside cabinet, on which was an ancient table lamp. She looked at the tiny sink and draining board, with its integral double electric hob, something that she found highly strange and couldn't imagine being allowed by law in the UK.

There was a drawer and a couple of cupboard doors in the sink unit and a small table under a wall mirror that served as a dressing table area. Extravagant it certainly wasn't.

"Charles, darling, it's perfect. What else, what more could I ask for? I have the perfect husband, the perfect view and I'm on a Greek island for three weeks." She takes the couple of steps needed to be right in front of him and slides her arms around his waist. He takes her in his arms and she buries her head in his chest.

Over the succeeding three weeks they live a kind of dream. They seek out a different taverna in which to eat each evening, occasionally choosing to return to one they'd enjoyed for a return visit. They walk for hours along the coast on the larger part of the island and swim naked in isolated bays, where they then lay entangled in eachother's limbs under the shade of the trees at the back of some tiny beach. They take tiny water taxis to Monastiri Beach and to Aliki Beach just along the coast from Galatas across the water and Claire extracts her watercolour pad from her rucksack, her glass jar of water and her paints and brushes and sits for hours capturing the Elysian scenes that confront them on a daily basis whilst Charles dozes under a small parasol that he'd invested in from a small tourist shop down the Mitropoleos, a steep, stepped street just below their room, lined with small businesses selling a cornucopia of items to tempt the browser.

With just two days remaining of their sojourn in this soporific place, Charles decides that this holiday has done what he'd hoped it would for his troubled wife's emotional and mental state. Over iced coffees in one of the *kafenions* near the quayside, he reaches for her hand and engages her eyes in a searching look. He hopes that Claire will understand what he's looking for in her soul.

She returns his look with intensity and tells him, "Charley, I've never had such a wonderful time in my entire life. This place is magic. I wish this could go on forever."

Charles smiles, but inside he tells himself, "Unfortunately, in the real world, it can't."

10. Claire, Alone, Wonders, June 15th 1990.

At two o'clock in the afternoon, Claire sips Earl Grey tea in the kitchen of a potential client in a country farmhouse near Wotton-Under-Edge. The weather for June this year is awful. There has been some sun this morning, but once again the clouds have seeped their way across the heavens and the shade of grey is darkening. The householder is a countrywoman who wants Claire to do a portrait of her two Great Danes, Bollinger and Chandon. Her children are at boarding school and her husband, a solicitor and a Freemason, is hardly ever home, so her two dogs are her main source of company during the week.

"I think that's acceptable," says the householder, in response to Claire's price for supplying the painting in question. It'll be oil on canvas and approximately 100 by 70 centimetres in size, portrait rather than landscape. Frame extra, but Claire has given her a price both with and without and the client, a Mrs. Brandonbury, has agreed that she'd like the frame included. Claire opens her folio and draws out an A4 catalogue of picture frames. She places it on the table for the customer to refer to.

"Do you have a family, if I may make so bold as to ask?" Enquires Mrs. Brandonbury, over the top of her half-glasses, which are kept from falling to the floor whenever she's not using them to read by a cord that runs from each arm around the back of her neck. Her part-grey, wavy, shoulder-length hair is kept from her face at this time by a red and white polka-dot cotton bandana, tied around her head from behind. Claire estimates that she's a fairly well preserved early fifties, maybe late forties. A pair of green wellies is parked just inside the barn door that leads outside to the flagged yard, beyond which is a garden that sweeps a long way down a gentle slope affording spectacular views over a verdant valley. There are woods too. Altogether, not a bad place to live.

Claire hesitates over her response, leading Mrs. Brandonbury to continue, "Oh, I'm so sorry. Have I asked the wrong thing? My husband's always telling me to engage brain before mouth. Do forgive me. I'd really rather…"

"It's fine, really. Thank you for your concern. I'm OK. I was nearly a mother once. I…" She doesn't now know whether she'll benefit from pouring out the story to this virtual stranger, but then thinks that it really rather may prove to be a little cathartic. "May I tell you the story? I know that it's really not anything that concerns you, but just maybe it'll help me to talk to someone. I haven't done so in a while."

Her hostess adopts an expression that quite clearly communicates the fact that she's all ears. After all, Mrs. Amanda Brandonbury is bored for 90% of her time. The local Parish Council isn't enough to keep her from going half-mad sometimes. In fact it's more the opposite. This might be just as cathartic for her too.

"I'm not going anywhere my dear, and it's only just after two. If you have the time then I most certainly do."

Claire begins. "Well, I got married in November 1981 and my husband, Charles, is everything I dreamed he would be. I know, I know. Sounds sugary, but it's true. I considered myself realistic when I got married; after all, I was already thirty years old and had lived a bit. Charles is slightly older. He'd have been thirty-two. One of the reasons we decided to marry was the fact that I wanted to start a family before it became too late and I wanted a real 'nuclear' family, with all the supposed security which that brings. You hear all these stories about hospitals calling you an 'old mother' if you have your first when you're in your thirties. How gross is that?

"Anyway, as I say, I thought that I was realistic and fully expected that our relationship would go through some degree of strain as we settled into married life. After two or three years I couldn't believe my luck, to be honest. Charles had a good upbringing, with stable parents, so I suppose that helped; but to be truthful, he's just a thoroughly wonderful man. He's considerate, loving, patient…" She stops, but then goes on, "…I know, I'm making him sound perfect, which he really isn't. But I suppose what I'm trying to say is that no one could have wished for a better husband. He's had a great deal to put up with in me, no exaggeration. As time passed, he didn't change. He didn't start taking me for granted, he stayed the same sweet man I'd fallen in love with.

"I've always been one of those who can't quite work out what it's all about. Does that make any sense to you, Mrs. Brandonbury?"

"Amanda will do now, if I might call you Claire too?"

"Agreed." Claire's face hints at a smile, a smile of gratitude. "Well, Amanda… Oh, I don't know. Perhaps you're already regretting this and would rather we changed the subject."

"Claire," Amanda reaches out a hand to lightly touch the back of Claire's, "Like I said, if you want to tell me your story, you go ahead. I'm hardly going to gossip to all your friends, since I don't know any of them anyway. My life's pretty formulaic to be honest. If it weren't for my dogs Bolly and Chand, I'd already be in the funny farm. My hub's a good man, but attentive he most certainly isn't. My children are good children, but they're already at that stage where the best thing about having a mum is that they can get their laundry done if they're home and there is a ready source of cash to be tapped when they need it. Interesting my life isn't, dear.

"More tea?"

"Oh, yes, please. All right, well I'll go on. But you must tell me if you've had enough. I can talk endlessly when I get going."

Her companion smiles and rises to go to the kitchen worktop, where a large china teapot sits, awaiting its opportunity to provide further liquid comfort. Amanda flips the kettle button to boil a little more water. She turns while waiting, leans against the top and folds her arms. Claire resumes.

"As I said, I've struggled for a long time with this whole existence thing. My brain feels sometimes like it'll explode the way it runs riot with my thoughts. So much doesn't make any sense to me. Rather than go on down that road, though, suffice it to say that it's the reason why we decided, correction, I decided, but Charles readily agreed, that I'd like to start a family. I suppose I thought that if I buried myself in the raising of a child, even children, at least for a decade or two, I could keep my mind off all the darkness, the emptiness, the doubt.

"Trouble is, nothing happened. From the day we got married until 1985, we didn't conceive. We went for all the tests; we spoke to all kinds of people 'in the know' as it were. The message that kept coming back was that sooner or later, we'd succeed and I'd fall pregnant."

The switch on the kettle gives a 'click' and Amanda turns to top up the pot. Claire stares around at the room. She looks out of the Dickensian window at the tiny spots on the small panes, which betray the fact that it's beginning to drizzle. Amanda says:

"I know. June, eh? Britain's wonderful in many ways, but you can't plan a barbecue too far in advance, that's for sure.

"So, …you said before that you were nearly a mother. What do you mean Claire? Did you miscarry?"

"I really don't know where to start with this. I'm not sure that you'll even believe me if I tell you what happened. It even feels slightly unreal to me now, after all, it's over four years…"

"It's up to you. But there's another cup of Earl Grey to get through yet, so it's OK with me."

Claire reflects for a moment; then decides that she'll tell this woman who, up until this morning, had been a total stranger, the story of how Charles encountered Marianna in the middle of Bristol back in July 1985. She says:

"I'll have to give you the entire story. If I don't then you'll definitely think I've made it all up."

An hour later, two empty bone china mugs sit on the table between the two women, Amanda Brandonbury still hasn't chosen a frame for the portrait of her two dogs, and Claire has related the entire story, right up until she and Charles watched Eric walk out of the house with the last of Marianna's possessions. She's even related about how Charles had to re-decorate the 'nursery' alone, as she couldn't bring herself to go into that room. She still can't.

"Tell you what," says Amanda, "I fancy a slightly stronger drink. How about you?"

"What do you have in mind?"

"What do you say to a G&T?"

"Pour away." Claire remains seated at the table, whilst Amanda retreats to another room and re-emerges carrying a bottle of Gordon's London Dry. She places it on the table, then lifts a lemon from the fruit basket in the middle of the table. She retreats to the area near the sink and sets about cutting a couple of slices and extracting a bottle of Schweppes Tonic from the fridge nearby. From the wall cupboard she pulls out two long, slim glasses. Claire watches all this before going on.

"So, what's your verdict? Were we completely and utterly stupid? Naïve, perhaps? Did Marianna take us in, thus providing herself with a nice, comfy place to live for the duration of her pregnancy? Ought we to have been a little more mature right from the start?"

"Claire, listen. You've told me, with a startling degree of honesty I might add, a tragic story. Well, tragic for you and your husband, certainly. The fact that I'd never come across such a story before is of no importance. I'd like to think that Bernard and I would have done the same, I really do. Fact is though; no one can say how they'd react, what they'd do in such a situation until it's thrust upon them. You and your husband displayed extraordinary human kindness in my opinion and, in answer to your question; questions, rather: No, from what you've told me I don't think that girl planned anything. There are too many aspects that wouldn't add up if that were true.

"Let's face it too, how old are you now? Thirty-nine, I'm guessing. Well, there's still a chance you'll catch. If not, well, sorry, I'm not an expert in all things philosophical, but you do have a great deal to still be thankful for. Sorry, no, that's not what you want to hear."

There's now a slim tumbler of gin and tonic on ice on the table in front of Claire, which she sips at through a straw, before responding,

"You're right. It's not what I want to hear, but it is what I need to hear. Perfect G&T by the way. No, Amanda, you ARE right. I have to get on with it. After all, millions have lived before me with no more idea about what the hell's going on than I have and they survived, they saw it through. Why can't I shut off all that other stuff from my conscious thought?"

"I'll take that one." Says Amanda Brandonbury, having picked up the catalogue of frames and flicked through it for a few moments. She thrusts the catalogue towards Claire, pointing to a plain washed oak frame, reproduced in colour on the page before them. Claire laughs. She looks at Amanda, their glances lock momentarily and they both collapse into fits of giggles.

"You've no idea how right that comment was at that moment!" declares Claire.

Two hours later, it's around 6.30pm and the afternoon's rapidly leeching into evening and Claire is back home in her studio, shuffling through some colour 6x4s of Amanda Brandonbury's dogs. Thank heaven for the one-hour photo service up the road from here, she's thinking. At least at this time of the year the sun's still way above the horizon at this hour, and it's even begun poking through the clouds again, a fact which Claire acknowledges thankfully.

The phone rings, clanging through the quiet of the house. She rises and crosses to the wall, where the extension hangs expectantly. She picks up the receiver and props it between ear and shoulder whilst still shuffling photos, searching for the best one to use as the basis for the painting of the two huge dogs. She speaks: "Claire Mason, what can I do for you?"

A voice enquires: "Mrs. Mason. I'm glad I've finally been able to track you down. My name is Clara Wilde and I'm a solicitor. I have some news for you, which is both tragic and potentially seismic in nature. I am sorry, but I would suggest that you sit down. I've been trying to track you down for most of the day.

"It would be better if we meet up fairly soon, but may I tell you the reason for my call?"

"Of course. You've got me baffled anyway. Fire away."

"Well, firstly, I'd be seeing you in person right now, were it not for the fact that I'm based in London and you, as I understand, are in Clifton, Bristol. Am I correct?"

"Yes, sure. Go on." Claire is now desperate to learn the reason for this unexpected call. What could a London solicitor be doing calling her, and at this hour too?"

"Mrs. Mason, I am in possession of a will left by a Mrs. Marianna Geesin, whom I presume you remember?"

Claire's mind races. It's the first time, apart from earlier this very day, when she'd talked with her client and new friend Amanda Brandonbury about the whole affair with Marianna, Eric and the baby, that she's even allowed herself to think about Marianna for some years. Now here is this voice, this disembodied voice talking about a will.

A will? That must mean, but, no, surely it can't. Marianna would only be about twenty-five now. Claire's legs go weak and she sits down on her stool, the one she keeps near her easel.

"Mrs. Mason, are you there?"

"What? Oh, yes, yes. But surely…"

"I should add that I am in possession of both the will of Mrs. Marianna Geesin, and that of her husband, Mr. Eric Geesin, of Croydon, South London. You may be very sorry to hear that Mr.

and Mrs. Geesin were involved in an accident on the South Circular recently, one that actually involved six private vehicles and a large lorry. I am sorry to say that both Mr. and Mrs. Geesin were killed in the accident. They were both certified deceased at the scene I'm afraid. I need..."

"WHAT? No NO. You must have it wrong. Surely there's a mistake. They're so young, they're, they're... They have a daughter, a young DAUGHTER. She's only four. Don't tell me..."

"Mrs. Mason. I understand how difficult this must be for you. For you and your husband. Is he present with you there?"

"Charles? NO. No, he's at work. He often doesn't come home until late. He called me lunchtime to tell me he'd be late tonight. This can't be. This can't be..."

"Mrs. Mason. Firstly, be assured that the young daughter to whom you refer is fine. She was rescued unscathed from the vehicle and is now in the care of the Social Services. This is really why I need to speak seriously with you and your husband. You see Mrs. Mason, both Mr. Eric and Mrs. Marianna Geesin stated explicitly in their individual wills that, should anything happen to both of them together, they would very much like - should the both of you be willing - that their daughter be entrusted to your care. Do you understand what I'm saying? I'm so sorry to be the bearer of such difficult news.

"Of course, you and your husband will need some time to digest this, then there will be a process to go through; but for the time being it was important that I get hold of you to give you this news. Let me give you my contact details..."

Claire is in shock. She's staring at the window and yet sees nothing except Marianna, sitting at her kitchen table crying, the two of them in the cinema stuffing themselves with popcorn. She sees

Marianna in the hospital bed just after she'd given birth. Images are swimming around and around and her head is full of voices, Marianna's as she says, "I think I shall take you up on your offer," she and the young expectant mother riffling through baby clothes and other paraphernalia in Lewis' department store, Eric's face as he turned around to look at both Claire and Charles when they arrived at the hospital so full of hope.

"Mrs. Mason. Are you all right?"

"Yes, well, in a relative sense. I don't know what to say, to think. It's so awful. They were so young. Are you quite sure..?"

"Quite sure Mrs. Mason, sad though the whole situation is." She continues to give Claire her contact details, which Claire scribbles on the pad on the wall next to the phone. It has a ballpoint pen hanging by a string nearby, so she doesn't have to move away from the phone.

After the solicitor has hung up, Claire remains where she is on the stool for an age. She can't move. She feels as though she is paralyzed. Her brain is in overdrive and her body shakes uncontrollably, as though shivering. After what to her seems like hours, but is in actuality only four or five minutes, she realizes that she must call Charles. She knows that she must do so, yet can't move. It's as if her body's been frozen in one position, apart from the trembling that is.

Finally, she is able to rise and go downstairs, where she pours herself a glass of Jameson's and sits on the sofa where there's a phone on the adjacent coffee table. She dials Charles' office number. It rings and rings for ages and she glances at the clock on the wall, which informs her that it's now gone seven and Charles is probably having a quiet drink with Alistair at their favourite wine bar. He only does this with any degree of regularity once a week on a Friday, or perhaps too on days when he knows that she's totally absorbed in a picture. Now and again he has business meetings with clients, or potential clients, which take place over a restaurant table, it goes with the territory. So, basically, she never worries if he's home late. Plus, he'd already called her earlier that day to warn her that tonight was one of those occasions.

She re-dials, this time trying his mobile telephone. He likes people to call him on the mobile. They're still quite rare in 1990 and as such a status symbol. Soon she's listening to the ringing tone, but once again, no answer.

A couple of miles away, downtown in Charles' office, the metallic trill of his mobile phone momentarily breaks the silence in the fading light around his office desk. He's forgotten it. He has a rather uncomfortable appointment quite late tonight and his mind was distracted when he left the office with Alistair. Tonight he'll hopefully get the Alan Evans affair out of his life for good. It's been bothering him for months, nay years now.

Sitting in the wine bar with Alistair, he says: "I need to call Claire" and opens his executive case. He curses the fact that his phone is not there and clips the case closed once more. "Where the devil did I leave that? Must be back at the office. I'll go back and get it later."

Alistair says, "Why not use the bar's phone?"

"It doesn't matter. Claire's got a new job on, which I'll bet a penny to a pound she'll have already started. She told me she was pretty confident that this woman was going to bite. She's already prepared a canvas so that betrays a certain confidence in her signing this woman up, if I'm any judge. Some lonely 'green welly brigade' wife from out in the sticks who wants her precious dogs immortalized on her chimneybreast. Those kinds are putty in

Claire's hands. She'll be OK. I'll call her when I get the phone."

Charles looks at their wine glasses and adds, "another one before we go?"

Claire can't settle. A cotton handkerchief wrapped around her fingers, she cries on the sofa as the light fades and wonders where Charles is. What will be his reaction to this sudden re-entry into their lives of Marianna, albeit posthumously? Posthumously! How can she use such a term to describe that young woman who was so recently full of youth and vitality? They say a pregnant woman is often in the bloom of health. Marianna certainly still has to be. How can she think about that dear young girl in the past tense?

She notices that she's thinking sympathetically about Marianna. Whereas up until this moment she'd never been able to shake off the view that perhaps in some way Marianna and Eric had staged the whole thing, however illogical it may have been, now she finds herself exhibiting only feelings of empathy and love. She lies down on her side on the Chesterfield, handkerchief still wrapped tightly around her right hand, which she now presses to her lips. her legs rise up and fold themselves at one end of the sofa, with her head at the other. Her eyes are still moist and her whisky glass is empty on the coffee table. She closes her eyes and allows herself to drift back along the timeline of her few months of happiness while Marianna was living with her and Charles. How could she really have allowed herself to believe that the girl wasn't genuine? They'd truly developed a bond that would have been lasting, had Eric not re-emerged from the woodwork like that.

In the cold light of this tragic development she realizes that it had been her way of facing the disappointment of losing the child. That was the real reason why she'd preferred to throw blame at Eric and

Marianna. It had no basis in fact, but it helped her make some sense of what she was going through after having been so sure that she was going to be a mother. The child would have been legally theirs, they would have been its parents. Birth mother or not, she would have cherished it and it would have always clung to her as its mother, her mother. 'It's not an "it", she thinks to herself, 'it's a "she". She's a girl and she might have been my girl.'

Despite feelings of deep chill, sadness and loss about what has happened, Claire senses a parallel feeling of hope once more springing up in her soul. What must this be telling her, this fact that both Eric and Marianna made wills in which they specifically expressed the desire that she and Charles take on the girl if anything ever happened to them? It has to tell her that, despite the fact that there had been no alternative but for them to bring up their own child, they both had felt a deep hurt inside over what the situation had done to Claire and Charles. It speaks volumes about the decency and love of those two young people. She finds herself warming to the thought that from the very start, the couple had entertained feelings of guilt, of responsibility, of regret about what she and Charles were going to go through, going home to a house that had a nursery already prepared, going home to face a future once again devoid of a child that they'd so quickly come to anticipate would be theirs to raise and cherish.

Why had she never heard from Marianna and Eric to let her and Charles know that this was their wish? There are all kinds of reasons, she tells herself. Perhaps one of them is simply that they'd only recently decided to make wills. Often people of their generation tend to think that such things are to be put off until later in life. Perhaps, too, they had found it difficult to find a way to approach the Masons, worrying about how they'd react to be hearing from them again after all that had passed between them. One thing is sure: she'll never be able to ask them. Eric and Marianna, dead. Snuffed out just like that. Did they suffer? Did they lie there twisted and broken in that vehicle for hours before losing consciousness? Claire now finds herself trying to push such thoughts away. She can't deal with such pain right now. She has to believe that at least they didn't suffer, that they were killed instantly. She didn't want to know, in case it was otherwise.

That poor mite of a girl. She's four years old and evidently without any close family. Claire knows already that Marianna didn't have anyone she could call close and such family as she has live way up north somewhere. Eric's parents, aren't they from Taunton, down that way she thinks? Are they aware of what's happened? Perhaps they wouldn't want to take on the child, or are not able to do so anyway.

Claire feels that she must talk to Charles. She needs his shoulder right now. She calls his mobile again. Still no answer.

Just at that moment Claire remembers. The solicitor forgot to tell her the child's name.

In the wine bar two old friends have run into Charles and Alistair rather unexpectedly. They've done a spur-of-the-moment thing and gone off to a pasta house to eat. Charles thinks that Claire won't mind. She's no doubt furiously mixing paint, sketching out with a charcoal pencil the shape of the two huge dogs that are going to earn her a tidy sum. She'll have put Suzanne Vega on the hi-fi and poured herself a glass of Pinot Noir and be quite happy to be alone while she works. She and Charles have such a trusting relationship that he really doesn't need to worry about her. She'll know that he's just staying out, something he does now and then. He has told her anyway that he may have a late appointment tonight, even though she may have expected him to come home for a few hours first. She doesn't know whom he's meeting or why, but then that's par for the course for his work anyway.

What she doesn't know, has no notion of whatsoever, is that she will never see her husband, her beloved Charles, alive again.

11. Two Callers and an Unfortunate Pedestrian.

It's early in the morning of Saturday June 16th at Bridewell Police station, Bristol. The hot steel urn is doing its usual morning job of supplying the staff just starting their early shift with hot, strong tea. Quite a few mugs, all with their distinctive advertising slogans or statements of how great a dad it is who drinks out of them, are gathered on the surface in close proximity. A carton of milk, which ought to have been placed back in the Station fridge, is there too, two thirds full and with its outer surface acquiring a mist from condensation, indicating the level of the milk inside.

"Bit of a drama in the gorge," says PC Trevor James. "Another bloke topping himself by the look of it. Some jogger saw something in the mud."

"Whether it is or not," replies Station Sergeant Frank Farrier, "the DI says you'd better get over there. Take WPC Batten. Time she learned about such things."

"Can I finish me tea first?"

The look the sarge returns him tells PC James that it's a 'no'. He reluctantly rises, grabs his mack and nods to the WPC as he walks out past the desk. His hot mug of tea stands untouched on his desk, steam rising, teasingly.

"CID prob'ly going to meet you there. Not sure yet quite what went on." Calls Farrier, as he watches the receding back of WPC Batten.

Claire is awoken by the sound of her front door being knocked with some degree of vigour. She comes around slowly, becoming aware that she's spent the entire night on the sofa. She hadn't switched on any lights; she hadn't closed any curtains. She'd simply worried herself to sleep after the phone call from the solicitor and the fact that she hadn't been able to talk to Charles.

Tap, tap, tap, the door goes again. She swings her feet on to the floor and rises. Still slightly groggy, she makes her way into the hallway calling as she walks, "COMING! HOLD ON!" It crosses Claire's mind that she's still alone. Charles didn't come home last night. What's going on?

She can already see through the opaque glass in the hardwood front door that there are two people the other side of the door and that they're wearing uniforms. Nothing makes any sense. She's still trying to clear her head when she opens the door. A policeman and a woman police constable are standing in the porchway.

"Good morning. PC Trevor James and this is my colleague WPC Batten. Are you Mrs. Mason?"

Alarm shooting through her mind like lighting bolts, Claire finds the presence of mind to answer.

"Yes, I am. What's this about? What's… Where's Charles?"

"Do you think we may go inside and sit down?"

"Of course, of course," replies Claire, stepping to one side for the two officers to enter. "That way, through there." She tells them, directing them to the lounge.

Once the three of them are seated, PC James starts again. "Mrs. Mason, I'm afraid we have some bad news. There has apparently been a tragic accident and we believe that your husband, Charles Ma..."

"NO NO NO NO NO NO!!!!" Cries Claire. "NOOOOO. Please, NO! You've got this wrong. You MUST BE WRONG!! I'll call my husb..." the WPC reaches a hand across to Claire's, she squeezes Claire's and says:

"Mrs. Mason, I'm afraid there can be no mistake. It looks like your husband died last night, apparently after falling from the Suspension Bridge. At present we aren't sure, but it appears to be have been a suicide. I'm so sorry. There really is no other way to break this to you." Trevor's a bit irked at how his colleague Jenny's handled that bit; but it's not the appropriate moment to chide her for cutting in. And the hand had helped, he has to admit. How he hates a fast learner. He adds,

"Mrs. Mason, for us to be absolutely sure as to the deceased's identity, we'll be asking you to come down to the morgue to formally identify him. We're terribly sorry to have to ask you to do this, but it is necessary. We can come back later today or maybe tomorrow and take you down, if that's OK?"

As though not having heard PC Trevor's words, Claire stares at the young policewoman in disbelief. Her mind is racing so fast that she fears it'll explode. First last night, the phone call from the solicitor about Marianna and Eric, and now this. What's happening? What's going on? This isn't right, it can't be. She must be still asleep. She's having a nightmare. It's all her fears piling up and throwing her mind into disarray.

Yet the two police officers still sit there, the WPC with her hand on Claire's, evident commiseration written across her face.

"Mrs. Mason, perhaps we should tell you what we know," continues Trevor James. WPC Batten interjects, "Would it be a good idea to have a drink? Point me at the kitchen and I'll be glad to rustle up a tea or coffee or something. Perhaps you'd like something stronger. We're not supposed to suggest that kind of thing, but we're only human. We really are very sorry Mrs. Mason." Now Trevor's really irritated. Wait 'til they get out of here. Damn girl's good though, that's the really annoying thing.

Without a word, Claire rises and shuffles into the kitchen, police constable Jenny Batten in tow. Once beside the kitchen table, Claire draws back a beech chair and sits. The young policewoman catches sight of the kettle, fills it under the tap over the sink and flips the switch on. She sits down across the table from Claire, who stares at her with a resigned expression that makes her feel that it's right to continue. Officer James follows and also sits at the kitchen table. He goes on, trying to add something to his voice that will tell the WPC to remember who's senior here:

"At dawn this morning a jogger was running along the Portway. He reported seeing something unusual in the uh, …in the mud, as the tide was still low and just rising at the time. He ran to the nearest phone box and dialled 999. The fire brigade were on the spot in eight minutes from the time of the call and they confirmed that it looked like a man's body on the mud bank. If they didn't act fast the tide would be rising to cover it. The firemen had to stretch ladders across the mud to retrieve the man, whom they hoped, however slimly, may still be alive. People have survived the fall from the bridge before, the mud being so …soft.

"Anyway, once they'd got him to the path on the roadside and inside the ambulance, which had arrived at almost the same moment, the paramedics confirmed that he was in fact deceased. Police also attended the scene, including a couple of CID officers. We have to try and establish exactly what made your husband fall Mrs. Mason. To all intents and purposes, it looked like a suicide. But we can take nothing for granted at this stage. His wallet confirmed his ID and it didn't take us long then to find out your address.

"Once again, we're so, so sorry to have to bring you this news Mrs. Mason."

The police explain to Claire that her husband's body has now been taken to the morgue, where she'll have to go to make a formal ID, and is under the care of the pathologists. They tell her, too, that a process has to ensue in such cases. There will be a post mortem to confirm cause and time of death, then an inquest. These things can run into weeks.

Before they leave, they rise; walk from the kitchen into the hallway and towards the front door. Once there, PC James, turns and asks, "Mrs. Mason. Please take your time, but think carefully. Was there any reason why someone would have anything against your husband? Or, did he perhaps show any signs or tendencies of late to indicate that he may have been unhappy, you know, depressed? You have that card we gave you. Please don't hesitate to call us if anything comes to mind."

And they're gone.

Claire stands in the hallway, then leans her back against the wall, her hands each gripping the opposite shoulder as if hugging herself to gain some comfort. She stares at the ceiling. The last few minutes of the visit from the two Police officers were just a blur. She'd hardly heard what they been saying. Now she can't get her mind to assimilate all that she's learned in the past twenty-four hours.

Three people dead. A young couple who'd oh so briefly passed through her life four years ago, now her darling husband, Charles. It can't be. It can't be. Surely Charles will come through that door in a moment, kiss her and squeeze her and suggest that they open a bottle of chilled white. He'll ask her about the visit with Mrs. Brandonbury yesterday and whether she had indeed started work on the commission last night. What the hell was he doing on the Suspension Bridge in the middle of the night? Exactly what kind of 'client' was it that he'd been meeting? He'd never ever given her any reason to be concerned about what he was up to when they weren't together. Why now, out of the blue, does he end up in the Avon mud? She shudders at the thought. Now all she can see is her husband falling, falling.

It's been her all along. She knows it has. All her angst about, well, ...about everything. She's been wearing him down and although he hasn't given anything away, he's had enough of it. That must be it. How many times in the past few years has she bothered to ask him how he's feeling? Can she now say that she honestly knows, ...knew how he felt about life, purpose, whatever else preoccupied his crazy wife continually? Will she now ever be able to forgive herself for this nightmarish outcome of her stupid, selfish neuroses? Her legs begin to buckle at the knees and she slides slowly down the wall. When she reaches the floor she falls forward, finally arranging herself in the foetus position on the hall carpet. There she sobs. She sobs uncontrollably and without hope. There is nothing. There is no reason to carry on. Come what may, she can't deal with anything in life any more. She moans like a banshee, but there's no one to hear.

These old houses are very good at preventing sounds travelling outside or through the walls.

The postman pushes some brown envelopes through the letterbox. They flutter and alight over Claire's back, like autumn leaves, fallen from their life source, dying all the while.

Several hours earlier, at not many minutes after midnight:

Following his successful encounter with the suited gentleman ('that fool who was so out of his depth, Charles Mason,' thinks the man in the overcoat), he walks briskly off of the Clifton Suspension Bridge and across the Downs toward Clifton "village". His car is parked somewhere near Whiteladies Road, a walk of some twenty minutes or so. So much the better. He couldn't risk anyone identifying his motor as having been anywhere in the vicinity on the night that this poor depressed businessman had 'taken his own life'.

Overcoat man thinks, 'Yea, '*Taken his own life.*' that's for sure what the Police, the numbskulls, will conclude. He recites over and over again under his breath the numbers that he is to deliver to his superior in the morning. Under no circumstances is he to commit them to writing. The Cayman Islands or something, he doesn't know and he doesn't care. All he knows is that he'll be receiving his customary executive case full of used notes (various denominations) under a café table within a day or two for another mission safely accomplished. There'll be more than enough to live very nicely on until the next phone call, with the next commission.

The drunk driver careers around the corner out of nowhere. His darkly coloured Jaguar, windscreen wipers moving rhythmically back and forth, mounts the pavement, sending a litter bin flying, as it clangs and bounces down the slope of the glistening road. Overcoat man just has time to turn around before the car strikes him full-body, sending him flying. When he hits the ground thirty feet away, a dark stain begins to spread across the road in the sodium light of the street lamps. The car hasn't stopped. Eventually a woman walking her Jack Russell up to the downs for its morning runabout discovers a stranger lying, not a bone of his body unbroken, according to the later coroner's report, dead, half on the road and half on the pavement. This happens at about the same time as PC Trevor James has to abandon his fresh mug of tea at the Station.

Unbeknown to Claire, the death of overcoat man means that the people who were expecting the return of a significant quantity of cash are never going to learn where it was resting. The only record of some very important numbers was in the mind of the man who was lying in the damp, Bristol street until dawn.

Claire is now a very wealthy widow.

PC Trevor stands and watches the paramedics loading the overcoated man's body into the ambulance. It's drizzling again. They've been sent to the scene shortly after having made the visit on Claire Mason.

"This is turning into a bit of an eventful day," he remarks to Jennifer, WPC Batten, who's mad at him for the way he'd had a go at her after they'd left the house up at Pembroke Road. "Come on girl, I did say you did good. It's just a matter of seniority, that's all. And I didn't chide you in front of that poor woman, now did I?

"You reckon this incident's got anything to do with the suicide? I mean, we don't know for sure that it *was* suicide yet, do we?"

"Nah, just some unfortunate bloke going home after his night out. Someone'll prob'ly spot the damage to the car that hit him and report it some time."

"There wont' be any human tissue or hair on the vehicle, though, will there? I mean, that's the trouble with winter. People are too wrapped up against the cold. 'Cept of course, it's bloody June. Never known it so cold at night as lately for June. I've had the heating on this week - in JUNE!"

"Yea, well, single girls haven't got anyone to warm 'em up have they? ...*Have* they?" This second comment is an awkward and fairly transparent attempt at prizing out of his colleague whether she has a current boyfriend. Trevor quite fancies his chances with her, truth be told. She looks up at him and rolls her eyes.

"I thought you were supposed to be married."

"No. That's where you're wrong. I'm separated and supposed to be divorced. Only it hasn't come through yet."

"That's all the info I need. I vowed when I got into this career that I wouldn't take up with anyone on the Force. They're all either married to the job, or bigamists, married both to the job and to another human, and the human gets the raw end of the deal in all cases."

Trevor's had enough of this conversation. "It'll be for the CID boys to decide that anyway."

"What? Whether being married to the job and a partner is classed as bigamy?"

"No, dope! Whether there's any connection between this and the Bridge faller. Come on, I'll buy you a sneaky coffee at Billy's before we go back."

It's over a week later, Monday June 25th, and a very fragile Claire sits at 10.30 in the morning with her husband's solicitor. She sips weak coffee from a cup and saucer and ignores the small biscuit that sits in the saucer. The previous Monday, the eighteenth, she'd been with the police to identify Charles' body, prior to which visit she'd hoped beyond hope that it was all some awful mistake. It wasn't. The police had told her that bridge staff hadn't seen anything, which was rather unusual, but people who are determined to jump sometimes choose a spot where they're least likely to be spotted before it's too late. There is no CCTV on the bridge.

"There are a few things that I need to appraise you of, Mrs. Mason, which you will probably find come as a bit of a shock. It's almost difficult to know where to begin."

Claire looks at the woman over the top of the cup. She's only in her early forties, but exudes a mumsy kind of vibe. Claire actually likes this. It makes her feel like the woman's a coper, that she's organized and focused and good at what she does. Of course, since Charles had dealt with her for most of his working life, Claire feels that her estimation of this woman is probably on the money.

Mrs. Mary Weaver, who specializes in dealing with wills, probate and estates, is forty-four and has three children. She likes gardening and going to flower shows. She watches *"Cheers"* and *"The Cosby Show"* and cooks Sunday roast every weekend for her husband and three children, all of whom are now in their teens. She holds down a demanding job and cares for a household. OK, so she does have a cleaner who comes in twice a week to do the house but, otherwise, she's a hands-on housewife. Her husband of twenty years loves classic cars and often goes to shows on weekends where petrol-heads peer under bonnets and discuss carburettors and the like. He runs a successful Ford dealership, which he's built up himself over two decades.

Mary can see that Claire isn't managing to deal with this whole thing very well. She decides to press on.

"Mrs. Mason, you'll be aware of course that every asset of your husband's passes to you. I have done as you asked and contacted the life insurance company and, since the policy is over ten years old, they've told me that they will indeed be paying out once the inquest is concluded. That sum amounts to more or less fifty thousand. Together with the fact that your husband had substantially healthy banks accounts with three high street banks, these points alone would ensure that you have no money worries for the foreseeable future. I know that's small compensation for your loss, but it's at least one less problem you have to deal with.

"If it helps at all Mrs. Mason, I knew and did business with Mr. Mason for a long time and had not only the utmost respect for him as a man of integrity, but also a great liking for him as a person. If I may offer an opinion, and do tell me to mind my own business if you want to, I shall never be convinced that he took his own life. So you really mustn't spend the rest of your life blaming yourself. I'm not even going to postulate as to what may have occurred, only to say that - were he to have made an enemy, however unwittingly, of the wrong kind of person - one of the best ways to deal with such matters and get away with it, would be to…

"I'm sorry. I ought not to be talking like this."

"No, it's all right Mrs. Weaver. I know you mean well and I know how much you've done for Charles over the years. He always spoke most highly of you and I shall continue to use your firm for all my legal requirements, rest assured. I'm afraid that, well, water under the bridge and that. The Police called by to tell me that they had absolutely nothing to indicate that he was, well, assisted in any way to fall. No joy from the bridge staff apparently, which they said was odd, but it has been known. So it's almost inevitable that the verdict at the inquest will be suicide. I…"

Claire can't go on. Her throat won't allow it. Mary Weaver

continues:

"Mrs. Mason. As you know, your husband kept some documents and some letters in a safety deposit box in one of the banks where he held an account. On your instructions I have been through the contents of the box and there is a rather large surprise, nay, conundrum, which arises. Inside that box Mrs. Mason, were details of several accounts in the Cayman Islands, wherein are deposited a sum in excess of one million Pounds Sterling. At present there is no indication as to where he may have procured such a large sum of money. Now, it could be that some appreciative benefactor or benefactors gave the cash to him as a gift. I understand that in his line of business, which I as far as I am aware and, I must say *believe,* he always conducted himself with the utmost diligence and attention to the law's requirements, some very large amounts of money change hands. Involved, as he was, with construction projects both at home and overseas that often involved housing, retail complexes, cinemas and the like, it's not rocket science to imagine how much capital would have been invested by some very wealthy companies and individuals. But I need to tell you that the authorities will have to be made aware of this money, if they aren't already. Should they find after investigation that there is no way of finding out quite where it came from and that nothing indicates any wrongdoing on your husband's part, then that money will be of course included in the estate, after death duties that is.

"Overseas investigations of this sort are extremely difficult. However that money came to be there, it's highly likely that nothing can be done about discovering what was behind it. If there is anyone who might lay claim to it, but perhaps would be rather anxious to remain 'under the radar' of the authorities, so to speak, then they'll probably have to write it off anyway. If they were to surface, they'd be apprehended right away and wouldn't remain free long enough to spend it.

"The fact remains, Mrs. Mason, that you will in all probability end up with enough capital behind you to live out the remainder of your life without worries. That is, without financial worries I mean."

Claire's eyes are now so open that they are in danger of popping out. She's trying to comprehend all of this, but not doing a very good job of it. 'Where are we now?' She asks herself inwardly, 'summer 1990. Just four years ago how different my life was. In February 1986 we thought that we were going to be parents. I was feeling so positive. I was painting regularly, Charles was really happy in his work and we both had Marianna to care for and indeed thank for what was looking like being a really fulfilling next two decades or so.

'Now, just four and a half years later, Marianna and Eric are dead. Charles is gone too. There's all this money, which I really don't want. There's a will that says that Charles and I could once again assume parental rights over that poor young orphan that Marianna and Eric left behind. But I don't have Charles any more. Where did all that cash come from? Did it have anything to do with Charles' death? He'd never let on to me that anything was wrong, or that he'd been involved in anything remotely shady. I know my Charles. He was straight as a dye. Either way it makes no difference. If it turns out that no one can ascertain where that cash came from, then it'll come to me. What do I want with all that? I'd rather be in a hovel and still with Charles. I'd rather he'd come home that night and that I'd been able to tell him all about the child and Marianna and the accident and… Oh, God!!!'

The solicitor waits a while, seeing that Claire is churning things over in her mind. Then continues:

"Mrs. Mason..."

"I want you to write to a solicitor in Croydon. Her name is Clara Wilde. I'll give you the address details, here." She riffles in her bag and draws out a fax. She'd received it from the Geesins' solicitor after they'd talked about the will in which she and Charles were named as preferred guardians of the little girl. She almost throws it across the desk at Mary Weaver. "Please write and tell her that, much though I appreciate the way in which the Geesins, those were her clients, ...though I appreciate the fact that they wanted Charles and I to assume care of their four year old daughter, following recent events I feel that I cannot accept the child. It pains me to say so, but I would be no fit parent now that I'm alone. The girl will do better with loving foster parents or something. I can't, I can't..." She tries to gather herself.

"Mrs. Weaver. I'm sure you can frame the words. The details you'll need are in that fax. I have to go now. Thank you."

Claire feels stifled. She's choking and can't breathe. Rising and shaking the solicitor's hand, she offers a half-smile and hurries out of the office. She arrives in the street outside and leans back against the wall. She is hyperventilating.

Where can she go from here?

12. Distractions.

We humans have a tendency to look for meaning in everything. It's how we cope with not understanding life. If there's no reason whatsoever for something happening, we find that deeply unsettling. We must have something to blame, or someone. It's innate.

For this reason, millions in the so-called "civilized" Western world like to suck the comfort blanket of fate when someone dies, someone wins a lot of money, perhaps just narrowly misses being run over by a bus, in fact just about every little thing that happens in daily life. If a person can say, "it was meant to be" then they can somehow remove the doubt, perhaps inject a little meaning into a predominantly meaningless existence. The centuries of religious brainwashing that have wafted across this world have left the vast majority of the populace with no real conviction about anything. Small wonder that the masses latched on to Darwin when they did, even though his theory doesn't hold with true scientific fact. But it's a better alternative for many than the fear of a divine being that plucks people from the earth capriciously to have them with him in heaven. A mother loses an infant, so her pastor assures her that "God has picked a little flower." 'Hmm,' thinks the woman, 'and with the other corner of his mouth the priest tells me that God is love?' Why too, if this God is love, are we to tremble at him, to worry all our lives that if we've been bad then he'll burn us for an eternity?

Claire is the result of centuries of religious and philosophical confusion and sits bewildered by everything. She feels deep down that logic says that there must be a designer. Too many things don't add up otherwise. How does the Monarch butterfly go on its three thousand mile pilgrimage every year from Canada to the exact same valley and exact same section of woodland in Mexico that its parents flew to the year before? Butterflies don't sit down over a nice cup of tea with a map and tell their kids where to go. How do tiny birds with brains that weigh less than an ounce do something similar, only over much larger distances? Why do we even feel love? Why do we build hospitals to care for the weak? If it's a question of survival of the fittest, then why not let the weak die off in the quest to build a stronger species, more able to survive? Why, in fact, isn't Adolf Hitler a hero, since he was simply a good evolutionist when you come down to it?

Claire feels like her mind is fighting to escape her skull. Where, or what is happiness? Perhaps it exists only for the dumb, those with such a simple mind that to eat, drink and reproduce is enough for them. For the first time in her life she understands the saying 'ignorance is bliss'.

The evening after she's been to see the solicitor, she prepares pasta, with pesto and sundried tomatoes. She lays two places at the table and places two plates of the steaming food in front of both her chair and Charles'. She pours two glasses of chilled Grenache and sits down, using a small lighter from the kitchen drawer to light a thick perfumed candle in the centre of the table as she does so. She sits down and stares at her plate, the fork and spoon beside it, the cotton napkin in the wooden ring, awaiting removal and placing on her lap. She can't move any more. She can't bring her self to pick up the cutlery. She finds herself willing Charles to walk into the room, she's fantasizing that he's been away and will do just as she wills, any moment. It's all been a nightmare, but she's about to wake up.

After about fifteen minutes, the telephone rings. She jumps up so quickly that she knocks the table and both glasses of wine tip over. Hers smashes, Charles' doesn't, but spills its wine across the waxed pine surface and rolls in a part-circle. She runs to the kitchen wall, grabs the receiver, thrusts it to her left ear and says, "Charles? Charles?"

"Umm, sorry. Claire? Is that you? It's Amanda Brandonbury. Only, as it's been about ten days now, I was just wondering how things are going with the portrait."

Claire is shocked into reality. "Oh, Amanda. Hi, I've... well, to be honest there's been... You don't know? There's been a... There's been a terrible..." She feels herself losing it again and can't frame any more words. Claire can't catch her breath. The caller at the other end cuts in:

"Claire? Are you all right? What's the matter dear? Has there been a problem? You do sound awfully upset. Tell me, please, tell me. Perhaps there's something I can do."

Claire summons her composure just a little, but it's enough to speak. "No, there really is nothing you can do Amanda. I, ...I don't know where to start, ...how to tell you this."

"My God, Claire! You do sound terrible, what on earth can have happened? Do tell me. I'm sure it can't be that bad."

Claire slides down the wall, leaving the telephone dangling. Amanda Brandonbury hears the receiver strike the wall, then only the faint sound of someone sobbing.

Wotton-Under-Edge is not more than half an hour from Clifton, give or take a little, depending on the traffic conditions. This evening it's fairly quiet, the main rush-hour having now subsided and the weather is calm and bright, if not as warm as it ought to be for the time of year. Since it's high summer there is still abundant sunlight streaming in through Amanda Brandonbury's kitchen window. Her husband, as always, isn't home. Her only company consists, as per usual, of her two Great Danes Bolly and Chandon. They lay stretched out near the Aga and stare up, wet eyed, at their mistress.

She replaces the telephone on its cradle at the corner of the kitchen worktop and stares at her two best friends. They return her gaze with apparent understanding. "You go," they say, "we're just fine here." She grabs her car keys from the hook near the kitchen door, shoves her feet into a couple of flat pumps, selected from the jumble of available footwear also near the door and marches out on to the gravel. Her 4x4 flashes its indicator lights and says "chock" in an electronic tone as she approaches it. Within a few more minutes she's off down the B4060 towards Wickwar and then Chipping Sodbury. Before much longer she's in suburbia and thumping the steering wheel at the umpteenth red light. She knows where Claire Mason lives. In fact she knows the whole area well and will have no problem finding Pembroke Road, just south of Clifton Downs.

Claire hears the front door. She wonders who it can be. After several more enthusiastic knocks, she rises and walks along the hallway. As it's late June it's still very light as it approaches 7.00pm. Claire slowly opens the door and seems confused to see Amanda Brandonbury standing in the porch. Her visitor instantly appraises the situation and marches into the house, sliding an arm around Claire's shoulder as she does so and guiding her back along the hallway to where she intuitively guesses she'll find the kitchen.

"Now, my girl, tell me what's the matter. Have you and your husband broken up? Is that it?"

"My husband is dead," answers Claire. Staring at Amanda's face, looking for a reaction. She gets it. Amanda Brandonbury's jaw drops and she's momentarily lost for words.

"What? Oh, I'm so sorry. How can this be? I mean…"

"Didn't you see the news? It's over a week ago now. He was found in the Avon Gorge, 245 feet below the Suspension Bridge. They say he killed himself. It's my fault."

The penny drops as Amanda recalls the story. She hadn't really paid that much attention to it, but does now recall something about a businessman falling from the bridge the weekend before last. She hadn't even dreamed for a moment of linking this story to her new artist friend, Claire Mason. She didn't even hear the man's name, as the sound was down on the TV that evening as she'd been talking to a fellow resident of Wotton at the time about the plans for this coming autumn's fruit and vegetable show.

"But," begins Amanda, "wasn't that the same evening after you'd been up to the house to discuss the painting of my dogs?"

Claire simply nods.

"Oh my God." Says Amanda, "How on earth must you be feeling you poor soul. I can't find words. Have you been here all alone since then?"

"I've spoken to my mother, but since my father's in the advanced stages of dementia she can't leave him for long, plus she doesn't drive anyway. I have a few friends, girls I was at college with years ago; they've telephoned, sent cards. I tell everyone I'm better left alone. I don't want to see anyone."

"Did your husband still have his parents? Haven't they been to see you?"

"They live in San Pedro de Alcantara. It's between Marbella and Estepona on the Costa del Sol. They're nearly seventy, the both of them. Dad-in-law can't fly any more, health problems. They've been out there ten years now. I haven't told them yet."

"My poor, poor dear. You do need someone to look out for you. You can't go through this on your own. I assume there will be an inquest? Were the police involved? What did they say?"

Claire, surprisingly, finds that she's glad to have Amanda's company. It's occupying her mind and enabling her to become articulate in her thoughts. She tells Amanda what the police have told her. Then continues,

"Alistair's been over a couple of times. He works with Charles. He's a brick. His wife's a sweetie too, but like I said, I've told people I want to be on my own. I haven't always answered the door, to be honest. You were lucky, Amanda, but …thanks for coming. You really shouldn't have, but I think I'm ready for some company."

Thus is it that a fast friendship begins that will last a long time.

On Tuesday July 17th, Claire sits across the desk from a pretty young girl in the travel agents at the top of Park Street.

In the past few weeks since Charles died, Amanda Brandonbury has proven to be a real friend and support. She's spoken to Alistair, Charles' business associate and he agreed to deal with Charles' parents, promising to inform them of the funeral arrangements as and when they were finalized; in fact, even choosing and dealing with the funeral directors on Claire's behalf. The Inquest had opened and very quickly closed with a verdict of "Death By Misadventure" owing to the fact that Charles had left no note and there were some doubts as to the certainty of whether it was a suicide. The Coroner had explained that, for a suicide verdict to be returned, there would need to be very clear evidence of this, owing to the possible financial, social and religious implications. In cases where there appeared to be no way of determining the exact circumstances, it had to be either an open verdict, or misadventure.

Alistair had explained to the Masons out on the Costa del Sol that Claire would talk to them as and when she felt she could deal with it, but they were quick to understand how she must be feeling and thus were prepared to be patient. They'd given their only son a good, balanced upbringing, though never had it been long on affection or tactility.

Amanda had checked in with Claire on an almost daily basis and even spent a few evenings with her, when they'd indulged in a few gin and tonics and the occasional bottle of wine, even drawing Claire into brief periods of warm recollection, during which she almost felt lighter momentarily. She'd been able to laugh at some of the things that she and Charles had done during their good times. One such event was when Charles had bought the Jensen. It was 1983 and the Jensen was a 1970 model FF, which had seen better days. He'd spent hours and hours out there in the garage with it, lovingly restoring it to its former glory and during the whole process she'd often threatened, though only half-heartedly, to leave him if he couldn't prove to her that he loved her more than the car. He'd told her that it was a close-run thing, but that she was probably going to prove marginally cheaper to run than the car, so in that case she was the winner.

Claire had also mused about her own childhood, telling Amanda about her times as a young child growing up in Tunbury, a small village strung out along one quiet country road on a ridge some seven miles outside of Bath. She'd vividly recalled where each of the other children in the village had lived and told Amanda about her best friend, Erica. She and Erica were at different schools, but she would often walk the three hundred yards or so to Erica's parents' bungalow on getting home on summer afternoons, then they'd play together before going in for their tea. One day, when Claire thought that she must have been about seven or eight, still sticks in her mind. She'd got off the school bus, run into the house, where her mother had made sure she'd changed out of her uniform, then skipped along the pavement in the quiet rural surroundings of the village, where everyone knew everyone else, to Erica's home. She couldn't work out why the front and back doors were both locked and evidently no one was home. Then it had struck her that, now and then, when her parents were both out for some reason when Erica got home from school, she'd go straight to her aunt Jenny's house, at the other end of the village.

Claire had felt a little happier on remembering this and so skipped her way back past her own home and a further five hundred yards or so up the gently sloping main road through the village, the B311-something or other (her dad would know), past a selection of chocolate-box homes and the village store to Erica's aunty Jenny's little two-up-two-down cottage with the roses each side of the front door.

Up until this point she hadn't noticed that what had started out as a fine afternoon was fast turning murky, as dark clouds had begun to gather above. When Erica's aunty had opened the front door it was to give Claire dismaying news.

"Oh, Claire my sweet, didn't she tell you? She had a dentist appointment and her mum's had to take her into Bath. She's not here I'm afraid."

This had left Claire feeling not only terribly lonely, but also at a loose end. After Erica's aunty had closed her front door, the rain spots had begun and there began a storm, with the first fingers of fork lightning illuminating the sky with their split-second brilliance that quite terrified the young Claire. As she'd begun running back down to her own home, the rains had very quickly become stair-rods and the thunder had boomed to such an extent that the young Claire was frightened out of her wits. It took her no more than five minutes to get back to the shelter of her own back door, but by that time she was hyperventilating with fear and soaked to the skin. Claire had never been out of doors before in a thunderstorm. She'd run the last hundred yards to home screaming and with tears flowing freely, though disguised by the rainwater that was falling with such ferocity on to her cheeks as to almost render her blind.

Her mother had opened the back door and thrown a towel around her child, but Claire was shivering and crying and there was no comforting her for at least an hour after that.

For the first time in Claire's life, she'd experienced unpredictability. Her stable little world had rocked just a little and it left her with an abiding unease that grew as the years passed.

Amanda had trodden carefully around the circumstances surrounding Charles' death, allowing Claire to set the agenda regarding what they conversed about most of the time. She really had demonstrated an extraordinary capacity for empathy and patience. And so it was that four and a half weeks after she'd lost Charles, Claire found herself aimlessly walking the streets and, almost without premeditation, she'd walked into the travel agents and taken the first empty seat across from one of the staff.

"Send me to Greece." says Claire, in response to the young woman's "Good morning, can I help you?" The young woman then replies, "OK, Greece. Do you have anywhere particular in mind, the mainland, an island perhaps? Hotel, apartment, village rooms?"

"I'll go anywhere except Poros. I can't go there. And I don't want a hotel. I want to stay somewhere where I can be left in peace. Sorry to sound strange about this."

"Not at all," replies the girl, warming to the task, "Will you be traveling alone, or with a partner perhaps, children maybe?"

Those last couple of phrases cut into Claire's heart like a knife. She thinks '*me*, have a partner, children? Life is determined not to allow me such things. I just need to get myself lost among a backdrop where I can find a little balm for my soul, at least for a while'.

"I'm travelling alone," replies Claire. She had discussed the possibility of Amanda coming too, but Amanda's schedule didn't allow her to depart at such short notice; a couple of Freemasons 'dos' to go to with her husband, then there was Parish Council business, that kind of thing. Plus who'd look after the dogs?

"OK. That's fine. There may be a single supplement, but let's see what I can find for you. When do you wish to travel?" asks the girl, making it quite evident that she knows her job only too well. 'How many times does she go through the same series of questions during one working day?' Claire asks herself. She replies:

"Right away, as soon as I can. My house in on the market and I don't want to be in it while people are shown around. Does that make any sense?" Amanda had helped her choose an estate agent. There's no way Claire is going to stay in that house now.

Whether it's intuition or not, the travel agent rep seems to catch on that something's not right with this poor woman. She makes the decision to simply press on with the job at hand. She taps away at her keyboard while studying the screen in front of her. It's convex and black with rudimentary coloured letters and numbers scrolling across it. State of the art travel agent software for 1990.

I've got village rooms or an apartment in Parga. Nice sea view. It's a quiet resort, quite pretty, very Greek, if you know what I mean. I'd suggest the village room if you're not too worried about luxury, because the apartment definitely carries a single-occupancy supplement. You could fly on Saturday, that's the twenty-first. Fortunately you can go from Bristol too. How does that sound?"

"Sounds perfect. Money's not a problem, but a village room sounds like exactly what I want anyway."

The young woman smiles to herself, owing to the fairly dismal weather this past few weeks, even though now, in July, things have begun looking up, with warmer days and much more sunshine, people aren't taking any chances. They want guaranteed sunshine for a week or two and so she's earning quite good commission right now. Claire sits quietly while the young woman taps away, then asks for her personal details, takes her credit card and seals the deal. It's Tuesday. Just three complete days to get through before Claire can look forward to the distraction of another Greek experience. Just for two weeks perhaps she'll be able to cope, to remain mentally able to function.

On Saturday evening the plane touches down at Preveza airport and shortly thereafter Claire sits alone in the back of a taxi for the several hours drive to Parga. She's told the reps at the airport that she wasn't going to go on the coach. They were very good about it and gave her the instructions for the taxi driver, who told her that he knows the rooms anyway.

Staring out of the taxi window at the Greek landscape of yellow soil, olive trees and bougainvillea-clad walls, of huge terracotta urns and small *kafenions*, their lights just beginning to come on, she tells herself, 'This is good. This is the kind of distraction I need.'

A couple of days pass by, during which Claire allows herself to be directed by the rhythm of the village around her. Antigoni Rooms are very near the front and within metres of the jetty that juts out into the bay whilst playing host to the succession of boats and craft that come and go incessantly. Claire can sit on her tiny balcony and observe in detail the petite island of Panagia out in the bay, which affords the town's seafront some shelter from the rougher seas of wintertime. To her right and towering above her is the headland on which sits a small *kastro* and which hides from view the huge beach known as Valtos on the other side. Looking out to sea and slightly to the right, towards the northwest, are the islands of Paxos and Anti Paxos, shimmering on a hazy horizon above a cobalt sea. She begins, now, after two days, to feel a little warmer inside. She's sliding into anesthesia and is glad of it. There is a small bakery not a stone's throw away and already she's visited it early in the morning, guided by the delicious aroma of baking bread, and made a mental resolve that she's going to do this every day from now on for the duration. She bought a couple of *Psoma'kia* and some *Kouloura'kia*, those delicious circular sesame seed covered bread rings that children often buy from street vendors while running to school in the early morning.

She's taken coffee once at a small *kafenion* where some old men apparently sit every day and put the world to rights over a game of dominoes or Backgammon. They sip their *Ellinikos* and fret, their left hands often tossing their *komboloi'a*, or worry beads, over the backs of their hands incessantly as their other hand hovers, perhaps a domino held between the first two fingers, while they tease their opponent about where they're going to place it.

Claire didn't know what to order when she first sat down. So she pointed to an old local's *Elliniko* and said she'd like to try one of those. It looked very much like an espresso and in fact there isn't a great deal of difference, or so she concluded, but she liked it.

She's already spent one afternoon on the beach, trying to read a book but failing abysmally. Her mind can't settle to concentrate on the words on the page. After having read the same paragraph more times than she can count, she gave up. She has a cassette Walkman, so she's tried to use Van Morrison to help distract her mind too, with not much more success than that which the book had brought her. She was doing OK until the player reached *"Have I Told You Lately"*, when she couldn't bear it any longer.

Charles had bought her the CD, which she'd transferred to cassette tape to play in her Walkman, on their eighth wedding anniversary in November last year, 1989. It wasn't long after they'd gone to Poros together. She was taken back in her mind to that evening when Charles had come home from work to find that she was up in the studio, zoned in on the piece she was working on at the time. She'd completely forgotten that it was their anniversary. Charles was always better at such things than she. He'd placed the CD in the player, selected that particular track and then come up the stairs with a huge bouquet of red roses and lightly knocked on the studio door. She'd flung it open, ready to tell him to leave her alone as he knew that when she was 'in the zone' he ought to know better, but then she'd seen the flowers. She'd smelt them, then looked at him and he'd simply nodded his head towards the stairs as if to say, "Just listen."

She'd listened as Van Morrison's voice drifted upstairs with the words,

"Have I told you lately that I love you?
Have I told you there's no one above you?
Fill my heart with gladness
Take away my sadness
Ease my troubles, that's what you do."

What could she do? Shout at her old romantic of a husband? She'd thrown herself into his arms, almost crushing the roses in the process, and cried. So here, on a Greek beach a world away from that time and place, she'd realized that it had been a mistake to try and play *"Avalon Sunset"*. The Sex Pistols might have been a better idea in the circumstances.

Now, though, on Tuesday July 24th, she's sitting on her balcony, newly purchased *Kouloura'kia* on the small round table before her, and she's making up her mind to go to that *kafenion* again, where she'll sit and see if anyone might engage her in conversation. She doesn't want to interact with fellow Brits, but she would welcome the distraction of a complete stranger, preferably a Greek - or Greeks, to try and get her mind back into that state of anesthesia again.

She rises and steps into the deeper shade of her modest little room, with its white walls, one of which bears a rather poorly framed sepia-toned photograph of the Parga seafront of the 1940's. She throws off her robe and steps into the tiny shower in the "en suite" in the corner. She showers quickly, emerges towelling herself dry and opens the small self-assembly wardrobe against the wall furthest from the bed and pulls out a knee-length cotton sundress. Once she's dressed she slips on a pair of flip-flops and exits the room, slips the key into her small shoulder bag, descends the marble stairs to the street, waves a courteous good morning to her host, *Kyria* Antigoni herself, who stands expectantly at the threshold of her modest little souvenir store, and strolls along the front toward the *kafenion* in search of another distraction.

After the proprietor has served Claire her *Elliniko*, along with a warm smile of recognition and a cool glass of water to accompany the coffee, he asks her:

"*Kyria*, is your first time in Greece?" He's a rotund, balding, jolly-faced man with bad teeth and a huge moustache. His hair, what little remains of it, is swept back, accentuating the fact that it's also receding at a rapid pace now he's turned sixty. He doesn't mind. He's brought up three children with his faithful wife of twenty-five years. One of his sons is doing his national service and the other is in Athens studying. His daughter is engaged to a local businessman ten years her senior, so to Athanasios all is right with the world. If a man has a good income, a good wife to warm his bed and a clutch of children to care for him in his coming dotage, what else is there?

"No," replies Claire, "I came to Greece last September. Not here though. We went to Poros. Do you know it?"

"Poro? Of course. My second cousin married a girl from Porou. I have been several times. It is very beautiful. Not as beautiful as Parga, though. You agree?"

"Well, they're both quite different. I couldn't make the comparison."

"Ah, you can go all over Greece, but you will never find another

Parga, kyria, …*kyria?*" Athanasios evidently wants to learn Claire's name. He is rewarded.

"Claire, Claire Mason, " she answers, extending a hand to shake his. He extends his also and she notes how clean he is. His crisp, white shirt impresses her. It says a lot about the man, she thinks, or perhaps, about his wife. He has a tattoo on his forearm, but she can't read it. It's something in Greek. He makes as if to beat a retreat (there are other customers taking their seats as they speak), but it strikes him that she'd said '*we* went to Poros' when he'd asked her if it was her first time in Greece. He turns back to her and asks,

"Your husband, he is with you? I don't see him yet."

Claire sits still and within seconds a tear begins to run down her cheek and she looks down to her lap. Kyrios Athanasios is mortified. He bends towards her, proffering a spotless white cotton handkerchief, and says, "Aach, I'm sorry. I say something wrong! I'm a complete *mala'kas*, you will forgive me *Kyria* Claire. My wife she always say, 'Thano, you're a buffoon! You always put your foot, you dolt!"

This can't help but make Claire smile. She dries her eyes with the proffered handkerchief, which she'd accepted with gratitude. Her host continues, "Kyria Claire, please, you wait here. I must hear your reason for to cry. I serve these people, but please you will stay, please."

Her affable host strolls away to enquire as to what his new arrivals would like to drink and Claire stares out from under the awning into the brilliant sunlight at the to-ings and fro-ings of Parga village and seafront. As she scans around from left to right she momentarily catches the eyes of one or two of the other customers, who consist mainly of Greek men of retirement age, and every time she does so they return her glance with a warm smile. One raises his tiny coffee cup to her before taking a small sip and returning his gaze to the Backgammon board on the table between him and his companion. She occasionally latches visually on to an individual, or a couple who may be walking along the road, or perhaps ambling around the harbour area. She finds herself musing about what kind of life each one is living. Do they have problems that resemble those which have afflicted her? They must do, yet most of them seem to cope, to deal with it in one way or another. Why can't she? There is, though, something about this place, this country, which eases her pain. Quite what it is she feels it's too early to put a finger on, but she knows that she'll be back in Greece many times in the coming years if she possibly can.

She sits in quiet contemplation for half an hour or so, unable to generate the resolve to do anything else. Athanasios is quite busy and so far hasn't had time to continue their little chat and she doesn't begrudge him that. He has a living to make after all. She finds herself ordering an Amstel, which her host places before her along with a small glass dish of mixed nuts. He's an old hand and knows from her demeanour that she's not liable to be leaving any time soon. He's also already decided that he's probably got a regular customer until she has to leave to fly back to the UK. This pleases him, but not simply because it's how he makes his business work and survive. Like many of his background and métier, he genuinely likes people and often finds himself caring for individuals to a degree. He has his regulars for this very reason, because his warmth shows through and there are those who, from the contingent of tourists who've found Parga to their liking, or perhaps are too scared to go somewhere else and not find that they like the location as much, come back to his *kafenion* year after year.

A smartly dressed man, who looks to Claire as though he's

probably a professional of some kind and possibly nearing retirement, walks in between the tables out front and sits down at the table beside Claire's, like her with his back to the establishment's front wall. He has wavy hair, which is naturally almost black, but the colour of which is now beginning to lose the battle with grey, especially around the temples. There are no signs, though, of his hair thinning at all, it's still an abundant mane, with one or two wisps skillfully arranged so as to tease his forehead in a manner that he, to Claire's way of thinking, believes excites women. He's OK looking, not handsome in the classic way, but Claire finds herself thinking of someone like the actor Liam Neeson, whom she'd seen in a movie about a Scottish man who turns to bare-knuckle fighting in order to make ends meet. As she recalls, the movie had unsettled her and she'd come out of the cinema wishing she hadn't seen it. But she had been rather taken by Neeson, although quite why she couldn't say.

She glances sideways in order to study her new table-neighbour better. She is grateful that her sunglasses have wrap-around lenses and very dark glass. She can keep her head pointing in one direction whilst her eyes point somewhere different. She feels fairly confident that he isn't too aware of being the object of her scrutiny. Not that she in any way is thinking of romance, relationships, or anything like that. She's just grateful for another distraction and finds herself wondering about this man. From the white cotton shirt to the navy chinos to the boat shoes, he oozes financial security. He can afford the best quality, a fact born out also by the watch on his left wrist, which is a Rolex if Claire's eyes don't deceive her.

"Can I help you?"

The voice cuts through Claire's reverie. The object of her careful scrutiny has spoken and allowed a half a minute to pass while she registers that he has, in fact, spoken to her. She feels her face filling up with a deep red blush and turns her head toward him.

The man is looking at her with the gentlest hint of a smile on his lips. He speaks again, "You know, you really only have to ask. I'll tell you anything you want to know."

Claire is so embarrassed that she wishes that she was anywhere but here at this moment. She'd become so absorbed in her curiosity about this man that it had become very obvious that she was studying him.

Athanasios arrives, smiles at Claire, then addresses the new arrival with the words,

"*Aaah, Kyrie Thanasse, pos eisai simera? Ola kala?*" It's immediately apparent to Claire that the two men know eachother. Mr. Thanassis answers, "*Mia hara, fi'le mou Athanasi'eh. Mia hara.*"

The conversation continues, Claire not understanding a single word, except that she deduces that Athanasia has asked the man whom she now knows is called Thanasse if he'll have his usual and the client has answered in the affirmative.

As Athanasios retreats inside to fulfill the man's drink order, Mr. Thanassis turns back to Claire and asks, "Are you alone? If so, would it be all right if I joined you. I can assure you," he extends both hands forward, palms down, in a gesture of assurance "I shall be on my very best behaviour. That is unless of course, you're waiting for someone, your husband or partner perhaps?" His voice betrays a North American brogue, quite where exactly Claire wouldn't know. She finds herself replying,

"I am a widow. I'm afraid I would wait for a very long time for my husband to join me now. He died recently." She tries to say this without sounding self-pitying. She succeeds to a degree, but Thanassis replies,

"Oh, no, really? Please do accept my very deepest sympathies;

what an awful thing to happen to someone as young as you. I am married too, although my wife is still in Toronto. I'm here visiting family. So I would be very deeply obliged if you were to allow me to try and lighten your mood slightly. I know that there would be nothing that I could do to remove your pain, but if you want to talk about it, or perhaps not, I am at a loose end and would be happy to be a sounding board."

She can't help herself. It's only 11.30am after all and she has all day. In fact, she has all of the next twelve days or so to fill. She nods and thus he rises, comes across and sits beside her, his body facing out toward the road and the sea, as does hers. Athanasios emerges, a tray balanced on his right hand laden with bottles and glasses and betrays surprise at seeing the two of them sitting together at the same table. He soon recovers, though, and places a long slim glass in front of Thanassis, the liquid within which is a sparkling, yet translucent red colour. As if reading Claire's mind, her new acquaintance says,

"Campari and soda, I'm afraid I'm rather addicted to it at the moment. Anyway, I think a formal introduction is called for, Thanassis Koutsob'oulos at your service. And before you ask, I'm from Toronto, but my family hails from Parga, which is why I visit often. I have, as you've probably already worked out, plenty of cousins, aunts and uncles, not to mention siblings here. I have spent my life running a chain of clothing stores in Canada, which I'm very pleased to say is now in the hands of my eldest son, Mike; although he's actually a Mihalis, but he hates to be called that. He's a Canadian through and through and has no interest in coming over here, much to my disappointment, although not my surprise. And that's really about it. My wife of thirty years is called Spiridoula, we love eachother dearly and, well, that's my life in a nutshell.

Interesting it isn't, but happy? I suppose one would say as happy as one can be, in the circumstances.

"Now, tell me about you. And once again, my deepest condolences."

"Claire Mason. I am English and this is only my second time in Greece, but I think I am rather growing to love the place. I came to Poros in September last year. It seems like a lifetime ago now, though. That was my first taste of Greece. My husband rather surprised me with the holiday, but it was just what I needed at the time. He died just over a month ago. I love, *loved* him very much. I think I drove him to it. I don't think I want to tell you more than that. Sorry to be rude, it's not meant to sound like that. I just don't know where to start, there's so much that's gone on."

"Mrs. Mason - Claire, firstly, may I say I am extremely pleased to meet you. And before we go any further, let me assure you that I am very happily married myself and have no desire to make you feel uncomfortable. It does seem to me, though, that you do rather need someone to talk to, or at least to distract you from your grief. I'm not suggesting for a moment that you shouldn't be grieving, of course, it's a natural process and must be allowed to run its course, I do believe that. But occasionally we need something to help us get a focus, to help us evaluate things. Life's a lottery it's true. But you can salvage something positive out of any situation, in my view. Call me naïve if you like, but that's how I look at it.

"Of course I haven't lost my partner, but I have had my share of tragedy. My brother died in an industrial accident when he was twenty-three and we lost a child many years ago. Everyone has his or her own tragedies to deal with and we ought not to compare one person's problems with another's, don't you agree? Whatever it is that you face is big enough for you and the same applies to me and everyone else on this unhappy planet of ours."

'This man seems to be talking some kind of sense' thinks Claire. For the first time in a while she allows herself a feeling of inner calm. 'Perhaps there *is* someone upstairs after all. But then, that can't be the explanation. In the time it's taken to start this conversation, probably a few hundred people have died in some war zone somewhere, or who knows how many children have died from hunger in some arid country elsewhere. For the Almighty to forget all those poor unfortunates simply to provide Claire Mason with a distraction from her grief would be asking rather a lot of the creator of all things,' she decides.

Yet she'll take what life offers and right now it's offering some soothing figurative Germolene for a nasty graze on her heart.

Since she hasn't yet replied, Thanassis continues, "So, only your second time in Greece. What do you make of us, we who proudly boast of having given the world democracy, even though we haven't always been that good at it ourselves?"

"So far I'm quite taken with you all," replies Claire, now allowing her mind to slip into the present moment, leaving all other thoughts to quietly tiptoe behind a cupboard door in the recesses of her conscious mind and close it behind them. "The people we met in Poros, and those few that I've met here this time, all seem to be friendly and welcoming. I can't quite get used to being so well treated by shopkeepers, restaurant owners and the like, I must say. Everyone seems to smile at me and treat me with the utmost respect. It's just not like that so often where I come from. Last year we stayed in a small village room, owned and run by a widow who was quite young. I couldn't get over how she'd keep presenting us with little gifts when we encountered her in her courtyard. Perhaps it was something she'd cooked, or even something as simple as a sprig of

Basil, or once or twice she'd invite us to sit down while she made us a drink and sat with us for half an hour or so. By the time we left I felt as though I'd known her for years. To be honest, if Charles hadn't, ...if my husband hadn't fallen..." she needs just a second or two to keep herself in check, but succeeding, goes on: "Anyway, if I wasn't going to find it too difficult to go back there so soon after losing my own husband, I'd have been drawn back there now. Seems that I'll have to go back some time because Mrs. Ioannou and I now have something in common, we're both relatively young widows. The only difference is that she has a son and I don't have any children."

Thanassis is nothing if not intuitive. He reads from the last comment that his new friend is somewhat disheartened over not having become a mother. He wonders whether it's wise, yet asks:

"And you would have liked them?"

Claire looks at him. In order to make eye contact she removes her sunglasses and places them on the table. She searches in his eyes for his intent and sees what she perceives as a really nice, caring person, with no hidden agenda.

"You know what I would like? In fact, what I really need?"

"I am sure you're about to tell me."

"I need a guide. I have the best part of two weeks still to spend in this enchanting place and I want someone who knows where to go and what to see to help me derive the maximum benefit from my stay here."

"Looks like you've found him, then," replies Thanassis.

13. Thanassis.

Claire is in no way looking for a new relationship. Her love for Charles still burns like an inferno and she is at that stage where to even think of a romantic relationship with anyone else would be tantamount to adultery. She is unaware now, at this time, that she'll remain in such a mind-set, or perhaps heart-set, for many years to come. This will be partly owing to the fact that she blames herself for her husband's death and, even though the primary reason for not seeking another relationship will continue to be the fact that she feels that no one will ever quite measure up to Charles, a powerful deterrent too is the fact that she fears that her own neuroses may well produce the same result in another possible mate. However ridiculous this notion may be, it's a thought that she cannot shake from the back of her mind. How often do we all find ourselves battling with feelings that we know don't make any sense, yet they persist in badgering us in those quiet moments.

So it is that she and Thanassis Koutso'boulos become fast friends quite quickly. They arrange to meet at eleven every morning in Athanasio's *kafenion* in order plan their day. Thanassis often doesn't arrive until twelve and when he does, can never understand at all why Claire is slightly irritated, though by the time the second week of Claire's stay arrives she's become used to it and realizes that it's a Greek thing.

Thanassis has the use of a car (that belongs to his cousin) for the duration of his stay. Stelios, the owner, rarely uses it, tethered as he is all day every day during the tourist season to his taverna at the back of the town. On one excursion Thanassis takes Claire up into the hinterland to the town of Ioannina, about an hour and a half's drive away. Claire is captivated at the opportunity to visit a working Greek town that's almost untouched by tourism. Thanassis seems to have an endless stream of facts and figures at his fingertips and explains to Claire that the population of Ioannina is somewhere just over 100,000. Claire can grasp this, as it's not dissimilar to the population of Bath, not many miles from where she was brought up. What really charms her is the fact that the town sits on the shores of a huge lake, the beauty of which quite takes her breath away. As they take a light lunch in the middle of the afternoon, with a view overlooking the lake, she interrupts him as he's telling her all about the fact that this area of Greece is famous for the quality of its feta cheese and its *baklava*.

"What is *baklava?*" Claire asks. Before her genial guide can reply, she adds, "Or rather, put that one on the back-burner, what I really want to know is, why is it that when a Greek says that he'll meet you at eleven o'clock, he doesn't seem to see anything wrong with arriving anything up to an hour late?"

Thanassis can tell from her tone of voice that Claire is only lightly chiding him. She is very intelligent and he works out quickly that she's coming to understand a few things about Greek culture quite quickly. She genuinely wants to get into the Greek psyche, since the people and culture evidently have an appeal for her and if anything, she just needs anything to keep her mind off of the fact that she's lost Charles.

"Where do I start?" he asks, not really expecting a reply. Claire knows this and so waits, content to gaze at the amazing view of the lake and its island a little further out. "It has something to do with the climate I suppose. When you get several months every summer of very high temperatures and endless blue skies, you tend not to want to do anything in a hurry. Over the centuries this has translated into a way of measuring time here. For example, if you ask a Greek what time it is, he or she will probably say it's - I don't know - say three o'clock, when it may well be either ten minutes to or ten past, but three o'clock is close enough. I think in Canada it's rather like the UK, isn't it? If someone asks you the time you'll say, after probably glancing at your watch, that it's almost ten past three, or perhaps twenty-five past six. A Greek more often will simply round it to the nearest half an hour. Even on radio stations here you'll hear an announcer say, 'it's two o'clock' and you'll glance at your clock or watch and see that it's three minutes to or as many minutes past the hour.

"I suppose we Greeks don't see why there must be this preoccupation with the exact minute. Who cares? It's too hot most of the time to rush anyway, so do what you have to do as and when you can summon the energy to do it. I understand that it's difficult for someone from a temperate climate to grasp this, after all, I've lived in Canada for most of my life but, here's another thing you have to get used to in Greece.

"Say, for example, you've asked a tradesman to call to fix something in the house. It could be someone you know really well and, in fact, in the villages that's sure to be the case. He'll say 'I'll be there at nine o'clock the day after tomorrow.' 'OK,' you reply and on the morning in question you'll await his arrival. Probably by about half past eleven you'll call him and say, assuming you can get an answer that is, 'I thought you were coming at nine o'clock.'

"He'll probably say, 'I'll be there soon, just had to do something else,' or maybe 'just had to take my mother to the doctor', I don't know. When he finally arrives two days late and in the afternoon, he'll be mystified if you're all angry about it. His genuine response will be, 'what's the problem? I came didn't I?'

"That's the Greek psyche for you. One does whatever one has to do, or perhaps whatever comes up and requires doing, without all that much heed being paid to schedules or appointments. If it's swelteringly hot it'll always be done at a very slow pace too. The Greeks aren't lazy, never think that, they're just very, very laid back about life."

"Well, they're certainly a friendly lot, from my limited experience I can vouch for that. They seem by and large to take everything in life in their ambling kind of stride. In the UK we're always rushing around everywhere. We rush our work, our food, we rush our shopping, we rush our recreation and we rush to visit family and friends. Everyone is ruled by their watch in Britain. My husband says, 'To go out without wearing one is to go out naked.' Sorry, I meant to say 'he said'."

She swallows and her eyes become watery. Thanassis starts a little, leaning forward, wondering 'will she start to cry?'

"I'm OK, don't worry. Being here and so far from my real life helps me to place everything in a kind of movie that I'm not watching at the moment, it's like I've clicked the pause button.

"Do you dance, Thanassi?"

"Every Greek dances, Claire. It's endemic in our upbringing. There are so many festivals and celebrations in our calendar that all the children grow up dancing from almost as soon as they can walk. The ex-pat community in Toronto, much like all Greek communities the world over, keeps to such traditions religiously. Everywhere you go in the world you find Greeks, as I'm sure you'll know. Did you also know that the vast majority of them are all living for the day when they can come home to Greece for good? They're not, by and large, living in the UK, America, Canada, Australia or wherever else because they want to be there. Greeks are fiercely proud and fond of their homeland. Do you know why so many are found in so many far-flung corners of the world?

"You've got me there. I have to confess to my ignorance of such matters. It's just something I've accepted without much thought. I suppose I would say it's something to do with the fact that Greece is a maritime nation."

"The primary reason in this century is the Second World War and what happened immediately afterwards. You do know that much of Greece was ruled by the Italians leading up to the war, yes?"

"Um, well, I can't say I was particularly conscious of it, no. Am I very stupid?"

"Of course not. Why would you know unless you'd studied Modern Greek history at school or college? Greece was occupied by the Crusader Knights during the late middle ages, then by the Ottomans all the way down into the nineteenth century. In the 1820's Greece finally achieved some measure of independence, but only for the mainland and the Cyclades Islands. The Turks ruled much of the country, especially the islands like Crete for example.

There were frequent insurrections, all of them put down by the occupiers. A lot of blood was shed during that time.

"The Aegean islands came under the Italians for the early part of the twentieth century, then the Germans, who also occupied the mainland and Athens, the capital. When the war ended the British were here, but they didn't do much to stop the bloody civil war that erupted as the world war ended. They stood here and watched, occasionally making diplomatic noises. Many thought that they were simply waiting to see which side would get the upper hand. Even before that civil war thousands were dying in Athens of starvation. There's not much point going into all that now, but suffice it to say that there was a huge exodus of Greeks after the war owing to the bloody fighting and abject poverty that afflicted the whole country. They went abroad in order to survive, but always dreamed that they'd come back some day to live out their dotage in what they hoped would be a more prosperous and peaceful homeland than that from which they'd fled.

"I'm sure that I'm boring you now. Would you like another drink?"

"No and yes. No you're not boring me. I feel I want to drink in all that I can about this country. I'm woefully ignorant about it. It's suffered and bled in a literal and symbolic way for centuries by the sound of it. Yes, I would like some more Retsina please."

Thanassis orders another jug of locally made resin wine and Claire continues: "I asked you if you danced and that opened the floodgates!" She is smiling and he knows that she is glad to have heard what he had to tell her. "I asked because when I visited Poros last year with my husband, we watched some local boys dancing several times. There was this outdoor club at the end of the bay where they'd play European and American music for half an hour at a time, interspersed with half an hour of Greek music and I was amazed by the fact that the tourists would clear the floor once the Greek music began and the local boys would get up, probably twenty of them at a time, and they'd dance these wonderful dances, sometimes with the leading man connected to the rest of the line by a white handkerchief and turning somersaults, sometimes not. Sometimes they'd gather in a circle around one person, all clapping in time as he'd whirl and jump and all kinds of other things, but always there seemed to me to be a passion and a fervour born of something in these people that we don't seem to have where I come from any more. Could it be anything to do with the fact that Greece as a whole has still so recently become one nation again? One thing I do know is that many of the islands were only made part of Greece again in the late 1940's, right? When I heard that I was shocked. I couldn't believe that I'd been so ignorant."

"Well, Claire, now you're touching on what makes this land tick."

She is so absorbed in this conversation that she has, for a brief moment anyway, pushed her pain to the back of her mind. Unconsciously, she's absorbing the anaesthetic that she'd been seeking when she came here.

"You have recently been bereaved. Sorry, I don't want to remind you and I don't want you to feel sad. But you, Claire, of all people, if you can learn from your adversity, will understand much about this country owing to your own experience. Do you see what I'm saying?"

Claire looks at Thanassi, takes a sip from her newly charged glass of Retsina and shakes her head slightly, a look of puzzlement drifting across her face.

"Claire, in the short time that we've known eachother, I deduce that you're having trouble coming to terms with what's happened to you and that's entirely understandable. You haven't told me much except that you very recently lost your husband and you loved him deeply. I suspect that you've had other trials to bear from small indications you've given me, probably quite unknowingly. But look at this nation, its culture and its people. You know why they're so laid back, why they're so generous hearted, why they're so philosophical about everything?

"They've endured centuries of occupation by successive powers, oppression and bloodshed, yet through it all they've come through with their language and culture intact. They've a stoicism born of endurance and gritty pragmatism.

"That, Claire my dear friend - and I shall from this moment on always call you that - is what you must learn. The Greeks are survivors, even under the worst circumstances. When you learn that, you'll come through with flying colours."

Claire stares at this man and wonders how on earth she could have come from just days ago wandering the streets of Bristol, trying to come to terms with suddenly being alone in life, trying to restrain her mind from totally letting go of all reason, not being able to see past the next few hours, leave alone days or months, to sitting here, in the middle of a country thousands of miles from home, with a man she's only known for about a week, yet feeling like she's learning all about life over again.

'But,' she muses to herself, 'I don't think I ever really learned about life before now anyway. I've just been muddling through, hoping that one day it would all make some kind of sense. Maybe that's what I ought to do, to précis Thanassi's word as I see it, grin and bear it, perhaps?'

All too soon it's Friday August 3rd and Claire is to fly home tomorrow. She'll fly back to the real world, to that movie she'd been watching yet had placed on 'pause'. She feels herself sinking under a creeping dread of being back in the real world. For the past two weeks she's been mentally anaesthetized and has been able to keep herself occupied with her guided excursions courtesy of Thanassi, who's proven to be the perfect gentlemen throughout. He made it clear at the outset that Claire was providing him with a useful way to pass the time, whilst he knew that he was helping her endure a tough period in her life. He'd gone to great pains to convince her that he had no intentions other than friendship and she is now satisfied that he meant what he'd said. Mr. Athanasios at the *kafenion* has also become quite fond of this melancholy English woman and had several times refused payment for her drink or drinks, much to her chagrin, as she really wanted him to accept her money. She finds herself almost dreading the wrench that she would feel when she departs tomorrow.

Athanasio's wife too, *Kyria* Spiridoula, a bountifully proportioned woman who seemed always to be fixing snacks and drinks at the back of the bar and saying *"Doxa to theo"* at every opportunity, had taken the time to attempt a conversation with Claire on several occasions, usually all the while stroking Claire's head and saying *"sillipityr'ia pedi mou"* a lot [condolences, or commiserations my child]. She assured Claire that God would protect her and guide her and that everything would be all right some day, see if it wouldn't. Whilst Claire doesn't share *Kyria* Spiridoula's simple yet immovable faith, she does appreciate the sentiments nonetheless.

She's been to several tavernas for her evening meal, one or two having been recommended by her landlady, *Kyria* Antigoni, and one the establishment run by Thanassi's cousin Niko, where she found herself being told that she was dining on the house, since she was a friend of Thanassi. Nikos had finished the evening once or twice by flopping himself down in the chair beside Claire at her modest little check-tableclothed table, lighting up a Marlboro' and clinking his glass of Metaxa with hers. Claire had been drinking in all the new experiences that she'd been having as the days passed until today and has come to the conclusion that she will come back to Greece at every opportunity. It may well prove to be the only place where she can find rest for her mind and heart, albeit temporarily.

Nikos had given off the vibes that he probably fancies Claire, but had comported himself with respect at all times, a fact for which she's very grateful. He is a handsome man, somewhat younger that his cousin, and not yet married. Claire would put him at about forty, perhaps slightly more, with a still black mane of wavy hair and deep-set eyes under dark, strong eyebrows. He puts her in mind a little of the actor Omar Sharif. In another life she may well have been beguiled, but not this one. Charles is so real to her that she still smells his cologne, hears his voice, can feel his face when he needs a shave, feels herself lying in his arms in their bed, all cozy and protected from her fears.

Yet, after two weeks of almost feeling calm and able to cope, she's becoming more and more aware that tomorrow she'll be back in Pembroke Road. The Jensen (which the AA had brought back to the house when the Police had found where it was parked) will be sitting there on the drive as she enters the garden gate. Charles' clothes are still going to be in the wardrobe. There are even some in the laundry basket, which she hasn't been able to touch for a couple of weeks. There are beers still in the refrigerator, Becks mainly. Claire doesn't drink Becks but it's one of Charles' favourites and he always likes, *liked*, to have some in.

His bedside cabinet will still be there. The book he was reading is still on the top beside the lamp and Charles' alarm clock is still sitting there too. The book is by a new author, an American called John Grisham. *A Time to Kill* it's called. Claire finds herself playing with the title in her mind as she packs her suitcase. "*Time to Kill*" would better describe her life now. She is still and always will be unaware of the fact that her husband was the victim of someone who'd decided that for them it was a time to kill. Charles Mason had been the victim.

As she closes the suitcase, she feels the day ebbing away as the light in the room begins to fade. She's going out to eat one more time before she comes back to her room, sleeps a short night and then takes her pre-arranged taxi back to the airport for the flight home.

Next day, as she walks up the steps to the aeroplane's door, the bright Greek sunlight bathing her in its heat, she resolves that she'll be back here, in this country, as soon as she is able. It feels after such a short time more like home to her than anywhere else on the planet now, after all that's happened to her.

14. Claire Moves.

At 11.30am on Friday August 17th, 1990, Richard Parry, the man from the estate agent that Alistair had engaged to sell the house, calls Claire, who's busy ramming things wrapped in newspaper into large cardboard boxes.

She hasn't touched any of Charles' things, since she still can't bring herself to face the fact that he won't be back to use them himself. It's two months and two days since Charles died and, for Claire, it's still an unbearable thought that he's not ever coming back. She gets through the days by willfully telling herself that he's away on a work assignment. Yet still, she must be acknowledging the facts to some degree, because she's got the house on the market and wants to get out of here as soon as she can. She's already found a Georgian house, a terraced affair just off of Whiteladies Road with what was once a shop-front on the ground floor. The idea is that, as and when she can bring herself to paint again, she'll convert the ground floor into a gallery, although the way she's feeling at the moment, it'll not be for a long time yet. She did manage to complete the portrait of Amanda Brandonbury's two huge dogs. It was a struggle, but she felt she owed it to Amanda, who's now become a good friend. They talk several times a week and Amanda insists that Claire come out at least once every week to drink coffee in a coffee bar downtown. "You mustn't sit there on your own and stew," she says. She really worries about Claire and Claire is grateful. In fact when she drove in her newly purchased Rover 200 up to Amanda's house in Wotton to deliver the canvas, replete in its frame and looking quite perfect for Amanda's chimney breast, which had been cleared of its previous inhabitant (a print of a generic winter scene), she insisted that it was a gift and wouldn't accept payment for it. She told Amanda that it was most probably the last work she'd be producing for quite some time.

Here, in Claire's studio, where she's been gathering what belongings she decides that she still wants to keep, which don't amount to all that many, furniture aside, she's taping up boxes in anticipation for her moving out of this house. This house that was once the warm love nest for two people who would face the world side by side and stare it out. Two people who'd almost tasted the happiness of being parents and raising a child before having that prospect snatched away from them at the eleventh hour, which in itself almost drove Claire off the rails.

'Where is that child now?' Claire wonders. She sips lukewarm coffee from a large mug and pictures Marianna in her mind's eye. All those delirious months of happiness as the child was growing in that girl's womb. All the cinema visits and late nights talking on the sofa with the TV burning silently across the room from them, ignored. The laughs as they sorted through the racks in clothes stores day after day or made the beds together, all the while growing closer and closer.

It was March 1986 when Eric Geesin had shattered their dreams and plans by turning up quite out of the blue at Marianna's bedside in the hospital. Now, here she is a little over four years later without her soul-mate Charles too. Marianna, Eric and Charles all dead. That poor four year old girl that Claire might, had things turned out differently, have been calling her daughter, where is she? Will she be in a good home? Is she still in care or may she perhaps end up in childrens' homes until she has to make her own way in the world. Will the experience make her into a misfit, someone who can't fit into this world and ends up a drug addict, a street beggar? The chance of having a balanced, secure upbringing was stolen from her by a moment's distraction on a motorway. Claire imagines again the mangled wrecks in the cold, damp, grey mist on the carriageway of the South Circular near London. Did the child see her own breath as she cried and sat in the wreckage behind her two lifeless parents awaiting discovery by the rescue services? Does she understand what's happened to her? 'Ought I' thinks Claire, 'to have accepted the responsibility, despite losing Charles, of bringing that child here and raising her alone? If she ends up with a poor, even a deprived childhood, it'll be because of me, it'll be my fault. Just like I drove Charles, with all my petty fears and neuroses, to go up to the bridge late that June night. Did I drive you to it Charles? Can't you just come back one more time to tell me what happened? Don't you realize what torture it is, the not knowing?'

Just as Claire is in danger of imploding again, she hears the urgent electronic clanging of the phone on the wall and turns to look at it. With great effort she rises from her knees, puts down her packing tape dispenser and crosses to the phone and lifts the receiver.

"Mrs. Mason?" Claire isn't sure who it is. Alistair had spoken to this man more times than she had up until now.

"Yes, can I help you?"

"Richard Parry, Clifton Property Partnership, I'm calling to tell you that you have received an offer on your house; a couple who viewed while you were away in Greece a couple of weeks ago. They didn't put in their offer before because they were awaiting a firm offer on their property, but they now have one and so want very much to buy Pembroke Road."

Claire feels her heart flutter. She so desperately wants to get this all sorted and behind her as soon as possible. The estate agent tells her that the offer is for the asking price, since the couple are so keen on her house and don't want to lose it. Claire can't believe it, but replies,

"Well, you'd better tell them that I accept then."

"Good, good. I hoped you'd say that Mrs. Mason. I shall get back to them right away and hopefully we'll put the wheels in motion."

When she's replaced the receiver, Claire calls the agent where she's seen the house she wants and puts her own offer in, after she's been told that the property is still available.

Claire sits in her mother's kitchen. She's looking down at the bone china cup and saucer on the red Formica tabletop and the side plate with a piece of Battenberg cake sitting sweetly and unappetizingly in the centre. There is a stainless steel knife lying across the plate beside the cake and a paper serviette with a blue flowery motif folded into a triangle beside it. Claire picks up the spoon from her saucer and absentmindedly stirs her tea. Her mother makes a good cup of tea, it has to be admitted. Always makes sure that she warms the pot, pouring a little boiling water into it before emptying it down the sink, spooning loose Brook Bond PG Tips into it and then refilling the pot with more boiling water from the kettle. She's just popped into the sitting room to see to Gordon, whose dementia has become more evident in recent years. He's now seventy-two and not in bad physical shape really. He does have a slight stomach, but not what you'd call a pot. It's just that he spends the majority of his time back in the Second World War these days, in his mind that is.

Marjory Barrett, who's been married to her husband for over forty years now, makes it her life's vocation to care for and protect her husband, her senior by nine years. He's been a good, no, an excellent husband and she wants him to be happy to the extent that's possible for as long as he can.

Claire is irritated by the fact that she's lost count of how many times she's told her mother that she doesn't like sweet things like packaged cakes bought from the supermarket. She's tried to explain that nutritionally they're non-starters and full of preservatives and sugar as well. Her mum persists, though, in the delusion that Claire simply denies herself these 'treats' in order to watch her weight. She resolves to have one bite and one bite only, just to show appreciation for the thought, but that she won't eat any more of it. Her mum's not going to allow herself to be educated at this stage in her life. At least for the most part of it Gordon was a gardener and regularly laid on the kitchen table vegetables and fruit that he'd grown himself. All that fresh produce must have compensated for the rubbish to some degree.

'It's all to do with the war,' Claire thinks to herself. 'Everything was wholemeal and basic fruit and vegetables were the staple then. Once the fifties arrived it was viewed as a luxury to have refined flour and lots of white sugar and a plethora of new culinary packaged 'creations' came on the market that now, decades later, are responsible for tooth decay, obesity and diabetes; goodness knows what else besides. My mum's generation can't seem to get out of that mindset.' Claire is still musing about the jolly-rolls and obscenely sweet packaged apple tarts that her mum buys in the supermarket and keeps a supply of in her kitchen cupboards, when her mother enters the kitchen.

"Sorry love, where were we? Oh yes, you think the house is sold then?"

"It is sold mum. The solicitors are now involved and the whole process is under way. Should have a completion date soon. That's partly why I came over today. I'd like you to see the place further down into Clifton that I'm buying. It has the potential to be turned into a studio if I ever want to do that one day."

"I'm not sure about coming out with your father like he is, Claire."

"He'll be all right in the car mum. He'll be with you the whole time. After all, he's usually OK when Sally comes in from nextdoor when you go shopping with Aunt May, isn't he? If you keep hold of his hand the whole time I'm sure he'll be fine. I really would like you to not only see the place, but be sure where it is too."

"Well, I suppose we can sort something out. A brief outing in the car might be a good thing."

"Great. Well, once I know I can get hold of the key I'll ring you and come over and get you.

"I'd better be going. I'm off over to Amanda's this afternoon."

"Do you have to go quite yet, pet? We don't see that much of you these days and with Charles gone we worry, well, ...I worry about you all the time. Most of the time your father just asks how you and

Charles are doing."

"Worrying won't change anything mum. I do love you and dad, you know that, but I have to deal with this on my own. There are still so many questions that I have no answers to." She stops, knowing that to go further down that road will do no good where her mother is concerned. Caring Marjory Barrett certainly is, but intellectual, or perhaps questioning, she probably isn't and such discussions only elicit such comments as 'What do you want to get all maudlin for love? Your father and I lived through the war you know and we just had to adopt a stiff upper lip and get on with it.'

Claire knows that her mother always means well, but is quite content to try and live in her own little world. She rises, lifts her cup to finish her tea, clatters the drained cup back on to its saucer, pulls her bag from the back of the chair and goes over to kiss her mother. "I'll pop into the front room and say goodbye to dad," she says.

In a tacky, pretentious room decked out as an office, upstairs in a "business unit" as they call them, somewhere off Feeder Road, between the Temple Meads area of Bristol and Barton Hill, Alan Evans, a self assured man who exudes an air of self-importance sits behind a desk that's far too big for both him and the room he's sitting in and puffs on a Black Russian. His pinstripe suite is expensive, as are his patent leather brogues, which are shined to a mirror finish at the end of his short legs, which are propped up on the corner of the desk, on the leather surface, dangerously close to a brass desk lamp. There is another, taller, more beefy man sitting in the swivel chair on the other side of the desk.

"I reckon she don't know." Says the man, who resembles one of those actors who always pop up in those gung-ho macho films where the people in the right use equally as much violence to win the day over the baddies as do the baddies themselves. His cauliflower ears reveal the fact that he was once a rugby player. A prop, hooker or a number eight in all likelihood; certainly in the scrum, anyway.

"But there's no way of tellin' is there?" Replies Evans, a cloud of smoke emanating from his nostrils and forming a nimbus around his head, "I mean he could well have never let on to his missus that he was minding it for us. Let's face it, he was frightened to death as it was, poor sod. Don't know anyfin' about the real world his sort. But on the other hand, he might have, but we must do somethin' alright. I'm feeling decidedly light of pocket and if we don't get it back then that whole perishin' job will have been a total waste of time. Months of plannin', a clean getaway, then this. That pathetic excuse for a human being McBroom was probably off in the clouds dreamin' about what he was gonna do with his fee, the ponce. Getting' himself killed like that. I mean, what are the chances, eh?"

"Very slim, boss. But I s'pose nothing's impossible. Like the infinite number of monkeys and…"

"See, let's look at it this way. We'll assume that she's heard. I mean maybe he left somethin' in his will, or maybe a letter or somat, then she'd have discovered it and where it was wouldn't she? Now, assumin' she has, then she might even be expecting someone to show up and ask for it back."

"Why would she even think it was someone else's cash, though? I reckon she'd just think he's salted it away from a few of his big deals. Had a few irons in the fire out in Dubai, or one a them Arab countries I shouldn't wonder. If some bloke out there wanted to be sure of something, then to chuck a million or so in the direction of the right people might just see them right. It has to be a possibility, boss. Small change to the likes of them."

"Has Renwick come up with anythin'? I assume he is actually keeping a lookout on her place, rather than kippin' in the back of his car and reading those grubby magazines of his."

"Just says he sees her comin' and goin'. Nuffin particularly unusual. Nothing to show she's suddenly struck it rich. Let's face it, her old man probably had a pretty good life insurance policy anyway. I don't see what we can do."

"Look, Gary, I know you're finkin' o me and that you don't want to take any chances, touching as it is, but if we just leave it then it's rather a big loss that I'm very, I repeat, very loathe to take on the chin."

"Yebbut, boss, you said yourself that if you turn up and the boys in blue get a sniff of it, you'll, correction, *WE'll* be inside before you can say 'money laundering.' Is it worth that kind of risk?"

"You're so flamin' practical Gary. That's your trouble. Listen, I've spent long enough thinking it all through. I've decided that I have to do something. We'll send Renwick in with some bogus excuse for callin' by. What about if he ponces himself up in a suit, we'll knock up a nice official-looking file and ID for him and he can ask her if she's found anything which might have made her suspicious about her husband's activities. If he plays it right she'll even give the tosser a cuppa while he pretends he's from the National Police Money Laundering Squad and he just needs to run a few things past her. He's investigating a few things they've heard, that sort of thing. He can even leave it so that she'll be willing to phone him if anything comes to light later. He can give her all the flannel about her being in the clear if anything should come to light. Has 'em eating out of his hand does our Tim when he's on song. What d'you reckon, then?"

"Sounds like it might work. 'National Police Money Laundering

Squad,' I like that. But there would be problems giving her a phone number. Traceable. He's got to clinch it on the first visit or forget it. She gets wind of anything, she'll call the law and we'll be in the sh…"

"I'm ahead of you Gary. OK, OK, you win. We'll have to prepare this very carefully. Any chance at all of there being a connection with me and we're doing porridge until I'm grey around the temples. Good point."

Evans already is grey around the temples, but his hairdresser takes care of that using a bottle every couple of weeks or so. Men like Alan Evans are nothing if not vain.

"If only we knew where the cretin put that money." He quips, mostly to himself.

It's now early September. Charles has been dead for over two months and patience never was one of Evans' best qualities.

"Mum," says Claire, who's on the phone in her kitchen, a room which is now looking decidedly bare, much of what makes such rooms look like someone lives in and uses them having now been consigned either to a charity shop or a cardboard box with copious quantities of newspaper. "I've got a completion date. September twenty-eighth, isn't that great?"

"It is Claire, love. So quickly. Well done."

"Yes, well, it's because there are only three in the chain and I'm the middle one. The people buying this are a couple who've only been renting up until now. Seems he moved around a lot with his job. Well, he's changed it now and that's why they told me they wanted to settle somewhere. He must be earning pretty well, that's all I can say. But then, I don't really care, I just have to get away from this house."

"I know love. I'm sorry though too, because you and Cha...., you put a lot of work into that house and I really love it. I know your father does too, when he can remember it that is."

"This was a home for me and Charles, mum. It isn't any more. It will never be a home for me without Charles here too. Plus, it's just too big for me. I'm lost in it. Anyway, I just wanted to tell you first. I'm going to call Amanda now."

Her mother gives her the usual assurances of how much both she and Gordon love her and they do a couple of 'mmwah' kisses, then hang up.

Claire is almost bordering on happy as she calls her friend Amanda. She's also glad that she asked the agent, well, to be precise, she'd got Alistair to instruct the agent that she didn't want a sign outside. As she'd hoped, the house had attracted a buyer really quickly and she can now at least divert her mind from the gnawing void that is always just a hair's breadth under the surface by focusing on the coming move and all it entails.

The night before the move, Claire is sitting quietly on the edge of her bed, reflecting on where she is in life. 'I'm frightened,' she thinks. 'I'm frightened and I think that's one of the reasons, missing Charles aside, that I can't deal with things very well. I've never been in this position before and would never, just a few short months ago, have dreamt that this would be my situation now, in September of 1990. I'm thirty-nine years old and I'm on my own. I'm a painter but can't bring myself to paint anything since Charles went. The only few moments of relative tranquility I've experienced since losing Charles were those two weeks in Parga, Greece.'

She lifts her legs and slides them under the duvet. It's late and she wants to sleep. She hasn't been sleeping all that well lately but, after almost two weeks of disrupted nights, when she's been up prowling the house, watching rubbish on TV and trying to read whilst sipping Earl Grey tea, or perhaps on occasion a glass of Jameson's, she thinks that tonight she may just sleep, she may just be zonked out. One can hope.

Charles is laughing. He's sitting on the patio chair in the back garden and he's shaking a bottle of Champagne. 'Here's to a great life in a wonderful house with a beautiful woman by my side!' he says and pops the cork, which flies clean over the trees into nextdoor's garden. A 'bonk' is heard as it bounces off the neighbour's greenhouse roof, mercifully without breaking any glass. He stands up, the bottle foaming and white bubbles falling from it as he does so. He approaches Claire, who's standing on the grass a few feet from him, and proffers the bottle, since she's holding a glass flute in each hand. It's the day they moved into the house in Pembroke Road. She laughs and spins around, but when she completes the full circle he's gone, the patio is gone, she is in Tunbury, the village where she grew up, and she's only nine years old again. She's playing in the road in front of her parents' modest Victorian house. She has a Lucky Bag, recently purchased from Benwell's store along the road, and in it she's discovered one of those slim, plastic propellers in a circular frame, it comes with a small plastic "launcher" and she uses it to send the yellow plastic toy hovering away from her. She's startled by the snapping sound of a "cap" going off. She turns to see Robert James, her friend from two doors away. He's playing with the little pink plastic rocket that came in his own Lucky Bag. He has a small round cardboard box, about coin-sized, that holds the paper tape of caps, those tiny discs of explosive that a child would buy from the local village general store, and you would rip a "cap" off, place it beneath the small sprung metal piston mounted in the nose of the rocket, then throw the whole thing up in the air and watch it drop.

As it struck the ground the cap would go off, "Snap!" Robert had thrown his rocket so that it landed right behind Claire.

Claire is mad at Robert, who laughs and shouts "scaredy cat, scaredy cat!!" He dances around her and she starts to cry. She runs in through her own front gate but the house isn't there. Instead she's running across the Clifton Suspension Bridge and there's a man climbing on to the rail. She hears herself crying out "CHARLES!! CHARLES!! DON'T, NO, PLEASE DON'T…"

She's sitting up in her bed in a cold sweat. She takes a few moments to realize that she's just had a weird dream. 'This house is doing things to me,' she thinks. 'I'm glad that by this time tomorrow I'll be gone. Perhaps once I'm somewhere that doesn't hold a memory of Charles in every nook and cranny and crevice I'll be able to take myself in hand.'

"She's WHAT?" Alan Evans can scarcely restrain himself. It's been a long time since he hit anyone and he misses it.

It's two weeks after Claire's move. In Alan Evans' office, there stands a lean man with a bony face and yet a well-proportioned frame. He isn't handsome, yet he does have something that seems to attract the girls, probably his expensive clothes. He's probably in his early thirties and he's standing, hands behind his back, in front of his employer's ostentatious desk. Evans is sitting on his leather swivel chair, feet under the desk, hands joined through the fingers as they rest in front of him on the blotter on top of the leather inlay of the desk. It's the type that has a series of brass-domed rivets all around the outer edge. Evans' fingers display several huge chunky gold rings, one of which has a gold coin set into it. His face is now almost puce.

"I said she's moved Mr. Evans. She isn't there any more."

"You're such a Dickhead Renwick, you prob'ly went to the wrong house. Get back down there and talk to the woman."

"Mr. Evans, sir, I didn't go to the wrong house, I'm very sure of that. You had me watching her for several weeks and I know the house very well. When you called me off a couple of weeks ago I'd been watching her on and off for over a month. There is no mistake."

Renwick knows that it's never a good idea to argue with his boss, but he has to stand his ground here as he has no alternative. It is the truth after all. He goes on, "Mr. Evans, I went along as instructed; briefcase, phoney files and fake ID all at the ready. To all intents and purposes I was the law. I knocked the door, but already it didn't feel right. There was one o'them people carriers and quite a lot of junk, boxes and the like, on the drive. Some bloke, prob'ly in his thirties, answered the door with a kid about eighteen months old on his hip. 'Can I 'elp you?' he says. I ask 'Is Mrs. Mason in please?' and he says right away, "No, she moved out coupla weeks ago and we moved in. Was it important?' like he'd a been able to help me anyway. Couldn't give me her new address there and then. What else could I do? I had to beat a hasty retreat, sir."

A couple of miles away and reasonably well concealed amongst the Georgian terraces of Clifton village, Claire is quite unaware of the interest being shown in her by Alan Evans and his cronies. She's sitting on the stripped pine floor upstairs in her new home with Amanda, both of them tearing open yet more cardboard boxes and deciding where to put stuff, hot mugs of coffee cooling on the window sill overlooking a busy Clifton street.

15. More Distractions.

Fifteenth of May 1991: Claire is again on an aeroplane, heading across Europe to Greece. This time she's only booked a spare seat on a charter flight and is going to Kefallonia, because she wants to sample different places with each visit to see if her impression of the Greek people is borne out all across the country.

Her house in Clifton is now ship-shape and tidy, albeit a little bleak in that she feels unbearably lonely when she's at home. Especially during all those long winter evenings did she struggle to keep her mind distracted as the months dragged by. Amanda did her best to give Claire things to do, places to go, but all too often Claire would refuse. She didn't particularly want to be on her own, yet she didn't feel up to smiling at the green wellie brigade either and making small talk about the village panto or the next fund-raiser or whatever. She's put on a little weight, having spent far too many nights watching mindless rubbish on TV and dunking chocolate digestives in endless cups of Earl Grey tea. At least she hasn't succumbed to alcohol. It would have been understandable if she had, but no, her vice remained McVitie's chocolate digestives and a hot mug of tea.

She has allowed herself to take coffee with Amanda during weekday mornings, when Amanda too is often at a loose end and her hubby's off running his branch of the NatWest somewhere down in the city. They've taken to walking Amanda's two dogs together once or twice a week, something which Claire has to admit to really enjoying. The chilly, often frigid fresh air in her lungs, the smells of a British winter landscape, the feel of thin ice breaking under her feet in country lanes, the sight of birds foraging about in hedgerows or sitting high in bare trees, such things do go some way to clearing Claire's mind, to helping her understand that the gentle natural rhythms of the seasons bespeak purpose, order, even some measure of design behind everything. It gives her a glimmer of hope that there is something, some purpose behind it all.

Claire is really very grateful for having befriended Amanda. She's slightly disappointed, though, that Amanda has again declined to come to Greece with her, but having got to know her better has decided that, reading between the lines, Amanda has a fear of flying and doesn't yet want to own up to it. Once again it produces mixed feelings in Claire's breast anyway. She rather likes the idea of being alone because it makes her seek company with the locals, and yet it can be a drawback when you just want someone you're close to, to pass the time or make plans with.

The aircraft's engines subtly change tone and the slight change too in the angle of the cabin floor tells Claire that they are beginning their descent. The Captain tells the passengers that the temperature at Kefallinia Airport is a balmy 29 degrees Celsius and the winds are light. They'll be landing in full daylight as it's May and still only about four o'clock in the afternoon anyway. Claire takes a long, deep breath and begins to feel that familiar feeling of approaching relief that she felt on both of the two previous occasions when she's visited Greece. The first was her visit to Poros with Charles, the second last year when she came alone to Parga.

The aircraft wheels screech at their first contact with the runway and Claire, sitting in a window seat near the front of the plane presses her forehead to the glass. She wants to begin drinking this place in even before she disembarks from the aircraft, she's that desperate for what she herself calls her anaesthetic. She's never been to Kefallonia. She just liked the sound of it when Judy, the girl she now feels she's starting to get to know at the travel agent's office, described it to her.

"It's a large island," Judy had begun, "with a buzzing capital called Argostoli. There are lots of small villages, some of them on the beach and seriously sleepy. There's also Melissani, an underground lake near the small harbour of Sami and there's the possibility of a visit to the legendary isle of Ithaca close by, from where Odysseus set out in Homer's Odyssey." On the wall in the agent's premises was a huge poster showing an impossibly white beach situated beneath dramatic cliffs and beside a deep blue ocean, the photo evidently taken from a mountainside nearby and affording a view of the entire beach, which apparently is called Myrtos. There is a huge area of hinterland waiting to be explored too, so Claire decided to give the island a try, since she didn't really want to lie on a beach all day, where she'd end up thinking too much.

Before long Claire is dragging her suitcase out of the terminal and a long line of black and white taxis is waiting there. She approaches the front taxi in the line and before she can even speak to the driver he's opening the boot and stowing her case. "Can I go to Poros, please?" asks Claire (she'd done a little homework and decided that she'd like to stay there for her first visit to the island). The driver hesitates for the merest microsecond, then nods, opens the rear door for Claire to climb inside and is soon pulling away and driving up the lane to the road. Taxi drivers are notorious for not always wanting a long fare, and the trip down to Poros from the airport is the best part of an hour each way. What sways the man is that he likes the look of his passenger. A Greek is always a sucker for a pretty woman. In this case Claire, at one month short of her fortieth birthday, is several years older than her driver, but he doesn't seem to notice. Any Greek *arsenikos* [red blooded male] will always argue the toss if someone tells him that the French or perhaps the Italians are the world's greatest lovers. "Amateurs!" he'll probably say.

The driver is quite tall and his name is Nikos. One thing Claire is soon to discover is that there aren't that many names in Greece. One comes across the same names so often it's hardly surprising that on Greek government forms which the populace have to fill out for such things as tax numbers, permits, in fact anything legal, ninety-nine times out of a hundred the applicant also has to write the forenames of both his parents. This is to hopefully differentiate him from all the other men with the same name. It's a fact borne of a culture where it's virtually compulsory to name the firstborn male after his *pappou* [grandfather] and the girl after her *yaya* [grandmother]. The net result is that precious few new names enter into the populace as a whole.

Nikos is in his early thirties, still single, which is par for the course, and quite handsome. His face perpetually sports a very dark five o'clock shadow and his rear-view mirror is festooned with a mixture of worry beads, a *ma'ti* [the evil eye], religious icons and a pennant declaring that he supports Panathanaikos. In Greece there are two religions, Greek Orthodox and football. Well, maybe three, since politics is in there somewhere too. It's quite normal when a Greek meets another male for the first time to enquire within seconds, "what's your team?" He drives with one eye on the road and the other perpetually scrutinizing the face of his passenger. He's adept enough at tourist-studying to know that she's British. He can't really read much more than that though. She's troubled, he can tell that much. Here he is, the great Nikos, ready and willing to ease her pain, lighten her burden, if she'll let him. He's confident that she will, but quite wrong.

He decides to try a conversation. "My name is Nikos. Pleased to meet you. Your first time on Kefallonia Miss, Miss..?"

"It's Claire, please, and yes, it's my first time on Kefallonia."

"Then you'll need a guide Miss Claire. I give you my number, you call me any time. I will show you the island. Anything you need, anywhere you want to go, you call Nikos. I am not expensive."

"Thank you, Nikos. That's very kind. I shall need to find a room, so can you help me? I have nothing reserved in advance, but rather thought that it wouldn't be difficult to find something for myself. Am I right or have I been stupid?"

"No problem Miss Claire. My cousin Poppi has very nice rooms, one hundred metres from the beach, upstairs with small balcony. Not too expensive, very clean. I take you there first?"

"Why not?" Claire is secretly very pleased. 'This freelance malarkey is easy' she thinks to herself. They converse on and off all the way down to Poros. As they pass through the village of Markopoulo Nikos explains proudly about the snakes that reputedly appear every year on August 15th, one of the largest religious celebrations in the Greek Orthodox calendar. He points out other odd facts and figures until they find themselves driving down through the gorge that cuts the village of Poros off from the plain behind it. Claire reflects on why she chose to come to the village of Poros. She really did so because she was bemused to find that there was a village on this island which had the same name as the first island that she'd ever visited. That was it really, purely curiosity.

As they enter the village from the rear she glimpses the sea, glistening a deep turquoise beyond the rooftops of the village. Nikos takes a left at a fork and halfway along a level street that appears to empty out at the far end on to the beach he pulls up on the lefthand side outside a building that looks like it has three apartments or studios on the upstairs floor and is a private house on the ground level. There is a metal gate and fence protecting a lush garden of hibiscus, Oleander and bougainvillaea, behind all of which is the front terrace of the building. To the left Claire glimpses an outdoor staircase leading up to a landing that's evidently around the back of the building, from where doubtless one enters the apartments.

Nikos jumps out and opens the rear door for his passenger and Claire steps out into the heat. It's at this moment she realizes that the air-conditioning in the car had given her a false sense of coolness. Although the afternoon is now imperceptibly becoming evening, the sun still shines and it still feels stiflingly hot after the temperatures she'd left behind in the UK. He leads her through the gate, towing her suitcase behind him and on to the terrace in front of the house. There is an oblong table dressed with a floral patterned oilcloth, in the centre of which sits a chunky, glass ashtray and around which is an assortment of different chairs. A few coloured plastic toys lay around betraying the fact that cousin Poppi in all probability has young children. Claire steels herself for the rush of feelings that she'll probably get when she sees them.

Before they reach the door a dark-haired woman of probably

similar age to Nikos exits the front door and kisses him on both cheeks. Nikos makes the introductions, assures Claire that she's in good hands and that Poppi can call him any time and he can be here within the hour and is on his way, Claire having paid him and added a generous extra amount as a tip.

Poppi speaks pretty good English, a fact which brings Claire substantial relief from anxiety. What if she'd been left here, in a small village at the bottom end of a Greek island, all alone and unable to communicate? She hadn't foreseen what she'd have done if that had happened, but fortunately, it hasn't. Poppi hugs Claire and, after kissing both cheeks, tells her the rental on the room and suggests they go upstairs and install Claire's case before they share a drink on the terrace. Once upstairs Claire is delighted with the studio. Entering the rear door, she sees a small kitchenette to her left, a door into a very clean shower room with sink, toilet, a selection of bright, clean white towels and nice clear mirror to her right and further inside a couple of beds with wooden frames, a modest dressing-table, fitted wardrobe and double glass door leading outside on to the compact balcony.

Claire can feel the anaesthetic kicking in already.

She spends a low-key couple of weeks on the island, during which she enlists Nikos' help on a number of occasions, during all of which he comports himself with the utmost respect. By the time he's pulling up at the airport terminal for Claire's departure she's visited the nearby island of Ithaca, which has one of the world's largest natural harbours and yet only about 3,000 inhabitants, climbed to the top of Mount Ainos and taken lunch in the village of Fiskardo, at the opposite end of the island to Poros. She's taken a swim at Assos and wandered alone on Myrtos Beach, the lane down to which is rutted and potholed, thus ensuring that the number of visitors actually getting all the way down to the beach itself is still few.

Claire has talked incessantly with not only her landlady, Poppi, whom she's found to be just as generous and hospitable as was Mrs. Ioannou on Poros Island, but also with the owner of the taverna that she frequented the most in Poros village (which was only a couple of hundred yards along the road and right on the beach), Kostas, who on several occasions had given her a lift along to the end of the beach or down to the tiny harbour at the south end of the village in his battered old pickup truck.

Claire once again feels slightly lighter of spirit. She feels deeply now that she's going to need these infusions of Greece in the coming years until something happens to either answer all her questions, or maybe she just stops asking them.

The years roll by from 1992 through to 1997, all the while Claire spending her time whilst at home in the UK planning her Greek visits. She becomes a close friend of Judy from the travel agent and simply calls her on the phone when she wants flights arranged. She's grown to understand much of the culture of the country and loves the quiet places where she can muscle in on a game of Backgammon among the old men in the local kafeneion, much to their surprise and delight, since the kafeneion is so often still a male domain during the morning hours. She visits Greece several times each summer and, when back home sees few people apart from her parents and Amanda. She loses touch with Charles' parents. They wouldn't have much to say to eachother anyway now and Claire feels pangs of conscience too, blaming herself for their son's death.

At least once a year from 1992 through to 1997 she returns to

Kefallonia, but eventually stays each time at a small block of village rooms on the town's outskirts, right across the road from the beach, which at that point is little more than a strand of rough stones and pebbles. Marina Rooms almost becomes a home from home for Claire and she stays in the same room each visit. She gets to know the landlady well and is greeted like long lost family each time she arrives.

In June 1998, she's leaving the plane on her arrival at Kefallinia airport when she encounters the young Alyson Wright, an apprehensive girl of not quite twenty years of age. Alyson is trying to stay away from the boy she really loves, owing to a complicated situation with his family. Claire has learned never to either judge or offer advice by now, but is adept at listening to other people as they talk. She and Alyson soon become close friends and, in another story really,* end up drifting around Greece for three years before finally settling in the village of Lindos, on the Aegean island of Rhodes. Claire feels very motherly toward Alyson in one sense and yet like a peer of hers in another. By and large, though, she likes to feel that each has benefited from the other. She had the financial wherewithal to drift around Greece and Alyson provided a much appreciated diversion for Claire's emotional state. For those three years and even after they settle in Lindos, she feels toward Alyson the kind of protective emotions that a mother would have for a vulnerable young daughter. Claire never really reveals much of herself to Alyson though, but the younger woman seems to understand that this isn't because she doesn't trust or love her, it's rather to do with Claire's own problems with dwelling on what her past contains and dealing with it.

The years roll on even further until Saturday June 18th, 2005. Claire is now fifty-four and she's been alone, apart that is from

*This is the basis for the story in *'The View From Kleoboulos'*, also by John Manuel.

Alyson's company, for fifteen years. Fifteen years almost to the day it is since Charles Mason died in a fall from the Clifton Suspension Bridge in the Avon Gorge in Bristol. For the past four years Claire and Alyson have now lived here in Lindos and during that time they have imperceptibly been drifting further apart. It's nothing intentional and there are no problems between them. Alyson is the much younger of the two and has acquired quite a circle of friends. She's become fond of going to the *Bouzoukia*, where young Greeks dance from midnight until almost dawn. Alyson can do the *Tsifteteli* like a Greek girl now. She's also dark haired and could even pass for one with her permanent tan too. She's been working for a number of years as a hairdresser for a small company that organizes weddings and is good at her job. Claire has taken more and more to sitting outside her front door when she has the shade to do so and reading books. In the evenings she does the same thing, with the occasional walk around the village when she'll sit usually in the Ikon Bar and watch the people passing by.

More often than not Claire and Alyson's paths meet these days at the Ikon Bar. It's during just such an occasion when the whole world turns upside-down for Alyson because, totally unknown to her, Dean, the young man she can never really get over, is in Lindos for his wedding to another girl. He finally gave up on ever seeing Alyson again and allowed himself to drift into another relationship, one which led him to this place and time. He's walking through the village when, by complete coincidence, his eyes meet Alyson's while she's sitting in the bar chatting with Claire. Claire is busy explaining to Alyson that she's made the decision to go back to the UK to try and start painting again. Her inner emptiness has begun to creep back over her once more and she feels now that after all these years perhaps the time is right to get back to what she's good at and immerse herself in it.

In Bristol once again, opening up the house and studio, she feels for the first time after many years that she wants to paint. She wants to create and to immerse herself in doing so. She already has a substantial body of work under dust sheets and so decides that the first thing is to work up a collection to try and exhibit. It's been seven years since she's returned to the house and she can't believe how good Amanda Brandonbury has been during all that time in regularly calling there, letting herself in with the key that Claire had given her, dealing with the post and keeping an eye on the security of the place.

For a while she and Alyson don't communicate. There's no rancour between them. Both know that when they next do so, then in all probability they'll be like a couple of schoolgirls. Claire knows that Alyson has a lot to work out and she is content to wait until Alyson and Dean have done so, when they're sure to let her know what's happening. In the meantime she resolves to buy Amanda an expensive gift to show her gratitude and also to meet up with her husband's old business partner Alistair, to see how he's doing and thank him once again for helping so much with the sale of Pembroke Road.

'I still can't deal with mortality,' thinks Claire, 'but I'm damn sure going to try and live my life.' When she thinks 'live', she means 'survive'. It's something she'll do despite herself.

16. Sunshine.

Tuesday September 14th 2010.

Claire and Julia have been running the gallery now for almost four years. Claire now exhibits all her work there, very rarely taking on exhibitions elsewhere. It's too much trouble and the gallery, which Claire has named "Sunshine," ticks over very nicely. She and Julia, whom she'd first met on Rhodes in 2006, work well together and Julia also lives in, each having their own bedroom and lounge, since the property has four floors when you include the roof rooms, which look out above the Georgian parapet from dormers in the sloping slate tiled roof.

Julia's son Dean is now back behind the wheel at his graphic design consultancy in Cardiff, working with his business partner Adam Hastings, and Alyson runs a pretty successful home hairdressing business. After their wedding in Lindos in summer 2007, they made the decision to return to the UK, since Dean's business was still a going concern, largely thanks to how Adam had kept it going during Dean's absence. Alyson's mum Christine had married Brian at the same time and they're now living in Bath, Brian earning an acceptable crust by playing his guitar and singing in the local folk clubs and live music venues.

Last evening they'd had a showing of a new collection of Claire's watercolours and there had been brisk business with quite a lot of the punters, having first been plied with wine and nibbles, placing orders. So now, at around eleven o'clock in the morning, Julia is seated in front of the iMac on the white desk near the back of the gallery processing them. She's printing delivery notes and address labels for those who are having their purchases sent out via courier. There's a huge roll of bubble wrap leaning against the wall behind her, standing sentry beside an equally huge roll of heavy-duty brown paper. The pictures that sold are stacked, corrugated cardboard separating each from the one both behind and in front of it, against the side of the desk and a packing tape dispenser sits beside Julia's mouse hand.

Claire is upstairs in the studio, sitting in front of a blank canvas and sifting through some photographs of yet another country house, the owners of which want a huge oil-on-canvas done to take pride of place on their staircase wall. It's not Claire's favourite aspect of her work, but commissions like this alone pay a lot of the bills. She sits studying the photographs while her mind wanders. She's thinking, as she so often does, about the huge amount of cash that was found in those Cayman Island accounts when Charles died. Since he'd left her more than well catered for financially, plus she'd been turning a very acceptable profit since she and Julia opened the Sunshine Gallery, she is proud to say to herself that all that cash is still sitting there. In spite of the fact that interest rates the world over have nosedived in recent times, she is also quite bemused to see how much more sits in those accounts now than on the day when her solicitor had discovered them. It's twenty years since Claire lost Charles and during all of that time nothing has ever happened to give her even the faintest hint as to where the money came from. One thing she was certain of, however, was that her Charles would never have become involved in anything corrupt or illegal. The conclusion that she most often comes to when she contemplates the whole thing is that some rich Arab businessmen must have given it to Charles as a gift, perhaps even a sweetener and possibly in smaller tranches, when he was doing some big property deals out in the gulf. That's the nearest Charles would ever have come to what could be termed "shady dealings".

She looks up and out of the tall sash window at the building across the street. The sun is shining and she congratulates herself on how she's been able to keep her morbid thoughts and fears at bay for a few years now, largely thanks to her new friend Julia. She still sees Amanda Brandonbury from time to time, but not so often as in the past. Amanda's husband retired a couple of years ago and so they tend to spend a lot more time together than when he was working. 'It's OK,' thinks Claire, 'life just continually changes. Nothing remains static for long. I'll always be grateful for the support and friendship she gave me when I needed it most. But she has her hubby to support now. So many men when they retire are at a loss as to what they're going to do with their time. Amanda seems to know that her job, well - one of her jobs - is to keep Lawrence amused.'

Claire picks up a stick of charcoal and begins to etch a hazy outline on the canvas of the scene that she'll be painting. She's let her hair grow again in recent times. For a number of years after she lost Charles and during her sojourn in Greece with Alyson Wright she'd kept it very short. It was a kind of sign of mourning in a way. She'd been determined to try not to look attractive, it fed her guilt. Now though, her hair has reached almost shoulder length, has been straightened and she's dyed it a striking red, what many would call henna. She still has a selection of earrings along her lower lobes and still verges on the hippy-chic side of fashion taste. It suits her. She has a face that's not aged significantly during the past ten years or so, and could still be described as pretty. She's a woman of fifty-nine, yet is often mistaken for someone at least ten years younger. She's grateful that she never really took up smoking in her teenage years, back when many of her circle of friends were smoking marijuana like it was going out of fashion. How many times had she taken a puff while the joints were being passed around and yet never inhaled? Whilst all those around her were getting stoned she would simply mimic their behaviour and usually get away with it.

Julia's voice resounds up the stairs, "Claire, darling!! Coffee's brewing, ten minutes, OK!?"

"OK! Be down in a while!" Claire replies.

They have a kind of routine when they're both at the house/gallery. Claire is usually upstairs in the studio while Julia minds the shop and whilst doing so keeps up to date with all the business stuff, like paying bills, cataloguing, invoicing and serving the occasional punter who walks in the front door. There is never a tremendous amount of footfall during the early part of the week and it suits Julia fine. If she wants to pop down the street to the local bakery or general store, she'll call to Claire who'll either drop what she's doing, come down and mind the shop, or she'll simply tell Julia to flip the closed sign for the ten minutes or so while she's absent. But at around eleven Julia will set the coffee machine going and fill the gallery with the aroma of freshly roasted coffee, then she'll call to Claire and, when the coffee's ready, Claire will come down and the two of them will have a natter for twenty minutes or so. Every afternoon they close the gallery at 4.00pm, except for Saturdays when they'll stay open until six. They don't open on Mondays during the day. If they're having a soirée to promote a new collection, then they'll often do it on a Monday night because it won't usually collide in the diaries of their potential guests. They have a fairly extensive database of regular buyers, people who simply love art, or perhaps are especially partial to Claire's work, or perhaps run businesses where they will exhibit a few works by local artists. The latter will come to the soirées although seldom actually buying anything; but it gives Claire the opportunity to thrash out deals where they'll take a few of her works and hang them in their craft shops or tea rooms and cafés on a sale-or-return basis.

Julia is glaring at her iMac monitor when she hears the doorbell tinkle. Looking up she sees a rather stylish young woman entering the gallery. She has long slim legs clad in tight expensive jeans, an off-white silk blouse, the top few buttons of which are undone and a very expensive looking gold necklace around her pretty neck. Her clutch bag exhibits a large Gucci logo and her suede stiletto boots look like they wouldn't leave one much change out of several hundred pounds. The girl's hair is auburn and very long, reaching down to well beyond her waist. Her heart-shaped face is made up, accentuating large eyes whilst not to the extent that it would make her look cheap. She looks anything but cheap.

'Hmmm' thinks Julia, 'could be a good sale here.' She rises, extends a smile and asks the young woman, "Good morning. Can I help you?"

"I really do hope so," replies the girl, without a trace of any regional accent that Julia can discern, "I'm hoping that this may be the gallery of Mrs. Claire Mason."

Julia replies, "It is indeed. May I ask how you've heard of Claire?"

"Umm, it's rather involved. I don't want to give any offense, but if you're not Claire Mason, I'd rather explain it to her myself. I am sorry to sound obtuse. No offense intended. Would it be possible to see her, or perhaps make an appointment to do so?"

"Well, I…" begins Julia.

"I don't see why not." Claire herself has just descended the stairs in anticipation of her usual coffee time chat with Julia. She's standing in the doorway and has overheard the past few comments. She walks forward and extends a hand to the young woman. "Claire Mason at your service and this is my close friend and business partner, Julia Waters."

"Pleased to meet you, Miss…?"

"Geesin, Sunny Geesin."

Claire hears an electric buzzer in the back of her brain. 'Wasn't Geesin Eric and Marianna's surname? How many years ago was it now? I believe that they died in 1990, about the same time as Charles. That would make it over twenty years ago. Feeling decidedly unsettled, she asks,

"Ought I to know you Miss Geesin? I've no idea quite why, though. Would you like some coffee, it's fresh and it's Illy brand?" Claire's mind is already racing and she is expecting a bombshell here. She doesn't yet allow herself to speculate though, but she feels her adrenalin rising.

Julia is already fixing three cups of coffee at the machine. "Milk, sugar Miss Geesin?"

"Just a little milk, please, thanks." Then, turning to Claire, she looks into her eyes, as if searching for something there, "You don't know me Mrs. Mason, but if I'm right, you once held me in your arms for a few moments. It would have been March of 1986, at Southmead Hospital. You see, my mother was Marianna and my father was Eric Geesin."

There is a thud as Claire hits the floor. She's fainted.

17. A History.

Claire's vision is still blurry. There are two heads coming into focus, each on either side of her own. The spotlights of the ceiling shine blindingly between them as she hears Julia's voice.

"She's coming to. Claire, Claire? Are you OK? Claire, talk to me!"

The other head has a long mane of auburn hair, which hangs almost to Claire's face. Its owner now sweeps it up and away over her shoulder. Claire thinks 'Yes, that's right, it's the young woman, it's Sunny, Sunny Geesin. Can it really be her, the child that I might have raised had my Charles not been taken from me all those years ago?' She makes an attempt to sit up and both of her companions extend hands to help her do so. She's sitting on the floor when she says,

"I'm so sorry. I don't know what came over me. Can I get up?"

Julia and Sunny help Claire into the one of customer chairs by the desk at which Julia had been sitting when Sunny Geesin had entered the gallery. They stand back and both display looks of deep concern on their faces. Sunny says:

"Mrs. Mason, I'm so, so sorry. I had no intention of causing you any distress. I have been trying to find you for quite some time and I want to explain things, a lot of things. Are you OK now?"

A few moments later, Julia sits behind the desk and Claire sits with Sunny on the other side, each of them clutching a bone china mug of steaming coffee in her right hand. Sunny begins:

"I'm really sorry if I shocked you; may I call you Claire?"

"Of course."

"Claire, I thought that you'd know my name, the name my parents gave me, because it's what you've called your gallery. I thought that it was in some way due to what you remembered about me. My name 'Sunny' isn't my actual name, it's 'Sunshine'. Rather unorthodox, but you know I quite like it. Didn't you call the gallery after me, Claire?"

"You know, I never even learned what your name was. When your parents took you away, for a long while I never wanted to see them again, I was so devastated. It was the right thing to do, don't misunderstand me, I understand that, but it didn't make it any easier for me to cope with. How much did they tell you about the circumstances surrounding your birth, Sunny?"

"They told me everything, but I lost them when I was only four. You don't either understand or retain a lot when you're as young as that. I still do recall the accident, though. I still can see vividly the scene inside that car when…"

The door tingles and two customers walk in, apparently a couple. After a few moments, during which Sunny and Claire sit smiling at eachother and maintaining a discreet silence while Julia shows some paintings to the middle aged man and his wife, Sunny suggests to

Claire, in a whisper,

"Claire. This isn't perhaps the appropriate place to tell you my story. Plus it'll take quite a while. Why don't I treat you and …sorry, what was your friend's name again?"

"It's Julia."

"OK. So why don't I treat you and Julia to an Italian this evening? There's an excellent one in Whiteladies Road, just around the corner from here, the Aqua. Do you know it? I suppose what's more to the point, do you like Italian?"

"Oh yes, we both eat Italian. We know the Aqua well and we've eaten there lots of times. But you can't…"

"Claire, I insist. Look, I've got stuff to do, business to attend to in Bristol this afternoon. So what say I meet you at the front door of the Aqua at eight o'clock this evening? I'll book the table. You two just turn up. Deal?"

"OK, deal. You really shouldn't…"

"I'll hear no more remonstrations! I owe you a huge debt, Claire. This is the first day of many in which I'll be attempting to repay it in some small way."

After the two women have waited for a further fifteen minutes, during which time it looks more and more like Julia is going to close a sale of one of Claire's large watercolours of the Avon Gorge, Sunny decides to leave them both to it, safe in the knowledge that she'll be able to explain her story at leisure during the coming evening. She rises, kisses Claire unexpectedly on the cheek while squeezing her shoulder, waves to Julia with a very brief, "I'll see you this evening," and a "please do excuse me" to the couple, and she's gone.

At eight o'clock sharp Julia and Claire cross the road in front of the restaurant and they see their newfound young friend waiting as she'd said she would be, right beside the door. The Aqua has some tables, rather continental-style, out front on a pavement terrace. Although it's the middle of September, the weather is surprisingly warm and, although there had been some rain earlier, it was now a fine evening. They decide to chance sitting outside and Sunny goes in to register their arrival and ask a member of staff to assign them a table.

They soon have aperitifs before them and, as they scan the menu, Sunny starts talking.

"So, can I tell you my story?"

"I'm desperate to hear it, please, do go on." replies Claire.

Julia knows that she's the gooseberry of sorts this evening, and so decides to keep discreetly out of things unless invited to contribute at some time. She's very content anyway to be choosing some excellent Italian food, which will no doubt be complemented by a bottle of Chianti in the not too distant future.

"I have vivid memories of being in this vehicle on the South Circular on the day of the accident. I don't recall the actual accident at all, but the immediate aftermath, yes. Some firemen had to smash away some window glass and cut away a window pillar to get me out of the wreck. I seem to recall that a very nice lady, a Policewoman probably, was talking to me the whole time. I wasn't crying, but I must have been asking about mummy and daddy, why they weren't answering me. I can't say that I even noticed the blood, or anything like that. It's a bit surreal, but that's that I suppose. I didn't sustain even a small scratch, it's a miracle really.

"Prior to that day I do remember snippets of my life with my birth parents. We had a modest semi in Croydon with a small front garden. It was mainly lawn with a few shrubs. Mum was always with me so I assume that she didn't work at the time. Daddy used to come home in a blue boiler suit usually. He was never late home though and seldom worked on weekends. The abiding memories I have of that time are warm and comforting. I think that they'd have done a good job of bringing me up, had the accident not killed them both so suddenly."

Claire is staring at this beautiful young woman and wondering how terrible this must have been for her. She was only four years old, bless her. She indicates by body language that she's eager for Sunny to go on.

"I can't remember a lot of the fine details, except that I was moved around quite a bit to begin with. My grandparents, for reasons best known to themselves, didn't want to take me on. That's my grandparents on dad's side, of course. I never knew any of my birth mother's relatives. I know now that she was from the north, but she never had any contact with any of her family, so naturally neither did I. My father's parents were from Taunton. I think now that their noses were put out of joint when they heard in the reading of my father's will, that you and your husband, Claire, were the preferred guardians, should you decide to accept the responsibility for me."

"Oh, dear child! I feel so guilty, it was, just for a moment, a thrill to hear that Marianna and Eric had wished for that, but of course I was devastated to hear the reason why we'd been contacted. I couldn't believe that poor Marianna and her husband were dead. But I also had dreadful news the next morning, and I..."

"Claire, it's OK. It's OK. I'm not telling you this to get at you. Anything but. I simply want you to hear the whole story, which I hope will help explain why I sought you out. The fact that my natural grandparents didn't want to take me on is why I ended up being fostered, something which, to be frank, I'm now extremely glad about and grateful for.

A waiter appears, notebook in hand, she's a young woman with a black skirt, black tights, white shirt and a badge declaring her name, which is Alana. She asks the women if they're ready to order. Julia nods, but Claire asks for a few more moments. She hasn't even glanced at the menu as yet. Well, she has, but she hasn't seen a single word on it. For a few minutes they all study the menu, before agreeing on what they're all going to order. They'll skip starters and go straight for the main course, following Julia's suggestion that if she eats a starter, then she won't have room for dessert, and she really would like a dessert, Claire and Sunny concur.

"Would you like a bottle of wine?" asks Sunny, glancing from Claire to Julia and back again. Their eyes meet as if they already know what their answer will be, which indeed they do. Claire turns to the wine list and, after a moment or two running her finger up and down, replies "Is it OK if we have a bottle of Chianti Riserva Piccini, from Tuscany? It's not the cheapest wine on the menu, but…"

"Don't even think about price tonight, the both of you," replies Sunny, glancing from one to the other. The Chianti it is, and to eat?"

Claire is first to reveal her choice, "I'd like the Pollo Limoni," a dish of chicken breast roasted with garlic, lemon & pancetta with green beans & mushrooms. Julia is quick to add, "Well, if it's OK, I'll go for the Penne Pollo," which is hand torn roasted chicken with pancetta, mushrooms in a white wine & cream sauce with a hint of chilli.

Sunny lightly chides Julia, "There's no need to keep asking if anything's OK, Julia. This is my treat tonight and there are no limits or conditions, got it?" Julia nods, sheepishly.

Alana the waitress having retreated to put their order into the kitchen, Sunny goes on: "Claire, first let me get something understood. I fully understand why you couldn't take me on. I understand now that you lost your husband at virtually the exact same time as my parents were killed. I've no idea how I'd have felt if I were in your shoes, but to lose your husband and then voluntarily become a single parent, well, not many people would be able to do such a thing.

"Before I go on, you may be interested to know how I found you."

"I hadn't even thought about that, but yes, now you mention it, how did you find me?"

Once I was old enough - and I'll come back to that later - I was given the contact details of my parents' solicitor, a Mrs. Clara Wilde, who still practices now, although she must be getting near retirement. She told me about how she'd spoken to you back when mum and dad died. She didn't have your current details, but she did have your solicitor's contact numbers. So I was able to ring Weaver and Weaver in Bristol, who were able to give me your current address once I'd explained who I was. When I first drove by the gallery I was thrilled to see that you'd named it Sunshine. I thought that it had to be because of your memories of me as a child, though it seems now that I was way off."

"Well, spooky though it is Sunny, like I said earlier I never actually knew what your parents had called you. But now I'm absolutely thrilled to find out what an extraordinary coincidence it is that your name is Sunshine. I can well picture Eric and Marianna coming up with that. You were a little ray of sunshine in their lives, there can be no doubt, even though at the start it looked as though they weren't going to make it as a couple. I think it's a lovely name and I'll not be changing the name of the gallery now, not ever!"

Sunny is well pleased to hear Claire's comments. Then, seeing that both women are exuding a palpable air of expectation, she resumes the account of her life.

"My parents died, as you of course know Claire, in June 1990. It was finally in January of 1991 that I was placed with foster parents. Mr. and Mrs. White, Terry and Sandra. They also fostered a boy, who I grew up calling my brother, even though we had different surnames. He's called Callum and you probably won't get to meet him any time soon as he's in New Zealand now and I get the feeling he's going to stay there. He's heavily into a relationship and she's a native New Zealander. He's taken up the challenge of sheep farming with her family and loves it. I have been over there to see him just the once.

"Callum was already in the White's home when I arrived. I'm told by Terry, who I've called dad for so long now that it's an immovable factor - after all, he and Sandra brought me up from the age of four until I left home at eighteen - anyway, I'm told by dad that I was a rascal when I first came to them. I was difficult to tame and they almost gave up on me. I don't remember any of this but they told me that I would have tantrums and would hold my breath until I was blue. They must have worried themselves silly. I don't know what it was, but something eventually clicked in my mind and I began to work with them rather than rebelling against them and they really did prove to be wonderful parents. I could never have wished for a better upbringing. I mean, how lucky was that, in the circumstances?

"Dad was a policeman, CID. He's taken early retirement now, but he was a Chief Inspector for quite a few years before that. Mum only ever worked part-time, a little shop work, some clerical stuff, but she always wanted to be at home when we got in from school. The last job she had was as a dental receptionist in Stroud, but only filling in, she never worked a lot of hours. Mum and dad knew the dentist as a friend, otherwise she probably never would have got that job. Sadly, mum died in summer 2006, breast cancer. She didn't go and get checked out until it was far too late.

"I still miss her, but it really hit dad very badly. They had a good marriage, something which filtered through to Callum and I. It gave us a cozy, stable home environment and, thinking back, I can't believe our luck that we were allowed to stay with them until we grew up. I don't know how all these things work, the system and all, but when they moved from Beckenham to Stroud in 1993, we went with them. As far as Callum and I were concerned, we were a regular family. We grew up with a safe home environment in Kingscourt Lane, which was virtually in the countryside. It was the kind of childhood that I'm sure others would describe as idyllic. I played in trees, chased horses around fields, explored the woods, skipped in the road and played hopscotch with my best friend Bryony. The school we went to was small and we never got into any trouble."

"Did you know during all this time," asks Claire, "that you were not with your birth parents? Did Mr. and Mrs. White tell you much about how you came to be with them?"

"They were always completely transparent. I'm only guessing at this, but perhaps it had to do with the fact that we, Callum and I, weren't legally adopted, only fostered. There may always have been the chance that we could have been taken away from mum and dad. I can't imagine what I'd have done if that had happened, how I'd have felt. Anyway, I'm very glad to say that it didn't happen and I owe a huge debt to Terry and Sandra, mum and dad to me. As I grew up they would sit me down from time to time and say, 'Sunny, we need to have a little talk. Just so you know who you are and why you must always walk tall and be proud.' They sound too good to be true, but there you are, they were I suppose.

"We even had a few cousins that we'd visit on weekends, or maybe they'd come to us. We had aunties and uncles, all of whom treated us as though we were the real children of the Whites. Never any grandparents, though. I think that both mum and dad had lost their parents when they were still relatively young."

By now the women have been tucking into their food for a while and sipping appreciatively at the Chianti. Sunny, pouring the last of the wine into Julia's glass, holds the bottle up and, through the glass of the restaurant's window, catches the eye of their waitress, Alana. Soon a second bottle is sitting on the table and all three companions are feeling very comfortable in eachother's company. Claire, especially, is fascinated to hear this story. This young woman, who could so easily have had her life inextricably bound up with Claire's, is telling the story of the years that passed during which Claire was quite lost and at least for part of the time finding her only true relief in her regular Greek visits. She looks hard at Sunny, hoping that the young woman doesn't feel uncomfortable under her stare, and contemplates about all the things that might have been and yet never were. 'This could have been my legally adopted daughter, she could have been calling me "mum",' thinks Claire. It's unsettling, threatening to drive Claire downwards, and yet she's buoyed by Sunny's vivacity and natural charm. Would she and Charles have done a better job of raising this girl and releasing her into the world? She doesn't think so. Sunny's done all right when all's said and done and that's what really matters now, all these years later.

Twenty years have somehow trickled away. Twenty years ago what a different prospect lay before Claire Mason. Now, though, she has to be grateful that this young woman has sought her out. Even though she hasn't been preoccupied by it, there has always been in Claire's mind a curiosity about what became of this girl. If she hadn't come out of the woodwork, Claire could well have seen herself adding even more guilt to her already overburdened conscience. She still thinks that she drove Charles to kill himself, but she could foresee herself wracking her conscience over the possibility that the child had been ill-treated, had a deprived upbringing, may have ended up a burden on society. Instead she now finds herself looking at this evidently self-assured, well-balanced young woman of, 'well, she must be twenty four by now' thinks Claire.

"Terry and Sandra, mum and dad," continues Sunny, "told us when we were probably in our early teens the reason why they became foster parents. They couldn't have children of their own. I don't remember now what the problem was, but anyway it resulted in both Callum and I getting the benefit. When I turned eighteen, in March 2004, mum and dad sat me down and told me something that they'd kept back until then. My birth parents had taken out life insurance. It was a pretty large sum. The cash had been paid out and my natural grandparents, in doing the only thing they ever really did do for me, had lodged it in a trust fund for me. It was due to be paid out to me on my reaching the age of eighteen. So, when I was not more than a few weeks past my eighteenth birthday, I had a five figure sum in the bank, thanks to my real parents and their foresight.

"You know, ...by the way, are you cold?" Claire and Julia exchange glances, then turn to Sunny and nod, "It is getting slightly chilly now, don't you think?"

"I do too. Let's get ourselves transferred to an indoor table." Says Sunny Geesin. She rises, enters the door and is soon exiting again and beckoning to Claire and Julia to follow her inside. Alana leads them past the stylish bar area to the rear of the restaurant and shows them to a comfortable round table in the warmth. They're soon seated and talking about dessert. Claire orders Tiramisu and Julia the sticky toffee pudding. Sunny asks for a dark chocolate brownie with vanilla ice cream and they all agree that they'll top the meal off with a filter coffee.

For a while they're all three preoccupied by their desserts, but Claire's curiosity soon surfaces again.

"Sunny, if you don't mind me asking, I know you inherited the trust fund, as you told us, but how do you make a living now? Sorry to be nosey."

"Not at all. That was what I was going to tell you next. Since I was first in my teens I became quite single-minded in my career plan, I wanted to run my own restaurant. The cash I received gave me the wherewithal to make my dream a reality. There were those who thought that someone as young as I opening a French Restaurant in a small backstreet in Bath was a recipe for disaster. But, you know, it's now over four years since I opened "La Jambe de Grenouille" and it's going well. I love running it and there have even been a couple of magazine articles about it. I was fortunate in getting a very good chef to come on board. He's called Raymond Doherty and he used to run the restaurant at the Royal Crescent Hotel, which is seriously prestigious. It's small, but I like that because it's also very intimate. We keep the lighting subdued to add to what my manager calls romantic, though I'd prefer to say 'conspiratorial', atmosphere. You two will really have to pay us a visit soon. It'll be on the house of course."

Claire and Julia exchange enthusiastic glances and both reward Sunny with warm smiles of appreciation.

"I think I've just about given you my potted history. I hope it's not been boring!"

Claire is quick to respond to this display of modesty on Sunny's part. "Boring? Are you kidding Sunny? I've spent the last twenty years wondering what happened to you and whether I'd ever see you again. I've also been punishing myself inwardly, never talking to anyone else about it, because I would often get frightened that perhaps things had gone badly for you and, if they had, I'd have been to blame. I mean, your parents, your birth parents that is, had entrusted you to me and Charles. OK, so I lost Charles and I'm never going to get over that, but to have been the cause of you having a nightmare of a life too, that would have finished me off.

"No, Sunny, I think the reason I fainted when I first really accepted that it was you this morning was the fact that I'd only ever seen you as a baby a few hours old. To see such a vision of loveliness before me not only gave me a huge sense of relief, but it made me wonder where twenty-four years had gone. I'll stop there. Julia will tell you that I'm a little too preoccupied with this whole 'life, death and existence' thing for most people's taste.

"But you've no idea how happy today has made me feel. You really haven't." Claire reaches out a hand and squeezes Sunny's, which is laying on the table, her fingers resting on the foot of her empty wine glass.

Julia smiles at both of her companions, still content to witness such a momentous moment in both of their lives. She contemplates her own life; how she'd had two great kids, Dean and Aimi. Neither had really ever been trouble for her. The only reason Dean had brought her any anxiety some years back was because of her ex-husband's intolerance. Francis Waters was a self-made man who expected too much of his children, especially of Dean. When Dean found Alyson, there had been fireworks between him and his father because in his view Alyson's background wasn't suitable for a son of his to marry. He'd had his eye on his son finding a nice middle-to-upper class girl with horses and a country estate. Alyson was raised by a single mother (Christine) on a council estate in Twerton. Just when Dean had thought that he and Alyson were going to stay together, which would have meant Francis cutting off all the help he'd been giving Dean while he started his fledgling graphic design business, Alyson had fled, mistakenly thinking that it would be better her giving Dean up for his sake.

She didn't ever tell Dean where she'd gone and, as it happened, met Claire whilst the two of them were getting off an aeroplane in Kefallonia back in 1998.

Julia carries on musing over all that went on. She remembers how Dean had finally got over Alyson. It had taken him a couple of years. When he and his Fiancée Fiona had arranged to be married in Lindos in the summer of 2005, on the Greek island of Rhodes, who would have ever dreamt that Alyson had been living there for quite a while, or that Dean and Alyson would bump into eachother like they had. Of course all hell had broken loose as Dean had absconded with Alyson and Fiona had returned home heartbroken. Francis, well, Julia had never, ever seen him so livid. One thing Julia was grateful for about all of this though was that these events had triggered in her the strength to consider for the first time whether she really wanted to carry on as the wife of 'Mr. Bombastic Society Climber', Francis Waters.

In July of 2006 she'd finally walked out on Francis and flown out to Rhodes to surprise Dean by turning up at his wedding, this time to Alyson. That's when she'd first met Claire and they'd become fast friends almost immediately. Boy what a time that was. Brian, now

Alyson's father-in-law, whom Julia knows well, had known Alyson's mum Christine way back in the late seventies and when he'd seen Dean's father quite by chance in 2005, the year before, when Dean was supposed to have married Fiona, he'd recognised him but couldn't remember where from. One thing led to another and it became very evident to Brian, wrongly as it all turned out, that Dean may well have been… well, what does it matter now? The fact is she and Claire have been in business together and also fast friends now for upward of three years. After many years of putting up with a man who evaluated everything in life financially, she now has a stable, happy, fulfilling existence. Yes, OK, occasionally she thinks about whether it would be nice to find another man, but she's really not all that bothered. She's fifty-six now and feels pretty good about herself. She can still get into jeans and dresses she wore a decade ago, so she's not let herself go. She runs on Clifton Downs several times a week, which surely must help.

All in all, she has a lot to be thankful for. She finds herself wondering, more out of curiosity than out of any lingering concern, what her ex is doing now. She hasn't spoken to him for a long time and, since both children had flown the nest when she left him, they haven't had much cause to communicate anyway. Aimi is living in Germany with Heinz, her professor husband and Dean is running his business in Cardiff. She makes a mental note to ring Dean and Alyson tomorrow to arrange to get together soon.

"Julia! Julia!!" Claire is almost singing Julia's name to bring her out of her reverie. "Old age creeping up, eh, love? Forgot where we are did we?"

"Ruddy cheek!!" replies Julia. "What's happening?"

"See? Told you. Haven't had our medication today have we?"

Claire seems in joking mood. Julia responds again:

"Listen here my girl, I still have three years or so on you. Last time I reckoned it up anyway! Never put down to old age what ought to be put down to several glasses of rather exceptional wine."

All three women laugh and Claire says, "We just wanted to tell you we've decided to all go back to the flat for a brandy and After Eights. Agreed?"

"Why on earth wouldn't I? I'm anyone's for an After Eight."

Sunny settles the bill and they all rise together. They take turns at thanking their waitress, Alana, and she sees them to the door, before turning to grin like a Cheshire Cat at her friend behind the bar owing to the exceptionally good tip that Sunny has left her. As she walks back through the restaurant, she says, to no one in particular, "Sometimes I looooove my job."

The women walk the five minutes or so from the restaurant to the front door of the gallery and Claire lets them all in. Without putting any more lights on, apart from the few night lights that are always on downstairs overnight, they proceed to the door which leads to the stairs and they make their way upstairs and into the lounge, which is all stripped pine floor and cream cotton loose-cover sofas with huge cushions, two of them. The large wooden shutters, original remnants of the Georgian era during which this place was built, are still folded neatly away in their purpose-built recesses each side of the high Georgian sash windows. They are painted a silk-finish olive green colour and Claire tugs them out and partly closes them across the windows to afford the women a degree of privacy. Not that it's really needed, as the building across the street, also a Georgian terrace, houses only offices on the first floor and there are no lights showing in any of the windows at this hour, late in the evening as it is.

"Stick some music on will you Jools? I'll fix us a Metaxa. Metaxa all right for you Sunny?"

"Can't say I've ever tried it. Greek isn't it?"

"Indeed it is. And I can't bring myself to drink any other Brandy since I fell in love with the country. You ever been there, Sunny?"

The sound of Lee Ritenour's guitar on the album *Rio* fills in the subtle, subdued hollows of the room as Sunny replies, "No, I haven't. I really must go there one day. I read somewhere that in the list of 100 things to do before you die the Acropolis in Athens features quite high up."

"Well, I'd say it's more like '100 places to visit', but yes, you're right anyway."

Julia and Sunny sink deeply into the well-upholstered sofas, one is a three-seater and the other a two. Claire arrives with three brandy balloons, each one almost half-full. She says, "I'll just break out a box of After Eights, won't be a mo'."

Sunny sees above the cast iron fireplace which faces her a large oil-on-canvas of the Clifton Suspension bridge. She gazes at it and asks, "Is this one of Claire's?"

Julia replies, "Yes, it is. She never goes up there these days, but seems unable to take it down, even though I sometimes think it hurts her to look at it."

"It's my penance," says Claire, arriving with the After Eights. She sits down beside Sunny and also looks up at her work. "Sunny, do you know how I lost Charles?"

"Your husband? NO! I only know that he died almost at the same time as my birth parents. Why, does it have something to do with..?" She looks back up at the painting.

"He fell, Sunny. He fell from that bridge." There is a silence,

Sunny doesn't know what to say or even how to say it and Julia watches Claire. She knows exactly how to deal with Claire's moments now. She'll pull herself together and perk up, which she does.

"Still, long time ago. But I must have that painting up there. Some day I'll tell you why. But now, drink that brandy and filch a few of these," she says as she waves the box of mint chocolates under Sunny's nose. Sunny obeys and finds her fingers lifting away from the box with three of the individually-wrapped wafer-thin chocolates dangling from them.

"I still have something more to say to you, Claire." Sunny says. Claire's face betrays the fact that she's all ears.

"Well, as I told you, mum died four years ago. Dad's doing OK, but he still misses her. He's still only sixty and, although he's my 'dad' to all intents and purposes, he's a good-looking, well-preserved specimen. Joking aside, he'd pass for someone younger, to my way of thinking. He's always taken care of himself and still goes out walking for hours several times a week. He won't leave the house in Stroud, even though I've suggested he move to Bath or the surrounding area, but I get to see him at least twice a month. He had a brother, but I don't know what happened to him and, as you know from earlier, his parents were long gone from as early as I can remember. My other aunts and uncles were relatives of mum's. There's not a lot of contact there now. Dad does have a few friends, mainly those he mixes with in the local pub, where he goes once a week on a Friday night, never more than that. He also has a couple of old work colleagues that he sees now and then, when they'll talk shop for hours.

"So, what I'm trying to get around to is this. With my mum gone, I have no one apart from dad. OK, so I have Callum, but he's settled in New Zealand so is not going to figure in my life all that much from now on. I have, though, been told the whole story about what you and Charles did for my real mum when she was desperate and pregnant with me. I can't begin to express how appreciative I am of the things you did. You took a waif in from the street, well, almost, and gave her a home, a wage, a couple of much-needed shoulders to cry on. You fed her and clothed her. You were willing, if I've got this right, to help her get her life on track even after I came along if my father hadn't turned up when he did.

"Incidentally, if you're wondering quite how I know so much of this story, it's because my birth-mother wrote everything down, all of it. She wrote the whole story out long-hand and left it with the solicitor. I think she'd have given it to me herself once I'd grown up, but she obviously wanted to make sure that I knew the whole story if anything ever happened to her. So the solicitor was instructed to give it to me on my mother's death. I suppose she thought that I'd likely be coming to live with you, perhaps the solicitor would have made sure that the story was given to you and your husband if you'd taken me on, so that you too might have been able to let me read it when you gauged that I was old enough to understand it all. It's very thick and all written in ballpoint pen on A4 lined paper. It's all in there Claire, even the times that you and my mother ate popcorn and drank Coke in the cinema together. She even wrote down the films that you saw together. She expressed her feelings very expansively about both you and Charles and it's abundantly clear to me that she always felt that she'd let you down by taking me away and bringing me up with my father.

"I have the whole thing in my car, Claire, it's almost a book in itself there's so much detail there. Reading it made me cry for hours, especially the part where she describes how you and Charles reacted when you arrived at the hospital shortly after my birth and found my father sitting at the bedside, but it also made me so want to find you. It seems that my mother sensed that you might even have thought badly of her, that perhaps you even thought that she'd planned the whole thing. This affected her deeply and, towards the end, she agonized over whether to get in touch with you to explain it all, to try to assure you how much she appreciated what you did for her. She was always going to get back in touch, of that I'm in no doubt. The accident so abruptly brought an end to everything, all her intentions, all her guilt feelings, all the plans. I know from what she writes about my father that he was entirely in agreement with whatever course of action she took. He'd given her his blessing if she wanted to talk to you, write to you, whatever. I think she kept putting it off because she knew you too well, Claire. I think too that she was frightened of hurting you even more. It's like she felt you were hurting to have lost me, but that you'd probably hurt even more to be reminded of the whole affair all over again.

"But above all, she knew how much store you'd placed on adopting me. She knew how much you'd wanted to start a family. My mother, Claire, for what it's worth now at this late stage, my mother, I think, loved you. She'd grown to understand you and she felt deeply your pain on losing me, on losing your chance to raise a child.

"How can anyone quantify what you and your husband did? It's extraordinary - to put it mildly. It was a superlative display of humanity and kindness, of love, that I think very few people would have shown."

Claire is now crying. She's grabbed a box of tissues from the coffee table and is blowing her nose into one. Her guilt has come back over her in waves, since she now wants to punish herself for ever thinking badly of the young Marianna.

"Claire, please don't cry. Don't you see? We may have lost twenty-four years, but now I want you in my life. I want you, Claire, as my very belated, call it surrogate if you like, but I want to see you now as my mother."

18. Full Circle.

"It's OK though," says Sunny, "I won't call you 'mum'. That would be too crazy. I've already had two mothers and, anyway, I've only now come to meet you after I've already grown up. But it's the feeling of gratitude that children ought to have if they've been well brought up, if they've had really good parents, that I feel I have toward you."

Claire is quite overcome and doesn't know what to say. She dries her eyes, but they remain moist. Then she feels a wave of elation passing over her. She doesn't care where it comes from, she's grateful to feel it. She's moved to say, with a degree of humour,

"Well, if that's the case my girl, you're not driving a car again tonight after what you've had to drink. You'd better stay the night with us. The spare room bed's made up anyway, so it's no trouble for us. Agreed?"

Julia is already standing up, "I'll go and turn the bed down anyway. Then I'm turning in if it's OK with you two." Sunny stands up and hugs Julia, who bids the other two goodnight with "Well, nighty night. Don't let the bed bugs bite. …Oh," she adds as she reaches the door, "thanks so much Sunny for a wonderful meal this evening."

"You're very welcome, Julia. Goodnight. See you in the morning."

Sunny has accepted Claire's 'command' with good grace and a fair degree of appreciation anyway. Not only is she quite sure that she is over the limit, but she feels much too drained to drive the twelve miles or so back to Bath this evening. "I'll send Jilly a text, so she knows where I am and when I'll be back."

"Jilly?" Asks Claire.

"Yes, she manages the restaurant. Very bright girl. Much more efficient than me. I do all the bookwork, order foodstuffs and wine, pay the bills, deal with reps, plan the menus and stuff. Jilly does the hands-on day-to-day. She keeps the staff in order and looks after the place every hour its doors are open. I can't get her to take time off; she seems to love the job so much. We both live upstairs, so she'll probably wonder what's happened to me if I don't let her know something.

"Claire, thanks for listening to my story."

"Sunny, thanks for telling it to me. I shall be honoured to be in your life and to view you as a long, lost daughter whom I've now found. Now, get yourself to bed my girl. I'll call you for breakfast in the morning."

"La Jambe de Grenouille" is only open during evenings from Tuesday until Friday. On Mondays it's normally closed, unless required for a private function. On Saturdays and Sundays, however, it opens at 12 noon for lunches and stays open until midnight. The petit restaurant is situated down a small side street in the downtown area of the Georgian city of Bath. It's just along a cobbled street a few yards from what used to be the Hatchets public house, but is now called The Raven. Its intimate and cozy atmosphere makes it a hit with everyone who dines there, that and the fact that the food is superb. Chef Raymond Doherty was trained in one of the top hotels in London and used to run the kitchen at the Royal Crescent Hotel, Bath, which is seriously up market. The Royal Crescent is where movie stars stay and leading actors in touring companies while they play the Theatre Royal in the city. The plaudits he received whilst there were many and from diverse sources, plus there were innumerable articles about him in the Sunday papers. He got bored though. The chance to jump ship and cook primarily food of a French nature was what lured him to work for Sunshine Geesin. The fact that his boss was a beautiful young woman scarcely past twenty years of age might have had a bearing too, but he is in fact much older than her and happily married. He's one of those chefs, one of those people rather, who has earned enough over the years to enable him to make such a change without regard to what his salary was going to be. He wanted the job satisfaction of helping to put a small, select restaurant on the gastronomical map. Judging by the way things are going, he's succeeding.

On Saturday September 25th, Claire and Julia walk up the narrow street to the restaurant's front door at exactly 1.00pm as agreed with Sunny. It's a bright, clear blue-sky day, though a little cold for the time of year. Both women are arm in arm and wearing thick woolen three-quarter length coats.

Sunshine Geesin has been anxiously watching from one of the restaurant's two Dickensian front windows and rushes to the door to open it and greet her honoured guests.

"Hi ladies! Come in, come in! Let me take your coats, you OK with this table in the window? It's my favourite to be honest, 'cos you can people-watch from here too."

Both ladies nod and murmur their agreement and are soon seated opposite eachother across the crisp, white tablecloth. Sunny retreats for a brief moment and returns with a bottle of Moet, which she pops enthusiastically and pours the contents into the three flutes that she's placed on the table in readiness for this celebratory moment. They all lift their glasses as Sunny says,

"Welcome to my humble establishment. May it be the first of millions of hopefully regular visits over many years to come!"

All three raise their glasses and then sip the sparkling liquid. Claire and Julia are soon introduced to Jilly, a full-figured young woman of about thirty, who nevertheless does still have a waist, thus making her figure look nevertheless well-proportioned. She's dressed all in black and her hair is short, blonde and frizzy. She has a pretty-ish face but, if one were being picky, one might say with slightly prominent, chubby cheeks. She's bubbly though and soon makes her special guests feel just that - special. Sunny to's and fro's, ever checking to see if her charges are happy whilst also spending brief moments talking to the other diners. There are several couples doing lunch today. Sunny has made it a kind of trade mark of the restaurant that she 'floats' among her guests, spending just enough time with each party to make them feel she's attentive, without overdoing it to the extent that they wish she'd go away and afford them the privacy that they undoubtedly came to this restaurant for. Diners often recommend "La Jambe" to their friends purely because they want them to see the young beauty who runs the place and feel suitably impressed.

Julia and Claire are tucking into a delicious lunch and sipping mineral water (Perrier, of course) and both are keeping a watchful eye on the street outside for passers by about which to comment. As it's a nice, bright day and it's also a Saturday, there is plenty of "grist for the mill" so to speak. One or the other will say something like, 'those colours - together! Yuk.' or 'why do women who are that shape wear such short tops and tight leggings? That bum ought to be covered up. Doesn't she realize how much better she'd look?' Then there's the occasional "Now HE looks good, a man with some taste for a change. Why are the British so generally lacking in that area?' along with 'Got to be foreign, Greek or Italian I'd guess. You'd never see Brits wearing such nice clothes!'

Julia's attention is grabbed by a familiar couple, strolling very slowly, engaged in an animated conversation. They aren't looking toward the restaurant at first, but as they draw level with it, they stop and both turn to gaze at the building's frontage. They're hand in hand and the man is a little older than the woman. This is only really made evident by his graying hair, but both are quite fit, slim and healthy-looking. They appear to be very close from the body language they're both displaying. The man's hair is tied back in a short ponytail and the woman's is shoulder length and very dark. Whether it's dyed or not, it's hard to tell.

Julia smiles, but the couple don't react to her. The bright sunlight out in the street prevents them from seeing clearly through the restaurant's windows. She pulls out her mobile phone from the handbag hanging on the back of her chair and taps a couple of buttons on the keypad.

Claire notices and also turns to stare at the couple, both of whom she too recognizes. She first met the man, whose name is Brian Worth, when she and Alyson Wright (now Julia's daughter-in-law) had been living in Lindos, on the island of Rhodes. He is a musician and used to play regularly in a bar there, just him and his acoustic guitar. She'd been to watch him occasionally at Alyson's request and found him mesmerizing, his mastery of the instrument having entranced many of those who watched and listened to him. His voice was pretty good too, rather gravelly, the kind of tone Claire likes in a singer, which is why she has plenty of Tom Waits, Leonard Cohen, Bruce Springsteen and John Martyn albums in her CD collection.

The woman is Brian's wife. They'd married in Lindos in July 2007. It was a double wedding. Her single name was Christine Wright. She's almost exactly ten years younger than her husband. Although they only married three years ago, they've known eachother since the late 1970's. Theirs is a story worth the telling. Indeed it is told elsewhere.

Brian reaches into his jacket pocket and pulls out his phone, which is playing "Money" by Pink Floyd in its attempt to attract its owner's attention. Pressing the green button, he holds it up to his ear and says,

"Hello Julia. How you doing sweetie? To what do I owe this inestimable honour?"

"Can't you see us?" Asks Julia from just a few metres away, inside the restaurant, "I'm looking straight at you."

"Spying on us, eh? Never could rid yourself of that dream of becoming the first female James Bond, could you! Where the devil are you then?" He chuckles at his own wit whilst casting searching glances up and down the street and Julia answers,

"Brian, we're in the restaurant you're staring at, you dipstick! Look a little closer." From her position behind the glass, Julia now sees the couple walk across the cobbles to the window, whereupon Brian shields his eyes with his free hand, having released it from his wife's grip in order to do so, and presses it against the glass. Immediately seeing Julia and Claire he steps back waves, nudges his wife Christine and they both make for the door.

Once inside Brian and Christine are immediately pounced on by the ever-vigilant Jilly. "Have you a reservation, sir?" She asks.

Claire calls to her right away, "They're friends of ours Jilly, send them over!"

Jilly immediately retreats, a warm smile spreading across her face, whilst also extending a hand to beckon the new arrivals to join Claire and Julia. Once at the table, Brian embraces both Julia and Claire in turn, each of whom rises for the ritual of saying hello. Everyone takes turns at a hug and mock kisses on both cheeks, something they've all learned from their Greek visits, and Claire says:

"You two got the time to join us? Please do, we'd be delighted. We haven't seen you in a while. You both look well."

Brian exchanges a quick acknowledging glance with his wife, who nods a smiley face at him and he thus answers,

"OK. Why not? We were only wandering around town to pass an hour or two anyway.

"You two don't normally eat in here do you? You've never mentioned the place to us before."

"No, it's our first time," replies Julia, who then defers to her close friend Claire to continue. So she does.

"It is indeed our first time in here, but I get the feeling we'll be coming here quite a lot from now on. The owner is a long lost friend of mine from twenty years ago and more."

"Twenty years?" asks Christine, incredulously, "But I'd heard the owner of this place is only in her twenties anyway. How could you have known her over twenty years ago?"

"It's complicated," answers Claire, "But Sunny Geesin, who as you rightly say Chris is only still in her twenties, came within a hair's breadth of being the adopted daughter of my husband Charles and I back in 1986, would you believe."

The faces of both Brian and Christine display complete amazement at this revelation. Brian asks:

"You've got to tell us the story, Claire! You've never even hinted about anything like this before! How could this have happened, and why didn't you adopt then?"

Julia interjects. "First, Brian. I have a question for you, because Claire's story may well see us way into this evening if you want to hear it all."

"Fire away." Replies Brian.

"As you walked up the street outside, you both stopped and stared at this place. I don't know, but it seemed to me a strange thing to do if you didn't know that Claire and I were sitting in here having lunch. What's the explanation for that, then?"

"Yea, that's a point," adds Claire. "You have us both intrigued."

"Well, at the risk of stealing your thunder, Claire, we have a long story that could take ages too. But I'll try and cut it down to the bare bones. You both know that Christine and I knew eachother from a long time ago, right?" The women nod, "Well, we both first met in Porky's Bar, when I used to work behind the bar and sing at the mike in the corner and Christine cleared tables and did bar work too. Julia, you know that there was a brief connection between Christine and your ex way back around that time too, don't you?"

"Yes, of course. He tried to keep her on the straight and narrow; some family connection that led to him looking out for her welfare. Couldn't forget that, after what happened in Lindos, now could I? We'd not been married long and Dean was only a baby."

"Did you ever know where exactly Porky's Bar was, the place where Christine and I both worked?"

Claire and Julia both stare back blankly shaking their heads in unison. "You're going to tell us!" Says Julia.

"You're sitting in it."

Both Claire and Julia are stunned by the coincidence. Looking from Christine to Brian, both of whom stare back with conspiratorial smiles on their faces, they are momentarily struck dumb.

"See that corner over there," continues Brian, pointing, "That was where the tiny stage was, only a couple of metres square, where I'd set up my gear and play on weekends. The bar used to be there," he continues, pointing to a corner where there are now restaurant tables, "so you can see why, quite often when Christine and I walk up this street, we stop and stare at "La Jambe de Grenouille," but what we see in our mind's eye is the frontage of Porky's Bar from way back in, what, must have been seventy-seven, seventy-eight. Quite a coincidence it now seems, eh?

"Your turn, Claire." Brian adds, with a broad grin.

"I can't believe it, what a weird thing is this life! OK, so where do I start? Well, when Alyson and I struck up our friendship and toured Greece together from ninety-eight until two thousand and one, I told her scant details about my past. She knew that I was pretty down about everything, that I used visits to Greece as my pick-me-up, or anaesthetic as I'd sometimes call it, but apart from the fact that I told her how I'd lost Charles, I kept a lot to myself.

"To be truthful, I couldn't even bring myself to address the past, let alone recount it all to Alyson, which would have just sent me down into a black spiral anyway. I only told her that my husband, who I'd loved unreservedly and deeply, had died falling from the

Clifton Suspension Bridge some years earlier. That single event had destroyed me inside. I've always had great difficulty getting through life without answers that satisfied me, but when I lost Charles my world imploded. But there were other events from before and even at the time that added to the maelstrom - which is the only way I can describe it - that surrounded me for quite some time."

A young waiter arrives and enquires as to whether Brian and Christine would like to order something. Before they can resolve what they want to do, Sunny herself arrives, having noticed that there were now four people at the table. She asks Claire,

"Well, seems you guys all know eathother well. Aren't you going to introduce us?"

"Of course," replies Claire, "Brian, Christine, meet my new spiritual daughter, Sunny Geesin!"

"Pleased to meet you both. Are you local, or visiting Bath?"

Brian is quick to respond. "Oh, we're very local. In fact, we both used to work in this very establishment way back before you were born!"

Sunny makes it plain that no one at the table will be paying for anything and has to restrain Brian and Christine from insisting that they must. Since the couple are close friends of her new "mum" she won't hear of it and they eventually acquiesce.

Several hours pass while everyone chips in various details about the events of the past that eventually brought them all together. Claire finds that for the first time in ages she is able to recount what happened with Sunny's mother Marianna and how she and Charles almost came to be the legal parents of the young restaurateur, without going to pieces emotionally. She finds herself contemplating, whilst others are talking enthusiastically, about how events in Lindos had resulted in them all becoming related by marriage, apart from herself, who nevertheless feels quite maternal toward Christine's daughter Alyson, with whom she'd spent so many years together in Greece. Christine, Alyson and Julia have all treated her like family anyway since they all returned from Greece.

As she and Julia reluctantly leave the restaurant and darkness falls in the small Bath backstreet, Claire finds that for once she can feel happy, contented, even emotionally stable.

After all, she finally now does have someone she can call her own, Sunny Geesin. And she silently thanks Marianna and Eric for their thoughtfulness in expressing their wishes so clearly in their wills all those years ago.

19. Terry.

"You ought to meet him some time. You'd like him," says Sunny. She's sitting on a stool in Claire's studio, watching Claire work. It's another commission, this time someone's Siamese cat. Claire sometimes feels like a sell-out when she does jobs like this. But they pay well and the customers always seem to rave about her work. This one's a referral from her friend Amanda Brandonbury, who still sees Claire a couple of times a month. Sunny is referring to her foster "dad" Terry White.

"He's rather good looking as it happens. Bit old for me of course, even if he wasn't the man who brought me up. But some woman out there could do a lot worse." Claire places a brush between her teeth, turns and looks at Sunny with that 'don't you start trying on anything like that young lady' look. She lifts her coffee mug to her lips and grins anyway. Sunny has her hands clasped around her mug as she giggles.

"How long have you been on your own Claire, Hmm? Hold on,

I should know the answer to that one. Of course, you lost Charles when I lost my birth mum and dad. So you've been alone for twenty years. Haven't you during all that time ever run into someone you could perhaps have fallen for, even married?"

Claire thinks for a while. She's fifty-nine now, but still in good shape. Perhaps…, but then she responds: "When you lose someone you've planned to spend the rest of your days with, someone you struck a deep chord with, someone you were so in tune with that you actually understood the expression 'two become one', you're absolutely determined that you'll never love another. You'll never find someone else who can measure up. You don't want to go on alone, yet you can't stand even the thought of anyone else taking up the place of your lost partner. It would be a travesty, a crime, to imagine staring across the pillow at a different face, to walk hand in hand through the park and not see the right face looking back at you when you turn to look at your mate.

"I won't say that I've never considered finding someone else, Sunny, but each time I've even thought about the possibility I've soon come around to feelings of guilt. I know I'll never get my Charles back again, least I think I know. To be honest, I'm not really sure what I believe, but I suppose like so many people who are in the same boat, there's this abiding feeling that some day perhaps, in some way, I'll be reunited with him. Fanciful probably, but it leaves me always thinking that, if I were to even go out with another man, I'd be betraying Charles because he loved me and I loved him. How dare another man occupy Charles' place in my life and my heart?

"Does it sound strange if I say that, well, it would be unfair on the new man in my life anyway, because I'd probably soon find myself comparing him to Charles, or even punishing him for being where Charles ought to have been?"

"I hear what you're saying, of course. But surely we can only go forward. We can't go back. You're still young enough Claire to find a degree of happiness again. Don't you think that Charles just might, if he were able to express an opinion, approve? Would he want you to carry on alone into your dotage, never really enjoying life any more?"

"I appreciate your concern, Sunny. Perhaps when you eventually find Mr. Right you'll understand me more fully. But for now, that's just how it has to be for me I'm afraid."

Sunny spends quite a lot of her time now thinking about Claire and her welfare, her right to experience again the happiness and fulfillment of having a companion in life. She's only twenty four and still feels she's got the time to find the person that's right for her, but can't see herself going right through life on her own. She believes that in the few short weeks that she's known Claire that there is a void deep down that Claire would be better off filling. She knows that it's none of her business, yet she can't keep from coming up with ideas. She's already getting into the habit of visiting Claire in the studio while she works and chewing the fat with her. She wants to get to understand Claire as fully as possible. She contemplates continually the circumstances around which she was taken from this woman's arms when she was only hours old. She tries deliberately to conjure up the feelings in herself that Claire must have experienced when, after all those months of planning and anticipation, everything had been taken from her. She even finds that on one level she resents what her birth parents did to Charles and Claire. This confuses her, because at the same time she finds herself thinking that were she the parent, wouldn't she have done the same? What other choice was there?

*

On Saturday October 23rd she's driving up to Stroud to visit her dad, Terry. It's a filthy day, as people in the West Country would say; grey, wet and windy. She's got the wipers going incessantly and occasionally has to switch them to the higher speed, then back to regular speed again. She's a bit fed up because up until a few days ago it has been one of the sunniest Octobers on record. There was even a report on the TV that 23°C was recorded in Devon at the end of the first week of the month. It has been a classic Indian Summer that everyone hoped would last a little longer than it has.

She'd hoped today to be able to sit out in her dad's back garden on his teak patio set and sip Pimms with him while admiring his roses, many of which should still be blooming, what with the good weather that they've had. Terry's been a widower now for over four years. He's a coper, a fact probably born of his years on the Force. He soon learned to cook when Sandra died. It was one way to keep himself occupied and not become too inward-looking, or insular. He carried on his regular Friday night visits to the local pub and his friends and neighbours came up trumps in trying to help him keep going and get over losing Sandra, his wife of nearly thirty years.

Sunny is soon driving up the lane to Terry's house, which is situated in that part of Kingscourt Lane where the houses look across the road to a rural setting of fields and stands of deciduous trees. It's a pretty, green area of gently rolling hills and, although Sunny would like him to move nearer to Bath now that he's on his own, she can understand his reluctance to leave this locale. His house, which was probably built not long after the war, has a substantial back garden too, which is quite private. It's long enough, in fact, for Terry to use it to practice pitch and put, since he's become quite a golfer in recent years. He loves Sunny as if she were his own and willingly gives up his usual eighteen holes (well, nineteen really) on a Saturday when she's coming over. She's entirely confident about leaving the restaurant in Jilly's hands now and again and knows that she'll be back there by early evening anyway, prowling the tables and working her guests, many of whom like to boast to their friends about being on first-name terms with Sunny Geesin.

Terry is already at the front door at around twelve noon when Sunny pulls up outside the drive. He's been keeping vigil at the window for some time, as he usually does. She bounces over to meet him, not bothering to lock her car, and plants a huge kiss on his cheek while bear-hugging him hello. He beams down at her and says,

"Hello Sunshine my girl. How's it going? Roads OK on the way up?"

"Oh, the usual. You know me, dad, I don't touch the M5, I always come up the A46, the Old Sodbury way. Got a bit slowed down by a procession of hay-bale lorries from just the other side of Nailsworth, but no real bother."

"I bet you're gasping for a drink, yeh?"

"Has the Pope got a balcony, dad? Coffee would be great. It's not the weather for Pimms today, is it."

"Already got some Douwe Egberts percolating, I kind of sussed you'd be in a coffee mood." Terry turns and walks back along the hallway and through the house to the kitchen, the window of which looks out on his impressive back garden of immaculate lawn and rose borders. Sunny, having closed the front door, is right behind and sniffs enthusiastically as her nose picks up the aroma of the freshly brewing coffee. Terry throws a question over his shoulder as he approaches the cafetière on the kitchen top. "What's happenin' then? What's the news about this Claire Mason you've finally managed to track down? Still good friends?" he adds the last part mischievously, knowing that his foster-daughter has a sense of humour.

"Y'know, dad, she's a really lovely person. It's not hard to imagine having been brought up by her. I'd so love to have met her husband. From what she tells me he must have been a rare one. Bit like you really!"

Terry chuckles as he plants two mugs of steaming, dark liquid on the table between them, where Sunny is already seated and waiting. He opens the door to his under-the-counter fridge and extracts a carton of milk, already opened. Pouring a little of the milk into a china jug with a flower motif on the side and placing that on the table, he then goes into the wall cupboard in search of some biscuits. He always gives Sunny McVitie's Chocolate Digestives, the plain chocolate variety. For all her preoccupation with wholefoods and organic vegetables, she's anyone's for a McVitie's Plain Chocolate Digestive.

"Oh, I don't think he'd have been anything like me. Lazy, selfish, boring..."

"Dad!! Stop it!! You're none of those things and you know it. Don't YOU ever think about trying again though? You must know a few old birds who'd like a bit of company as they push their walking frames about!"

"Sometimes you're too cheeky for your own good. I bet I could still beat you in a race to the shed and back."

Sunny's instantly projected into a brief reverie of when she was maybe nine or ten years old. She and Terry used to race to the shed at the bottom of the garden and back, when he always let her win by a nose. That was when she was going to grow up and be an athlete and win an Olympic Gold medal.

"You always *lost*, if you get your facts right." She replies, gazing with genuine affection at the man across the table from her. "Seriously, though, dad. I know four years isn't that long, but has there been anyone who's crossed your sights that you may have wondered about? Can't be that much fun holed up here in the back of beyond all on your lonesome."

"The back of beyond just happens to be where I want to stay, thank you very much. But, well, you might have a point. I've got to say that I don't think I'm a good one for living on my own permanently. Trouble is, how would I replace your mother? Sandra was the one for me. She and I had something that I'm not sure I could ever find elsewhere."

"That's just it, dad. See, I think that it shouldn't be about replacing the one you loved and lost. It should be about moving on. Time's the enemy of all of us. It's like, well, as we go through life, a series of plate glass panes is being pushed down behind us perpetually. We can turn and look back, but there's no way we can break any of them and actually go in reverse, go back. We can see things from the past when we look back through them, but as more and more glass is put between us and the past, the more vague it becomes until, well, it's indiscernible. That make any sense?"

"I know what you're saying sweetie. Perhaps you're right. They say you can't put an old head on young shoulders, but occasionally it might be a good idea to try and put a young head on slightly older ones, eh?" Terry White sips his coffee, extracts a chocolate digestive from the packet and dunks it, before deftly bringing it to his lips before it falls in two, the damp part falling back into the coffee. He's evidently an expert, as is his foster-daughter, who does something similar. They both savour the flavour of the melting dark chocolate, mingled with digestive biscuit, before carrying on with their conversation.

"Anyway, back to Claire. I at least think that you two ought to meet some time. You know, you might at least become friends. I would like that, really I would, since you're both going to be playing major parts in my life from now on. What do you think?"

"Well, OK. Some time. But I don't want anything contrived going on OK? None of this, 'well, I'll just leave you two together while I…' malarkey!! Maybe some time when I'm down in Bristol you can show me her gallery. Who knows, perhaps I'll want to buy one of her paintings."

"Or sit for one!"

"I dunno what I'm gonna do with you, I really don't."

Thursday November 4th 2010. Claire picks up the phone. It's 10.45am. Sunny's voice greets her at the other end.

"Sorry to be a bit last minute about this, but do you and Julia fancy eating in the Aqua tonight? I'm in Bristol all day and I just thought it might be a good idea. I'm not going to want to eat when I get home. Work and all that stuff, you know, slaving over a hot restaurant. What do you say?"

"Hold on," answers Claire. She puts her hand over the phone, pulls at the studio door and calls out, "Jools!! Aqua tonight with Sunny! You up for it?"

From the bottom of the stairs there's a muffled "Why not!" and Claire takes her hand from the receiver and says,

"Looks like you're on. You booking a table or shall I?"

"Aah, well, I already did. Can always cancel if you couldn't make it, but I wanted to be sure we got in. See you in there at eight?"

"OK, Sunny. See you later then."

Claire Mason is quite intuitive and is fairly sure that something's afoot. She felt from the tone of Sunny's voice and the fact that it was the first time she'd done anything impulsive like this since they met, that there might be a hidden agenda. Still, she doesn't mind, she loves to see Sunny and she and Julia don't need much excuse to go to the Italian.

It's warm for the first week of November, but overcast. November in the UK for many is the worst month of the year. The entire winter is still ahead and it always seems that the sun has vanished forever. It seems that November is top month in Britain for grey skies. The nights are drawing in and this fact is emphasized by the cloudy skies, which mean that lights in people's homes are quite often being switched on at 3.30pm, owing to lack of brightness from the sun. There had been a brief moment of sunshine over Clifton during the morning, but Claire doesn't mind. She's basking in the glow of her new young *almost*-daughter, Sunshine Geesin. The gallery is now closed as it's past 6.00pm and she and Julia are in their respective rooms getting ready for their evening out.

As is quite often the case, the two women carry on a conversation from behind open bedroom doors. Claire asks Julia,

"Jools, you ever thought about finding another partner? I mean, how long have you been separated from Francis now?"

"No, not really. And as to your second question, the answer is just over four years and counting. Never say never though, that's how I reason on the matter. Problem is, we've got such a cozy little life going on here now, it would take a superman to drag me away from it!"

"I suppose I think the same. But you know something? I think that during the past year or so I've finally noticed that the pain from losing Charles has lessened. They say time is a healer, maybe that's what it is. I'll always love him, of course, goes without saying, but that horrible emptiness that affects your every waking moment? Gone. At least for most of the time. What does that mean Jools? D'you think that perhaps I ought to be looking around?"

"Claire, love, you should do what you want to do. If you did decide that you'd found someone and it meant us changing the living arrangements here at the gallery, I'd not stand in your way. I'm sure we'd work something out for both of our benefit. Don't ask me if I think you should do this or that, though. I think I've learnt from you that to offer advice is to offer to take partial responsibility for what happens if someone follows it and comes a cropper."

Julia looks around to see Claire leaning on her doorpost, hair all wet as she half-heartedly rubs it with a towel. She's in her bathrobe.

"Jools. I don't have any plans and I don't expect to have any in the foreseeable. It's just something Sunny said recently. 'We can only go forward. We can't go back,' she said. It left me thinking, maybe that's been my problem for a couple of decades. I've spent far too much time trying to go back and one can't, can one. I mean, it doesn't matter how much one longs for things in the past, they will always remain there, in the past. If we spend too much time pining, it messes up the present and the future too, doesn't it?"

"That girl has a wise head on her shoulders for one so young. So, what say we go out this weekend on the pull?"

Claire looks shocked, then she sees Julia break into a grin and they both laugh. Claire says,

"Yea, I'm gonna look out my old mini skirts, or maybe hot pants and knee-length suede boots. Remember them?"

"Of course not, silly. I'm far too young!"

At just after eight the two women are walking arm-in-arm across the road toward the Italian restaurant in Whiteladies Road. The warm glow of the lights from within is seductive, there's a crowd in and both women are glad that they have a reservation. They step into the door and their eyes search for Sunny. She's still not arrived, but Alana the waitress is soon beside them and asks,

"Hello you two, under the name of Geesin this time are we?"

They respond with happy nods and are led to a table deep inside the restaurant, where the atmosphere can be described as private or intimate. They're relieved of their coats and they sit down at a table laid for four, with a small black 'reserved' sign placed in the centre. Both Julia and Claire notice that there are four places laid, but decide that it's simply due to the fact that it's a square table and they lay them this way as a matter of course. They've soon ordered Campari and lemonades as aperitifs and before long Sunny walks into the room, followed by a tall slim man, with a full head of once dark hair which is now flecked very liberally with grey, almost completely so at the temples. His slim face and dark eyes put both women in mind of a slightly older George Clooney, so both begin hoping that he's going to be spending the evening with them, whilst also concluding that he only walked in behind Sunny as a matter of coincidence.

Sunny's face is flushed after the cold outside and the contrasting warmth within. She also is relieved of her coat, as is the man behind her, to whom she now turns and whispers, pointing toward the two women seated at their table. The young woman looks radiant in a tight woolen sweater, charcoal in colour, over leg-hugging black silk trousers and patent stilettos. Her long hair sheens under the subdued lighting and flows all the way down to the small of her back. She looks every inch the model. The man, who's definitely over six feet tall, wears a navy sweatshirt with something indistinguishable printed on the chest and expensive chinos over a pair of tan Timberland desert boots. Quite independently of eachother Claire and Julia find themselves having difficulty taking their eyes off him.

The pair arrive at the table and Sunny declares, "Hi ladies!! I hope you don't mind but I've brought Terry along with me, since he was at a loose end too tonight. He's my foster-dad who brought me up. Terry, Claire, Julia - Terry."

Julia and Claire reply with their "pleased to meet you's" and the company is complete as Terry and Sunny sit themselves down.

"So, let me guess," says Terry, "Umm - you're Julia and you're Claire. Don't shoot me down if I'm wrong, but Sunny told me that Julia's blonde and Claire's a henna redhead. A bit of a giveaway, maybe. Anyway, please excuse my gatecrashing, but this young minx thought it would be a good idea." He says this looking sideways at his foster-daughter, who blushes and adopts a shy attitude with her head.

Claire looks daggers at Sunny, but only half-heartedly. She makes as if to slap her cheek, but only in jest. "You, young lady, are incorrigible," she says.

"Terry needs to expand his social circle a little, that's all!" protests Sunny, "So I thought you wouldn't mind if I introduced you both to him. After all, to be honest, he and mum did such a good job of raising me and Callum, that…"

"In whose opinion?" Asks Claire, tongue firmly in cheek.

"I'm sorry?" Asks Sunny.

"In whose opinion did this charming man do a good job of raising you then?"

Sunny knows that Claire's having a joke at her expense and laughs. She decides to join in with the joke, "OK," she says, "…did such a bad job of raising me that I decided to punish him by helping him to get to know you two! Terry, say hello to Morticia and Cruella!"

"Charmed. I love a woman who terrorizes," says Terry, but then decides that he's been a bit forward and worries a little.

The evening wears on and, much to Sunny's relief, seems to be a success. Terry seems to charm both women and they warm to him perceptibly. As it draws to a close, Terry invites the women to come over for Sunday lunch with Sunny some time. They agree on Sunday the 28th, the earliest that all four could make it, and are soon all standing outside the restaurant, their breath visible in the November evening air, saying their goodnights.

By the time Sunny has driven the three of them up to Stroud on the pre-arranged Sunday, it's very cold and flecks of snow are falling, dancing downward and upward, this way and that in the strong winds. During the night it had dropped to -10ºC, a record for the South of England in November. Terry rustles up a very respectable roast dinner, followed by a delicious apple crumble with custard. All four of them are feeling well sated and rather sleepy when Terry breaks out the Port when he's got them settled in the easy chairs in his conservatory, which looks out through patio doors to his rather impressive back garden.

"I'd quite forgotten how beautiful the countryside is," quips Claire. "I've lived in town for so long that I can't remember what it's like to have a back garden with grass, roses, a pergola and shrubs. You must be proud of this Terry, even in this weather it looks wonderfully restful."

"Well, I must say it would be a wrench to have to leave it." He's looking at Sunny and hoping that his thoughts are not lost on her when he says this.

"What he's getting at," she says, "is that I've been running a campaign to get Terry to move closer to Bath. There are lots of areas around the city where he'd find something like this. But the stubborn old fool won't budge." She reaches across and squeezes his hand as she says this, to be sure that he accepts the comment with the affection that she intends. He does, of course.

"I can well understand where he's coming from, Sunny," Claire responds. She looks to Julia for support and receives a smiley nod of the head from her languorous friend for her trouble. All Julia wants to do, after a couple of sips of her Port, is drift off, feet tucked up on the sumptuous sofa and dream of nothing much; maybe Greek beaches.

Claire goes on, "It really is a lovely house in a beautiful area. It's not all that far from Bath really, is it Sunny? Plus, Terry doesn't look to me like he's about to keel over just yet. You can get there in about an hour, that's not too far really, is it?"

"OK, I give in!" replies Sunny, secretly wondering now whether Claire may be thinking that a weekend up here might be a good tonic, in the right company too…

Claire and Terry carry on talking about both of their experiences as widow and widower, so much so that Sunny sees an opportunity to slip out into the kitchen to sort out the dirty dishes and tidy up in there. Julia is almost snoring flat out now on one of the conservatory's sofas and Claire has to admit that she's not only enjoying the chat, but hasn't really noticed Sunny's absence. She really likes this man, he must be about the same age as her and he really is in good shape. He's handsome too, not that that's a good enough reason to take to someone, but it helps.

"So, Claire," ventures Terry, "You've never met anyone you

thought that you might be happy with since you lost your husband then?"

Claire ponders as to whether there's anything behind this. She decides to take it on face value.

"No, not really. For many years after I first lost Charles I studiously avoided anyone who might remotely have held an interest for me. Eventually, after a few years of living on Rhodes I..."

"You lived on Rhodes? How great is that! How long were you there and where exactly were you living? I have been once. We stayed at, what was the name of the place now? Kolymbia I think. That's right, I remember now because I spent the whole first week pronouncing it Columbia before someone eventually put me right. Can't say I thought a lot of the resort, but the hotel was excellent and the beach there was lovely. We went to visit Lindos too. What a place that is. It's got to be one of the most beautiful places I've ever been." From Claire's face Terry registers that she'd lived in Lindos. "You lived there? In Lindos? Wow, tell me about it, do."

"It's a long story. It's really how I came to meet Julia.

"The young woman I was travelling with, and eventually settled in Lindos with, well she married Julia's son, but there's a whole lot more to the story than that. I moved back to Clifton in 2005. I'd not painted, not even touched my oils, my watercolours, nothing since I lost Charles. That's fifteen years. I finally felt that if I buried myself in creating art again I could shake off my preoccupation with death and this whole mortality thing."

She pauses. Terry waits, staring into her eyes. "I'm getting heavy now aren't I? I do this sometimes. Sorry." She adds.

"Don't apologise. I'm rapt, believe me." He realizes that he's staring and decides that it's time he created a diversion. Turning to look out of the window, he says, "The snow's sticking. Look."

Outside the landscape is turning, nay, it's already turned into a Christmas card. Everything is white. The narrow road out front is now under a blanket of white and it's still snowing. Out in the lane Sunny's car has six inches of snow on its roof and windscreen and, gazing at a now white lawn, it dawns on Claire that they probably won't be driving back to Bath or Bristol tonight.

By the time the road is clear enough for the women to make it back to the main road and hence attempt the drive back to Bristol for Sunny to drop off Julia and Claire, it's Tuesday morning. Terry gave Julia and Claire his bed, Sunny slept in the spare room and Terry has spent two nights on the living room sofa. When the three women are leaving, everyone exchanges hugs and cheek-kissed and all agree that the snow's been a blessing rather than a curse. None of them can remember having had a better time for years. They've been walking knee-deep in snow in places and had some furious snowball fights. They've built a huge snowman on Terry's back lawn and spent several hours down in the local pub swapping stories with a few of Terry's friends.

In the car driving southwards along the A46, Sunny's behind the wheel and planning to take a right at old Sodbury in order to drive through Yate, then down through Frenchay and Eastville and over from there to Clifton. Claire says,

"Y'know girls, it's been like a holiday this last couple of days." The other two murmur words of agreement. Sunny's been on the phone to Jilly and they agreed to close "La Jambe" for a few days, so she had no urgent need to get back quickly. "Sunny," Claire goes on, "You're forgiven."

"I am? For what?"

"Don't give us any of that '*butter wouldn't melt*' rubbish my girl!

You've been scheming and conniving and well you know it. Your father told me yesterday that he'd warned you about getting up to anything. It was a warning you evidently ignored."

"But Claire, I only..."

"I said you're forgiven! Ease up. It's OK. Don't worry, I'm actually quite glad now because Terry is a genuinely nice bloke. What do you say Jools?" Claire is sitting beside Sunny in the front and Julia is behind, sitting amidships and gazing first to her left and then right at the white, winter wonderland that surrounds them. Apart from the long snake of shiny black that is the road, well salted and quite clear of snow, everything is white. It's as if there's been an explosion in a nearby icing sugar factory. This kind of weather in November is extremely rare in the UK nowadays. Julia answers,

"I've had a fantastic time and Terry was the perfect host. All in all I'm feeling more laid back than I've been for years. Thanks Sunny. How on earth did you organize that snow right on queue too?"

"We aim to please." came Sunny's reply. Inside, she was feeling well pleased with herself.

20. Claire and Terry.

Alan Evans is a very patient man. He's not a very nice man, but patient, yes, he can be described as such, at least in some things. He's sixty-two now, as it's July 2011, and he's been counting the years since he last saw Charles Mason face to face. Of course, when he'd sent the idiot McBroom to retrieve the account details so that he'd be able to get hold of the money that Charles had been minding for him, he could never have foreseen McBroom getting himself knocked down and killed before he could share the account details with his anxious boss. Nothing in writing, it's the rule that has to be followed, even though in this case it cost him over a million Pounds Sterling.

Since late 1990, now twenty-one years ago, he's had no leads as to the whereabouts of Charles Mason's widow. The real possibility of getting caught if he'd put his henchmen on to finding and talking to Claire has kept him from pursuing it too enthusiastically up until now. The fact is he's managed to live quite well on his ill-gotten gains over the years anyway, never quite allowing The Law to feel his collar. He rather fancies himself now as unassailable. Yet to have had to say goodbye to such a large sum has always galled him and not a week goes by that he doesn't ponder about it.

OK, so its real value in purchasing power has somewhat diminished over the years, yet it's still a sum that he'd very much like to get back. Imagine what the interest would be on that amount over so many years. There's no guarantee, of course, that the widow will still have it, but he so wants to know for sure.

It was just the other week when he got lucky. One of his "employees" came across the Sunshine Gallery in Clifton and noticed from a small sign in the window that it was the place where the works of a certain Claire Mason were displayed and put on sale. He reported this back to Mr. Evans, who became rather excited at the possible prospect of "closure" after all this time.

Quite a few people who've dealt with Alan Evans down through his "career" seem to have died prematurely. There's never ever been a hint of his being involved, of course, but it's pre-occupied a number of very good Policemen over the years, not to mention angering a few too, those who've just known that he was behind such events, yet couldn't quite nail him. "Slippery bastard" would be the way a lot of CID officers would describe him. One scalp that they've never so far been able to apprehend was that of Mr. Alan Evans and it's a source of rancour to them.

'It's been such a long time' muses Evans to himself as he slouches in his Captain's chair at his desk at home, which is a large house in Shirehampton. He's long been divorced from his third wife and his two grown-up children don't see him all that often. Patient he may be, but bitter he most certainly is as well. They've never understood, not his wives nor his children, what sacrifices he's made over the years for their benefit. And what thanks does he get? That's how he reasons. Now, though, he's consumed with thoughts about the length of time that's passed since both Charles Mason and his lackey McBroom met their deaths, surely it can't do any harm to pay this Mrs. Mason a visit. The trail must have gone cold by now. Anyway, an old school friend of her husband stopping by to pay his respects, where's the harm in that? Yes, he has to do it himself now, no half-witted 'employee'. Alan Evans Esquire will visit Mrs. Mason.

He just has to decide the appropriate time.

He calls out "Charlene! Bring me another Whisky Mac, there's a dear!" His young, slim, blonde, thirty-something companion, who's far more attracted by the cash he supplies her than she is in Mr. Evans physically, is quick to oblige. She knows where her bread's buttered.

Claire and Julia have seen Terry White quite often since last November, the time they spent a couple of nights up at his place when they'd been snowed in after Sunday lunch. Terry is most definitely attracted to Claire. Julia knows this and doesn't mind a bit. She's very happy on her own. Maybe it has something to do with the fact that she ended it with Francis. She's not a widow pining over a mate she'd really loved. Whatever, she's OK with it and even thinks that she may be wise to help things along a bit. She's talked to Claire about him, trying to subtly evince from her what her feelings are about Terry. Claire, though, is playing her cards close to her chest. Julia knows from experience, too, that Claire has never even considered another relationship up until now, so it's still a long shot.

Yet Julia can't help thinking about Terry and Claire as a couple. She thinks that they'd be very good together. Terry doesn't need to work any more, yet is very fit and young-looking for a man of sixty. They've discovered that he plays squash too, on a ladder in his local sports centre. He doesn't smoke and only drinks moderately. He can cook for goodness sake! He's mister perfect. 'Perhaps I should throw my hat in after all' she thinks to herself, but then chuckles and dismisses that thought as a joke.

On Saturday evening January 22nd, there's a big get together planned. They've booked a restaurant out in the countryside between Bristol and Bath and Dean and Alyson are coming over from Cardiff, Brian and Christine will be there too, plus Claire, Julia, Sunny and Terry. No special occasion, just the opportunity to catch up and talk about Lindos days and things that happened in the past, things that through convoluted ways, brought them all together.

The evening arrives and Claire and Julia arrive by taxi and meet Brian, Christine, Dean, Alyson, Sunny and Terry in the restaurant's very cozy lounge, where guests can take aperitifs and peruse the menu before walking through to the dining room. The lushly carpeted lounge has a huge log fire, which has the effect of tipping the company into a torpor even before they reach the point of deciding what to order. Eventually they drift into the restaurant at the bidding of a smartly dressed waiter in a dickie bow and they set about the appetizers, attack the main course and are soon on to a naughty but delicious dessert. By this time chairs have been swapped a few times as members of the group want to strike up clandestine conversations with one another, taking advantage of the bathroom absences of others in order to do so.

Terry manages to finally get into the seat next to Claire as the cheese board arrives and they order two bottles of Cockburn's Special Reserve to go with it. They're all rather glad that this restaurant is attached to a comfortable hotel and the option to stay overnight is there if they want it. Already Brian and Christine and Dean and Alyson have ensured that they have rooms reserved.

"Claire," says Terry, almost by way of a question, "can we talk?"

"Of course we can, Terry. Or do you mean 'talk' as in 'let's get down to some kind of serious business'?"

"You're ahead of me. But, well, yes. Claire, you remember when you stayed over with me when it snowed back in November?"

"Of course, a winter wonderland. We had a really good time in the end."

"You remember too that I asked you about whether you may ever feel ready for another relationship? I think we got derailed from that subject by your mentioning Lindos, right?"

Claire feels herself becoming warm, and it's not just from the wine, the heat of the room or the Port. "I remember," she replies, not at all sure of how she wants to handle this.

"Well, I've been thinking - and shoot me down here in flames if you want to - but, well, I was wondering if you and I could, well, not anything too drastic for now," Terry instantly regrets those last two words, owing to what they may imply, but decides to press on, "maybe go out now and again. Just as friends, of course, but it might be fun. What do you think?" The expressions 'just as friends' Terry had added quickly, showing just a little desire to offer Claire some reassurance.

"Oh, Terry, I really don't know. I kind of think that if we did that then perhaps I might be holding out some kind of hope to you that things would progress further. Sorry, I hope that doesn't sound like I'm reading you wrongly. But I don't think I am. Am I?"

"No, Claire, you're not. Look, when Sandra died I was absolutely one hundred percent sure that I was never going to so much as look at another woman, ever. I loved my wife and still do, but time throws a different perspective on things, don't you agree? To be honest, I'm not a good one for being alone."

Claire makes as if to speak, so Terry hurriedly goes on, "No. Sorry. That sounds wrong. I don't mean to say that, because I'm not the type to remain on my own, that I'll hit on the first eligible woman I take a fancy too. The fact is, Claire, I have had a few chances since becoming a widower, but I've let them go. I never expected to come across anyone I'd remotely feel I could make a go of it with. But that's changed recently."

Claire knows what Terry is saying. It's very easy to read between his lines. She's confused inside. "Terry, you're really nice, OK? But you really don't know me. You've no idea what you might be taking on. I'm neurotic, depressed, guilty, hopeless, negative… the list goes on. There are days when if you were around me you'd want to top yourself. I…" She's now filling up because what happened to Charles is flooding back, along with all her guilt about being to blame. She's uttered some words that now stab back at her. How often has she told herself that she drove Charles to kill himself? How often has she deliberately castigated herself and told herself that she doesn't deserve to be happy? She's convinced herself that she's been sentenced to living out her days paying for what happened to Charles.

She doesn't deserve to find happiness, to glimpse a moment of sunshine in her life any more.

The evening eventually draws to a close and Terry decides to drive home. He hasn't drunk much and the evening is dry and not too frosty. Everyone says their goodnights, Claire and Julia climb into their pre-ordered taxi, Sunny's driving home alone and the others are ready to retire to their hotel rooms. As they're all circling around eachother kissing and hugging and promising to see eachother again soon, Terry gets the chance to whisper a couple of words in Claire's ear.

"I hope I haven't spoilt anything, Claire. Please tell me we're still friends."

Claire is rather perturbed inside. She has rising feelings for this man and yet tries to persuade herself that it wouldn't be fair to inflict herself on him. It's her old habit of self-flagellation coming through and she succumbs to it. She's not deserving of this man and he doesn't deserve the torment she'd put him through if she acquiesced. She forces herself to try and sound settled, and replies:

"Terry, we will always be friends. Nothing you've said tonight would change that. It's just me, I'm afraid. Maybe we'll talk another time, OK?"

Terry finds himself driving northwards with the sinking feeling of having blown it.

21. Old Friend?

On July 14th 2011, which is a Thursday, when the weather's drier than it has been for a while, yet still predominantly cloudy, Claire is at the desk in the Gallery. She's minding the shop since Julia is over in Wales for a few days with Dean and Alyson, her son and daughter-in-law. It's a long overdue break for Julia and, since Claire hasn't too much commission work to be getting on with at the moment, she's told Julia 'be off with you' and to come back when she wants to.

Staring out at the grey day, Claire is reflecting on the sunshine that is sure to be blessing the Greek Islands right now, while she sits here and wonders if the temperature will rise over 20ºC today. Her right hand is moving the iMac's mouse around while her left clutches a mug of cold coffee. She's perusing holiday websites and wondering whether she ought to just book a holiday in the sun and close up for a week or two. The beauty of this kind of business is that you can place a laser print-out on the Gallery's front door, stating the dates between which it will be closed and you don't really lose all that much business. It's not an "instant" kind of trade to be in, selling works of art.

Claire finds herself mentally walking the streets of Lindos, perhaps sitting in the Rainbird Bar, with its stunning view across Lindos Bay. She can visualize the Tomb of Kleoboulos, where she and Alyson used to have their "funny five minutes" now and again. The warmth of a Greek sun on her skin and rope-soled sandals on her feet, wearing light strappy tops and cotton shorts, gazing at a cloudless sky day in, day out for months on end, all this is wafting across her mental movie screen. She imagines walking through the maze of tiny streets in the Medieval Old Town of Rhodes, window-shopping in the fascinating stores that sell the kinds of jewelry and accessories that you just don't seem to be able to find in the UK. She's walking up the *Kali Strata* to the village of Horio on the tiny nearby island of Symi, where she'd taken a few short breaks just on a whim during the years that she'd lived out there.

Somehow she now finds herself wondering whether it all really happened. Her fragile emotional state was so well served by being in Greece. She found that the whole place, with its climate, its people, its scenery, its ancient history, its food and its Retsina and Metaxa - it worked like a comfort blanket on her psyche and she could bury the anxiety that's haunted her perpetually. The time she spent out there finally gave her the strength to come back here and start work again.

And now, so much more has happened in the six years since she's been back here in Bristol. There are plans in the pipeline that she'd never have dreamt she could make just a few short months ago.

Claire is plucked out from her reverie by the "tink" of the bell on the shop door. She turns to look and sees a man entering the gallery. He's not very tall, probably only about five-five, but does look quite distinguished. His hair was once a mousy brown, but now exhibits plenty of grey around the temples. His face is oval and bears the lines that betray probably around six decades of frowning more often than he's smiled. The man is wearing a blue and white striped shirt with starched, white collar, which is open to make room for a polka-dot cravat. It makes him look like a throwback to the sixties. His navy Chino's are crisply creased and his shoes are very expensive pumps, the kind you'd expect to see on someone just walking down the gangway of a cabin cruiser in Mandraki Harbour.

He has a pair of Ray-Bans perched on his head, their arms dropping vertically to just behind his ears. Claire finds herself feeling irritated by the sunglasses. No way is it a day for sunglasses and people who wear them for effect, especially when they're at least Claire's age put her on edge with their air of the vainglorious. She gets the impression that, despite this man's attempt at looking suave, he has a streak of ruthlessness about him, even cruelty. Still, she's never met him before and hopes that she's quite wrong. She rises, comes out from behind the desk and attempts a gracious smile.

"Good morning, can I be of any assistance?"

The man doesn't answer immediately, but rather casts his eyes along the watercolours and oils along the walls, then appears to take in the ambience of the gallery, examining the spotlights, the magnolia walls, the white desk with its rather chic iMac sitting on it, the original stripped-pine floor, then runs his eyes up from Claire's feet to her face, without any hint of hurry or embarrassment, before responding,

"Well, perhaps yes, who knows? I'm rather slow at making decisions I'm afraid."

His accent is decidedly West Country, but he's making a poor attempt at sounding more middle class than he likely really is. Claire isn't at all fazed by his having run his eyes all the way up the length of her body before speaking - the fact is she's flattered to think that he decided it was worth the exercise with a woman of her age - but she is irked by his audacity. She's taller than this man, which she feels is making him compensate with bravado. It's something he's done ever since he was at school. She takes herself in hand, musters up a degree of grace and replies,

"Well, please take your time looking around, Mr.?"

"Evans. Alan Evans. I'm pleased to meet you. Would you by any chance be the artist herself, or do you mind the shop, as it were?" He's going to take this very slowly and very carefully. Take no unnecessary chances, that's one of his mottos.

After Evans has made a show of examining a number of Claire's pieces, she asks,

"Perhaps you'd like a coffee? There is some freshly brewed." Evans accepts, black, no sugar. A few moments later Claire hands him a bone china cup and saucer, steam rising from the hot dark liquid within. She senses that in some way there is a symbolic steam rising from this man's dark interior too, but she couldn't say why she thinks this. He's simmering over something, but who is she to guess what that may be? 'We all have our demons,' she concludes. Not many minutes later, she decides to try a conversation again. He might just be the man she's to expect.

"I don't want to bother you if you'd rather just browse, but perhaps I ought to tell you that I do commissions too, portraits, paintings of people's pets, houses, that kind of thing; oils, acrylic, pastels or watercolours. It can make a great gift for a loved one."

"Hmm, yes, perhaps," Evans replies. He's not in the mood for small talk this visit. Finishing his coffee after a while, during which he's made a show of browsing, and handing the cup and saucer to Claire, he says, "I thank you, Ms. Mason. I shall return soon." Then he turns and walks purposefully toward the door and out of the gallery.

Once Evans is probably a hundred yards or so away, the door to the stairs at the back of the gallery opens and Terry emerges.

"Hmm," he says, "perhaps we're gonna have to be very patient."

The following Tuesday, at about the same time of day, Claire is again in the gallery, having suggested to Julia on the phone that she extend her stay in Cardiff if Dean and Alyson aren't fed up with her yet. She hadn't taken much persuading. Once again, while Claire's fiddling around on the internet, the door bell tinkles and the same man, Alan Evans, enters. This time he's wearing black denim jeans over trainers and a white polo shirt under a dark expensive-looking leather jacket, but the cravat's the same. The weather's taken a turn for the worse and it's decidedly grey and cool for July. So the Ray-Bans are missing.

"Hello again." Says Claire. "Perhaps you saw something you'd like to take another look at? Or, if you'd care to point out a work that you quite like, I may have similar pieces up in the studio if it's not exactly what you're looking for."

"Ms. Mason, I think you're a very talented artist. Do you mind me asking if you have a family? Surely they all have examples of your work on their walls, I'd imagine."

"I don't have much of one I'm afraid." Again she asks, "*Was* there something that caught your eye the last time you were here?" with some emphasis on the word 'was'.

"Well, yes and no. I'm undecided. I do rather prefer watercolours to oils though, that I will say. I am in the process of acquiring a collection of work by local artists, purely for my own pleasure, you understand. But I often look at something many times before deciding to buy. May I ask, does your husband work in the business with you?"

"I don't have a husband, Mr. umm, was it Evans?" she replies, "I have been a widow for some years now. It's one of the reasons that I threw myself into my work. We were very close. I still miss him to be honest, but anyway, that's of no relevance to the here and now."

"It may be a coincidence, but you know I was at school with a 'Mason'. He was always a bit posh for most of us. Must have been, what, from about 1970 to '76. May I ask where your husband went to school, if it's not being too nosey? I reckon our ages must be similar."

"Well, if you'd really like to know, he went to the City of Bath Boys' School. He was born in Cheltenham, but moved to Bath when quite small. His name was Charles and I think he would have been at that school between the years you mention. Where did you go to school, Mr. Evans?"

"Well, Mrs. Mason, I'll be damned if it probably wasn't your husband I was at school with, then. I went to the City of Bath and Charles "Charley" Mason was in my class for five years. I left before sixth form, but I think he stayed on. Tall lad, quite blonde and always had his hair swept back, a bit *à la* Errol Flynn, if you know who he was."

"Well, pleased to meet you anyway, though I don't recall Charles ever mentioning your name."

"Well, you know, the class was probably about thirty-strong. There would be quite a few names he probably wouldn't have told you about. I'm sure you wouldn't have spent all that much time talking about your husband's schooldays, eh?

"Well, I'll be… Quite something bumping into Charley's widow after all these years. I don't remember ever hearing what he did for a crust once he went into the big wide world. I don't doubt it was something lucrative though." Evans says this almost as a question, as if hoping that Claire will oblige him with the answer, though he knows it anyway. "Sorry, I'm afraid I'm a naturally inquisitive person, so you mustn't mind me. No offence intended, it's just quite something, that's all. Well, well, Charley Mason's wife. If you don't mind my saying so Mrs. Mason, it looks as though Charley landed on his feet when he found you. That's meant as a compliment."

"I really believe it's the other way around, Mr. Evans." She knows that she ought to remonstrate a little about his forwardness, yet also wants to put him at his ease. "Charles was the perfect husband. But I'm afraid I can't talk about the subject any further. It does me no good, I'm sorry.

"Anyway, what about you? What have you been doing 'for a crust' as it were for all these years? Do you have a family, children perhaps?"

"I'm not very lucky when it comes to women I'm afraid. Married three times and divorced three times. Got two grown up kids from the first wife. I'm not too good at picking them I suppose."

Claire is wise enough to deduce from this that what he means is he doesn't know how to treat a woman. She keeps her counsel to herself.

After a little more small talk, during which her guest finally expresses interest in a watercolour, a landscape of about A3 size, of the Avon Gorge in Clifton with the misty outline of the bridge taking centre place, he says he'll give it a little more thought and leaves.

*

Two days later, in he walks again. Evans has now decided that it's safe to go for the jugular. But begins by approaching the watercolour he'd expressed interest in. Claire doesn't like to look at it. She painted it a long time ago, came across it in her stacks of unshown work upstairs and decided to try and get shot of it. She's not fond of looking at the bridge, so she's hung it out of sight of the desk.

"You mentioned that your husband never talked about knowing me, Mrs. Mason." He begins.

"Well, firstly, as I'm sure you'll understand, with the passing of the years one loses the contact details of so many people. It's only now, after learning of your whereabouts that I thought, why not offer a hand of friendship to my old friend's widow. Maybe there's something I can do to help, if not now, then perhaps in the future."

Claire can't help hoping that there will not be a future to this relationship. She thinks inwardly, 'He's, I don't know, fulsome I suppose, smarmy.' Her guest continues, "I would imagine from what I see around me that Charley left you well set up, if I may be a little bold. No offence intended."

"He had adequate life insurance, if that's what you mean. I'm sorry Mr. Evans, but you're not making the purpose of your visit very clear. Do you feel that you have something, some way, of helping me out? If so, then don't worry, there's really no need. Or are you just here to 'touch base' again with an old friend's widow? Are you going to make a purchase, perhaps?"

"No, well, you know how it is Mrs. Mason, Claire." A sickly smile creeps across Alan Evans' face, but it doesn't reach his eyes. "We were in a class of about thirty boys, I can't say I've kept in close touch with many of them, but that doesn't mean that we weren't good mates while at school together. Got up to all kinds of pranks did Charley Mason and me you know, me and him were like *that*."

He holds up a hand with the first two fingers wrapped around eachother.

"No, I was wondering if he ever mentioned something of mine that he'd been looking after, ...minding, if you like."

Claire knows what he's getting at. The money. All that huge amount of money that Charles' solicitor had discovered out in the Cayman Islands. The only reason she found it was because Charles had left some details in a safety deposit box at his bank. No explanations, just some account numbers. On studying the accounts it became apparent that the money had been deposited there over a period of a couple of weeks from various sources. All numbers, no names. Claire never could fathom where it could have come from at the time. Finally then the answer to the riddle. Without having ever met him before just last week, Claire knows that he came across it through foul means. 'Frankly,' she thinks to herself, 'however he acquired it isn't any of my business anyway. But I get the feeling he's still hankering after getting it back, after all, it is a huge amount of money. If it was legitimate though, surely he would have come out of the woodwork back when Charles died. He'd have turned up and asked for it, for sure he would have. So, no, he must have had reasons for keeping a low profile. Things are dropping into place.'

Claire decides to play dumb for a while.

"I'm not sure I follow, Mr. Evans. Why would my husband have been looking after something belonging to you? It's rather late after more than a couple of decades have passed to ask for a birthday present for your wife back, isn't it?"

"Claire, look. I'm not keen on pussyfooting around. Do you have insurance?"

"Insurance? What kind of insurance? Is that what you sell, insurance? My gallery is well covered if that's what you mean, as is my life. So I'm not shopping around at the moment I'm afraid. I don't believe you did tell me the other day what you do for a living."

"Claire, what I mean is, if you are holding out on me, then I ought to explain that I can offer you insurance, or rather the assurance, that your gallery will remain open for business, that it won't - say - have to close indefinitely owing to, you know, perhaps a fire or something. These things do happen you know."

Claire now most certainly picks up a menacing edge to this man's demeanour. There can be no doubt in her mind as to what kind of character he is. One thing's for sure, if Charles had been looking after that money for this man, then he'd probably been persuaded to do so under duress. Why else would he not have told Claire about it? She knows that she needs to hear Evans make himself even more clear. She has her reasons.

"Holding out on you? Why would I be holding out on a man I never even met before a few days ago? You're making me feel rather uncomfortable. I'd rather like you to leave now, if you don't mind." She knows he won't.

Evans' charm is now rapidly crumbling, to reveal the ruthless character hidden beneath. "Look, Mrs. Mason, you know and I know that you found a whole load of cash tucked away somewhere when your old man died. There, now I've come out with it. All I want is what's mine. Now, I know that it's been a long, a very long time. But the fact is, if you still have it, or even some of it, then I want it back and I want it quick. If I were to charge you interest on over a quarter of a century of holding on to my cash, you'd be well broke in seconds. I went to a lot of trouble to get that cash, took risks, and I'm still not writing it off. I don't care how much time, how long it takes, but if you're sitting on a bundle of my money and you're gonna pretend you don't even know it's there, then things might just turn a little unpleasant.

"Now I don't mean you any harm and I wouldn't like to see you come to any. But here I was, coming in here in good faith, thinking that Mrs. Claire Mason was a woman of principle, so that if she finally found out who it belonged to then she'd be only too pleased to give it back, but what I find is someone who's way out of her depth dealing with me, thinking she can blindside me. Well, it ain't gonna happen I'm afraid. Like I said, I can give you insurance. You play ball with me and I'll make sure that your precious little art shop stays fire and smoke free, understand?"

Claire knows that she just needs to extract a little more information from this man. So she changes tack.

"OK, OK, I'm sorry Mr. Evans. Look, I did find a large sum, just over a million Sterling in fact, and the Revenue investigators drew a blank, nothing made any sense, but still there it was. I presume you do know what trade your *'old friend'* my husband was in?" She doesn't wait for his reply, "He was in property development on a big scale. He was dealing with some seriously rich Arabs out in the gulf, some rather well-heeled Americans from across the Atlantic. Charles' solicitor told me that it wasn't at all unusual for such people to show their appreciation for the kind of help they may have had from the likes of my husband by lodging rather large sums of money in an account of their choosing. So I left it there anyway, because I didn't really need it. As you were bold enough to ask me earlier, how well set up did Charles leave me, well enough thank you very much. Oh I've been tempted, believe me. There have been occasions when I've almost succumbed and splashed out a huge sum on some vain whim. But you can be thankful for the kind of person I am, Mr. Evans. I'm a simple soul who doesn't really hanker after material things. My life is more ephemeral than that. I don't see the need to acquire things, rather I seek answers.

"Anyway, what I'm telling you is that I never in the end touched the money and it's been accruing interest over all these years. I'll let you have it if you'll tell me where it came from."

Evans senses a glimmer of hope here, yet he's not happy about the condition Claire has laid down. "You what? You gotta be joking, lady. My kind of business is very discreet. I go telling you things like that and your life could be in danger. I don't exaggerate, believe me."

Claire realizes that this last comment may just be a clue as to what happened to Charles. She doesn't want to let on though.

"Now you're threatening me, Mr. Evans. I'll remind you that if anything happens to either my gallery or me personally, you'll never get your money back. End of story. You don't know where it is. The only person who does is my solicitor."

"And who would that be then?"

"Ha ha, you don't expect me to tell you that, do you?" Though she's fairly sure he could find out if he wanted to. Nevertheless, she goes on, "No, I'm just curious. I'll make a deal with you. You tell me how you could afford to drop over a million Pounds on my husband to 'mind' for you and I'll give you some numbers that will make your day. I only have to call the solicitor's office to get the numbers. Then I can give them to you.

"Mr. Evans, out of my depth I may be. But stupid I most certainly am not. I'll give you my word that it won't ever pass my lips. You must see that it's in my best interests to keep my promise, because once the money's back in your hands, I have no bargaining chips left, do I? I could well see my gallery burn to the ground, if not something nasty happen to me. But when you consider what you asked my husband to take on, don't you think I deserve an explanation?

"Come on Mr. Evans. Do we have a deal?"

"Bank jobs. …You're gonna keep this to yourself, now, right?" One thing is for sure about Evans' type, they really can't resist a brag when they think it's safe to do so.

"I can promise you on my life, which is rather apt right now I'd say, that I shall never breathe a word to anyone. Why on earth would I? Now, just satisfy a cranky woman's curiosity. You're a bank robber yes? How exciting." She's warming to her task now. Flattery is always a good idea with the likes of Evans, who in truth are always looking for an audience whom they can impress.

Evans smiles, this time right up to his eyes. "S'a long time ago, but do you remember a series of jobs on banks all across southern England back in the eighties? Prob'ly not. All over the papers they were though, for a couple of months…"

"In actual fact I do remember the TV news going on about this, back in the eighties wasn't it?"

"You got it. Anyway, the Law spotted a few things about all six jobs that were similar, but were never really able to link them. That's my forté see, Claire. I'm a careful man. I am methodical. Leave nothing to chance. Plan everything down to the finest detail. Do dry runs. Bide my time. In the end the law gave up on all six investigations. They were chasing their tails, poor sods. I, on the other hand, netted over a million, after expenses. I just needed to keep it somewhere untraceable for a while. The boys in blue were sniffing around, see. They've known me for decades, Claire. They've been dead certain that I've been involved in all kinds of activities that they'd like to have felt my collar for. But they never have, see. The last job a bloke died. It was collateral damage. No one intended for that to happen. Think he had a wife and a couple of kids. Shouldn't have been in the Lloyds branch when we hit it, but he'd gone in out of hours for some reason or other. Very unfortunate, that. Still, risks have to be taken sometimes.

"If your husband hadn't gone and died, I'd have had the cash back a long time ago." He didn't want to mention his lackey and his unfortunate accident, not wise in the circumstances.

"Fact is though, I'm too clever for the plods. I hate to boast," he loves to, "but there it is."

"You WERE too clever, Evans. But not so much now." A male voice emanates from the doorway leading up to Claire's studio and living quarters. Terry White, ex Detective Chief Inspector Terry White in fact, is standing there. Well, he's now leaning on the doorpost and smiling broadly.

Evans is dumbstruck. He decides to brave this out.

"*Snowy!!* DCI Snowy White! What the hell are you doing here? 'Course, you didn't hear any of that, did you? Me and Mrs. Mason just talking about old times. I'm gonna buy a painting, see…"

"Every word Evans, every single word. In fact, I've got it all on this here." He holds up a Dictaphone and waves it at Evans for effect.

"But… But…" for the first time in his adult life, Alan Evans is at a loss for words. Then he finds a few, "How can YOU be here? How the devil can you be? It doesn't make sense. You CAN'T know this woman, how can you?"

"This, 'woman', Claire Mason, just happens to be my fiancée. We got engaged a couple of weeks back and I've been filling her in on some of my old cases over the occasional glass of wine and dish of pasta in the past few months, Alan. Just so happens she told me about a sum of money she'd discovered when her husband died. Of course, you'll know that I was working on a lot of cases that we knew you were involved in way back a while. As you so rightly said, we could never actually pin anything on you. But when my future wife told me about this cash and how it baffled her, well, it didn't take long for me to go back over some old notes, pay a visit to my old station where we checked out lots of gen about you. See, we know just about everything there is to know about you, Alan, including who you went to school with. You wanna see the size of that file, you'd be proud. Amazing how easy it is to look up stuff now it's all been transferred to computer archives. Isn't technology wonderful, eh?

"I reckon that now I've got your confession on this tape, you will be going down for the rest of your days."

Evans is about to bolt for the door, but as he turns toward it, he sees a pair of Police cars pulling up sharply, one from each direction in the street outside, their blue lights flashing and their front bumpers almost touching as they lurch up and down on their suspension while four uniformed officers leap from the doors and block the gallery exit.

"Oh, and…" adds Terry, "Since I've been eavesdropping for a while, I took the liberty of calling a few old mates to come and give you a lift." he nods in the direction of the Police officers, "Nice of me, eh?"

Not long after the meal that they'd attended at the country hotel and restaurant back in January, Claire had had a change of heart. Sunny and Julia had both been on her case about her perpetually beating herself up about Charles. She'd come around to Terry's suggestion that they simply see eachother once in a while. This has become a weekly night out. Sometimes to the cinema, occasionally they've attended a production at Bath Theatre Royal, or been out for meals, that kind of thing.

Claire soon realized that she was developing a love for Terry and she finally admitted it. One night she explained to him once again why she'd felt it was something she couldn't do, but he finally persuaded her that he was willing and able to take the risk. Over the course of their growing relationship she'd told him everything about Charles. It had been for her a cathartic experience anyway, plus it had given Terry an idea. However long the chances may have been, he'd talked with some of the guys still working in the local Bristol CID and asked them to keep an eye out for any goings on that might relate to their old foe Alan Evans. They'd always thought that he'd been behind the six bank jobs back in the 1980's. Terry didn't necessarily think they'd be able to get him, but they made sure that one of his cronies became aware of the location of the Sunshine Gallery. It was a simple matter of an informant bumping into the man in question and walking the streets with him exchanging gossip, just street stuff, nothing major. But in the course of the stroll, he'd led the man past the gallery and deliberately made his excuses and left the man right outside Claire's window. Within the hour Evans knew where to find Claire.

All Terry had to do was be in the gallery as often as he could, Dictaphone at the ready. Claire had been only too willing to help play her part, since she had every confidence that no harm would come to her while Terry was behind the door and anyway the Police would be on their way as soon as she'd extracted enough information out of Evans. This was why she'd encouraged Julia to go off and see her son for a while. Not that Julia would have been in any way a problem, but why put her at risk and involve her in a situation that just may have turned unpleasant? They'd tell her the whole story when she returned.

It was just as expected. Finally, Evans couldn't keep away. After only a week or two of waiting, once their insider had told them that Evans was planning a cultural visit to an art gallery, they struck gold.

22. Sunshine.

Charles is smiling. He's driving the Jensen along a sunny country lane near the coast. All the windows are down and Claire has a hand out of hers, feeling the warm wind flowing through her fingers. She lifts her other hand and brushes her husband's cheek with the back of it. He glances at her and grins even more. Within what feels like seconds they're parked up above some sand dunes and they're running down towards the clear, calm sea on a beach of golden sand.

Then they're clutched in eachother's arms in the foam, his mouth seeking hers as they kiss, the salty taste of the water mingling with the taste of her husband's lips. He draws away and looks her in both eyes. They're back in the house in Pembroke Road, seated at the kitchen table. Charles rises, picks up his executive case and car keys and walks towards the hallway door. Reaching it, he turns, gives Claire a little wave, jangling the keys in the process, and says, 'You'll be alright, darling. You're going to be fine. I'm off now. Goodbye.' Charles never ever leaves by saying 'goodbye', that was odd. Then he's gone and she feels as though there is an earthquake going on, yet in Bristol such things don't happen.

Claire comes to. She's been sleeping on the sofa in her lounge and Julia is gently shaking her by the shoulder.

"Your tea's gone cold. You dropped off sweetie. You must think you're back in Greece, it is siesta time after all!"

It's November 2011 and Claire Mason, now sixty years of age, is happier than she's been for twenty years and more. The dark doubts she nurtures deep in the recesses of her mind are still down there, but she's learned of late to keep them locked in a mental cabinet while she gets on with the present. She and Terry are planning to get married next year. She's already called him today to ask if he'll come over tonight, when they'll talk about making firm plans.

At 6.30pm Terry lets himself into the locked gallery door, closes and locks it behind him again and crosses the now dimly-lit room to the door leading upstairs. Julia is cooking tonight, she's in the kitchen preparing Chilli and sipping white wine. She's got the mini hi-fi on in there and Tom Waits' gravelly voice is crooning out *"I come calling in my Sunday best, ever since I put your picture in a frame"*. She's happy to leave the lovebirds to it in the lounge.

Terry enters the lounge, where Claire has already crossed to meet him at the door. They hug and share a big kiss on the lips and then make their way to the sofa. On the coffee table there is a MacBook, a pen and notepad and some brochures.

"Glass of Harveys Bristol Cream, love?" Asks Claire, already pouring from the dark blue bottle into a couple of schooners.

"I don't mind if I do," replies Terry, plonking himself down beside his fiancée on the sofa. "Right then. What are we doing? I presume you've got it all planned out in your mind."

"I do indeed." She smiles, sips her sherry, then begins. "Terry, you know I lived in Rhodes for a number of years and I've always hankered after going back there again?" He nods, knowing smile already gracing his handsome face, "Well, how about we get married out there? I know people out there who can arrange the whole thing, the paperwork, the service, the reception, even the hair do's. All I'll have to do is e-mail my friends at 'Flight of Fancy' where Alyson used to work, give them the date we want and they'll do the lot. All we do is fly out there a few days before the big day, so that we can sign some stuff and get acclimatized, then we do it, in Lindos! What do you think?"

"Sounds good to me. Does that mean we start the honeymoon the split second we say 'I do'?"

"Of course, if you want. We needn't have a huge crowd anyway. Small and intimate is what I'd prefer, I reckon you would too, right?" He nods, "So," she continues, "I have made a list of the guests if you agree. We could just have the Worths, Dean and Alyson, Amanda, perhaps my mum," her father is still alive, but now in a care home, "Callum, if he'll be able to make it, and your brother if you want. It would be nice to meet him some time after all. Sunny of course, and any of your friends from the pub if you like. Well, what do you say?"

"Sounds like you've got it pretty well sorted. Let's keep it really small, though. Peripheral friends and relatives could all come to a wedding dinner at Sunny's place when we get back, what about that idea?"

"Wonderful! Even better. In fact, I think my mum would prefer that, she's not going to feel like flying now anyway."

And so Claire composes an e-mail to Sally at Flight of Fancy, the wedding coordinators based in Lindos. She puts everything in it, including a request for Alyson's friend Linda to do the womens' hair before the big day. She and Terry arrive at a date, because Claire would like to have it coincide with the *Rhodes Rock* festival that takes place every June. So, having checked out the website, she suggests Friday June 22nd, the day before the rock extravaganza kicks off out at the far end of St. Paul's Bay. She's thinking more of Brian than she is of herself, because he knew a lot of the people involved in the event and is addicted to live music. But Terry says he's also interested in experiencing the whole thing too. They select the brand new Aquagrand Hotel in Psaltos Bay as the place to stay, where they can also have the wedding ceremony too if they wish. Claire's not so keen on using the little church in St Paul's Bay, simply because it's so busy at that time of the year that it's a bit like a conveyor belt, with sometimes one wedding group waiting at the parking area above, where the Rhodes Rock stage will be erected anyway, whilst the previous one goes through the ceremony below. 'One out, one in,' feels Claire.

As the next few days go by, e-mails are exchanged and the wedding confirmed. Claire now begins to get quite excited about going back to Rhodes with Terry. It'll be a bit strange in some ways, but it's the right thing to do, she's sure.

The winter of 2011-2012 passes and it's by and large a good one. Temperatures are mild for the most part and Terry and Claire get into the habit of driving to Clevedon to walk the cliffs. Julia visits Dean and Alyson more often than she has for a while and the conversations all revolve around arrangements for the group to fly off to Rhodes in June for the wedding.

Sunny is beside herself, even quite ecstatic about the way things have turned out between the man she calls "dad" and the woman who may well have been her legal mother, had things gone differently. Terry and Claire are often to be seen seated at the window table where Claire first sat with Julia on their first visit to "La Jambe de Grenouille" not much more than a year ago.

Claire and Julia have discussed the future living arrangements once the wedding has taken place. Claire and Terry are both as they term it "old fashioned" and won't begin to live together until they are married. There's still lots of stuff to be sorted out anyway. The two women have agreed though that Julia will carry on living in the gallery in Clifton, whilst Claire will move up to Terry's house in Stroud. She now feels that it would be an excellent location for her studio and Terry has already begun converting an upstairs room for her to use, with a glorious view of fields and woods affording excellent natural light and a healthy dose of tranquility too.

Sunny's actually really pleased about this development, because she knows that Terry will no longer be alone. The distance isn't all that great when you know someone's got company anyway. It's only huge when that person is alone. She's confident that she won't fret about her foster dad any more once Claire is ensconced in the house with him.

In May of 2012, Claire and Alyson, her young companion from 1998 to 2005, through all of the time that she'd lived out in Greece, decide to take a week and fly out to Rhodes to see all the gang they'd known when they'd lived there. This also gives Claire the opportunity to make sure that everything is going to be ready, with no last-minute hitches, for the wedding in June. There are a few things that she can sign in readiness, documents she can show and she can visit the hotel as well, even talk to the photographers, Chris and Karen, who'd worked often at weddings where Alyson had been involved in the past.

It's a strange feeling for both women to be walking the tiny streets of Lindos again, this time in such different circumstances. The last time they'd both been here together was the summer of 2007, when Dean and Alyson finally tied the knot, but that was only a couple of weeks and Claire and Alyson had had precious little time to talk. Prior to that the last time they'd been here as close friends had been in 2005, now almost seven years ago.

Not much has changed in the village itself, apart from one thing that saddens both women, the Ikon Bar is closed and doesn't look like it's going to reopen any time soon this season. Although it's still only May, the Greek sun and the warmth of the air infuses Claire with the same vitality that it always used to. Once again she can feel the weight of her anxieties lightening, even though her general mood of late has been much more positive than for more years than she cares to reflect on. She can sit on the beach, at one of the taverna tables very near to the water's edge, and gaze out at the seemingly endless expanse of blue and marvel at just how much water there is on this planet. On their second day here, she and Alyson have agreed to spend their time apart as Alyson catches up with a number of her old friends, people she used to hang out with during the evenings, Greeks and UK ex-pats with whom she used to dance the *Tsifteteli* well into the small hours.

Claire is glad to have some time, hours in fact, to simply stroll down past her old apartment toward the beach and find herself a small table, where she orders a jug of Retsina and a glass and sits contemplating everything.

Where do all the years go? How strange it is that sometimes the mind can concertina the time so that events of decades ago can feel as if they took place only moments before. She sips her resin wine and can hear voices, smell aromas, feel sensations that she'd actually experienced far back in the past. When was it now, it was incredibly almost twenty-three years ago, when she and Charles had spent that glorious few weeks staying at Mrs. Ioannou's modest little house of village rooms on the island of Poros. Closing her eyes she can relive intimate moments when she and Charles sat in places like this, while she struggled to overcome her neuroses about what had happened with Marianna and the baby, that baby that's now grown into the young woman Sunny. Where would she be now, Claire wonders, had that young woman not sought her out when she did? 'Can I really be engaged to be married, all these years on, to Sunny's foster father Terry?' She wonders. Well, she is, and she's quite sure that she's doing the right thing.

Sunny, for all the fact that she's still so young, had helped her to finally see the sense of letting go of the past, of releasing all those ropes that tied her to feelings of guilt, remorse, responsibility, doubt. Terry has turned out to be just the man she needed to rebuild her life with. Yes, she may be (and she also finds this hard to come to terms with) entering the seventh decade of her life, yet she still feels young inside. She's glad that she's in such good health and still slim. 'OK, so the hair colour comes out of a bottle these days, but if that's all I need to worry about, I ought not to complain' she thinks and smiles as she does so. Can Claire Mason, she who's always struggled to come to terms with her mortality and with finding answers to her questions, actually be starting to think positively? Surely not and yet, why, yes, she does believe that she is.

Sunny Geesin is also of the opinion that she's seeing a few pieces of the jigsaw of her life dropping neatly into place. She's grateful beyond belief that, following the tragic death of both parents in that awful pile-up, she ended up being placed with Terry and Sandra White. She often contemplates the possible outcomes had she ended up growing up in childrens' homes, or worse still, getting placed with a family that didn't give her the security, the love, the happiness that she'd enjoyed with the Whites. How often do people that aren't one's natural parents, usually the men, end up abusing the girls in their care? Probably not anything like as often as one would think. She blames the media for that, always highlighting those cases that do show abuse, neglect, violence and so on. It doesn't matter now, she's full of fond memories of a happy childhood and wants to see Terry rewarded for his kindness, especially since he too lost his dear wife Sandra, whom he'd love unquestionably for all their lives together. So much for the "experts" who nowadays say things like "well, men are genetically programmed to be promiscuous," or "you can't expect two people to remain together for a lifetime, it's asking too much." Terry and Sandra wouldn't have seen it that way.

She's still single at twenty-six. Plenty of time yet, she reasons. She's had a few short-term relationships, but really is quite happy to leave it a while longer before she finds her Mr. Right. 'How nice it will be,' she thinks, 'if I do eventually tie the knot and I've a full set of parents at my wedding. Terry even giving me away.' OK so they won't be her natural parents, but that's not so important really. She reflects on how strange her history is. How many people can there be who've had three possible sets of parents? How many lives had she lived in a parallel universe where she's been brought up by Charles and Claire, or Eric and Marianna? What would her life had been had she been brought up by Marianna as a single mum?

Sunny's disposition well reflects her given name. She's even more bright and cheerful than normal with the prospect of Terry and Claire's wedding looming large this coming June, now drawing so close.

Her iPhone is ringing. It's Thursday May 10th at 2.00pm. She's seated at a table toward the back of the restaurant, going through possible menus from handwritten suggestions of her chef Ray. There is a glass of Perrier on the white tablecloth beside her. She picks up the iPhone and looks at the screen. It's not a number she recognizes.

"Hello, Sunny Geesin." There is a pause while she listens to the caller. "Uncle Gordon! Wow, this IS a surprise, how long is it since we last spoke? Are you…" the caller interrupts her, he apologies but explains that he has very urgent news. She may want to drop everything."

It's about 6.00pm and Claire is now sitting with Alyson in the Rainbird Bar, both of them looking across the bay to the Tomb of Kleoboulos, a place that holds many memories for them both, most of them pleasant, though not all in Alyson's case. They are both feeling happy though, sipping Campari and Soda and talking about their day. Tomorrow Claire is scheduled to meet with Sally and Anthoula, from the wedding organizers "Flight of Fancy". She says:

"Do you ever wonder what would have happened if you hadn't been sitting with me that evening in the Ikon Bar when Dean walked by? Well not so much 'walked by' as stopped dead in his tracks when he saw you?"

"Yea, of course. But what happens happens, eh? I'm just glad that finally things came good. What I remember most about not only this place, but the years we spent like a couple of vagrants wandering around Greece, were all those deep conversations we used to have about the meaning of it all. I'm glad, Claire. I'm glad that you seem to be less, …what, …less, I dunno, weighed down I suppose, than you were then. It's so important to be able to enjoy the moment, isn't it?"

"Well, I suppose you're right Ally. I still fight myself now and then, but, yes, I am enjoying the moment now. I don't just mean this 'moment', I mean the whole time since I met Terry and the thought of what we're doing next month. I am finding that I can bury my mind in the 'present' enough to function normally. So I'm grateful for that.

"Do you still get a 'buzz' from being out here Ally? You know, Greece I mean?"

"No doubt about it. Not that I'm the world's greatest experienced traveller, but I always feel so chilled out when I'm here. I feel sad about people who might have changed their plans about coming over here after all that talk about the economic problems, social unrest and stuff. They don't know what they're missing. Anyway, where do you want to eat tonight?"

Before Claire can answer, Alyson's smartphone plays something by Coldplay and she tugs it out from her bag, strung over the back of her chair.

Looking at the screen, she sees that it's Sunny calling from the UK.

"Hi Sunny, how's it going?" Alyson listens as Sunny speaks. All Claire can hear is a chirping from the region around Alyson's ear, just about discernible as Sunny's voice. For some reason, from its tone it sounds alarm bells in Claire's mind. She feels a cold dread creeping over her as Alyson's face betrays that her feeling is justified.

"He's WHAT? But When?" She listens again as Sunny evidently is explaining something urgent.

After what to Claire seems like an hour, Alyson taps the close button to finish the call. She looks at Claire and her eyes fill up. Her expression tells Claire that the news isn't good.

"WHAT? Ally, WHAT IS IT?"

"Claire," begins her friend, "It's Terry. He's had a heart attack.

He's been taken to Stroud General. He's in Cardiology. He's unconscious. Sunny called me because your phone's off."

"I left it in the room! I'VE GOT TO GO!! GO NOW!!!"

"Claire, Claire. Hold on, OK? It'll take you a couple of days at least to get a flight back, and that's if you're lucky. We fly back in four days anyway. I'm sure it'll be OK."

"You're not, are you. That's just something we all say at times like this."

"Claire, perhaps I ought to tell you everything Sunny said. Try and keep calm, there's nothing we can do from here right now. Sunny told me..."

"Oh my GOD! He needs me. He needs me now. What can I DO ALLY? There must be something..."

"Let me tell you what happened. *Please*, Claire, drink some of that Campari and calm down." Claire doesn't feel like complying, but slumps back in her chair and takes a long sip from her straw. She hyperventilates, then says,

"OK, OK. I'm calm. Tell me."

"It's a good job he was out in the garden. His neighbour saw what happened. He was just deadheading roses, talking over the fence when he clutched his left shoulder, dropped his secateurs and fell to the ground. The neighbour rushed round there, tried to get him comfortable and rang for the ambulance. They turned up in about ten minutes. They took him to Stroud General and straight into Cardiology. He's had a major coronary apparently. No warning, nothing. Sunny is there with him now. It was her uncle Gordon, Terry's brother, who called her. They hadn't seen eachother in years apparently."

"I haven't met him yet. We did say hello on the phone once, that's all. Seems a decent bloke. They're just not that close I suppose. Terry said they were, years ago, but you just get on with your life and suddenly a long time's gone by. At least he's come through now, though. How did he hear about it? Did Sunny say?" Claire is having difficulty keeping her head from bursting.

"The neighbour said that Terry was able to tell him to look in his wallet, which was in his back pocket. His brother's number was in there. Terry's mobile was in the house somewhere. He wasn't able to explain to the neighbour where it was. Then apparently he went unconscious.

"Sunny says he's all wired up with electrodes and things. They can't tell her yet what's going to happen. If ...when he's going to come out of it.

"Claire, look. Try and keep calm. You won't do any good by getting into a state. I know, it's easy to say that, but hell, it's true."

"Does Julia know?"

"Sunny didn't say. Look, I'll call her now. What time is it in the UK? Twenty past four, a Thursday today. Right, she'll be in the gallery."

Alyson taps her phone and places it against her left ear, brushing her long dark hair aside in the process.

"Julia? Hi, it's... Oh, good. OK. No, she's here with me. Not feeling good at the moment. Right, will do. Talk soon, bye." She puts the phone on the table and looks at Claire, "She knows. Sunny called her right away. She sends her love."

Later in the evening Claire and Alyson are sitting on the balcony of their room at the hotel. Neither was hungry after the news and so they didn't go out to eat after all. It's now about 10.00pm and it's been dark for an hour or so. Neither is talking much. Claire has a novel on her lap, but hasn't read a word of it. Alyson is merely keeping Claire company and is afraid to leave her on her own. The moonlight glistens on the dark shimmery sea and a thousand bright stars twinkle in the inky black heavens above them. The night looks absolutely beautiful.

Claire's mind is there beside Terry. She can see him in her imagination, laying there under a white sheet, One of those electronic gismos beeping nearby, attached to his chest by wires and suckers, or plasters or whatever it is they use. She's certain that Sunny is there too, sitting beside him, probably holding his hand, maybe talking to him in whispers. Both Claire and Alyson are listening to the sound of a Lindos summer night, yet not really hearing it.

"All this beauty," begins Claire, "and yet so much pain, so much pointlessness. I can't bear this, Ally, I can't bear it. I'll call Sunny. I have to."

Alyson doesn't try to talk Claire out of it. She just watches as Claire fishes her phone out from the pocket of her shorts and punches the screen to call Sunny.

Two thousand miles away, Sunny Geesin is indeed sitting in a chair beside her foster father's bed. Her head is resting on her arm, which is lying on the side of the bed. She's fallen asleep. The monitoring machine is indeed close by. Every so often someone in white has been popping a head around the door to check on things, but for the moment she's alone with Terry. The electrocardiograph's display shows several lines, all of them horizontal. It is emitting a continual single electronic tone.

Sunny's phone bursts into life, still clutched tightly as it is, in her other hand. She comes around, dazed, slightly disoriented, she holds the phone up to her head, tapping the 'answer' button. It's Claire, who says "Sunny! Sunny? How's he doing love? Please tell me he's

OK, please do…"

Sunny glances at the electrocardiograph in disbelief. She needs a couple of seconds to register what it's telling her. Then she drops the phone and runs out of the room screaming for help.

Claire sits there on her hotel balcony. She hears the phone crash to the floor and behind that the electrocardiograph. Alyson stares at her, eyes popping out of her head. She knows something awful is happening, has happened. Claire too now drops her phone on to the hard floor of ceramic tiles and rises from her chair.

"I'm going for a walk, Ally. Please let me go alone." She says.

Alyson nods. She's not sure what to do, but decides not to challenge Claire. She decides that she'll follow her friend at a close distance, so that she can look out for her welfare.

Moments later, Claire Mason is walking purposefully down the lane that leads to the far end of Lindos Beach. She then strikes left and up along the ridge that leads past the overflow car park, past the stone monument, to the rough goat path leading out to the Tomb of Kleoboulos. It's dark, but she doesn't notice. Alyson, a few metres behind, follows Claire, still not sure what exactly she ought to do. She watches her friend stumble often, as her feet kick rough stones and rocks on the path. It is evident that she's only half aware of her surroundings.

Claire Mason is walking out to the Tomb. It's madness at this hour without a torch, but it's been done before. She knows the path well. She's walking out there, which will take her probably an hour or so, but she hasn't yet decided whether she'll ever be walking back.

Just for a brief time, a moment really in the great scheme of things, Claire Mason experienced a little sunshine.

It's gone now, though.

23. Outlook Fair.

Sunny's in a panic, but as she exits the room in which Terry lies, the electrocardiograph showing no heartbeat, she charges headlong into the leading member of the 'crash team'. Unbeknown to Sunny, if the machine records an unprecedented change in readings, an alarm goes off at the nurse's station down the ward and they spring into action. Three doctors and an anaesthetist are running, one pulling a trolley laden with electronic equipment.

They run past her, almost knocking her over, the last doctor throws an apology over his shoulder and within seconds they are bedside. Sunny walks back to the door of the room and watches in disbelief. The team works like a well-oiled machine and within a further few seconds one of the doctors has a couple of paddles on Terry's chest and the others stand back. Another member of the team operates the machine and, after three attempts, the electrocardiograph resumes its steady beep, beep, and the screen shows a regular jump in the white line running across it.

Sunny is drained and dazed, she doesn't really understand all of what's just gone on, except that she knows they've saved Terry's life. They carry on talking for a while and she thinks that someone gives him a shot, but she's more preoccupied now with what's happening in Rhodes. Where is her phone? Looking around she spots it under Terry's bed. She asks if she can retrieve it and a kindly doctor who's probably thirty-something and rather good-looking extends a hand as if to say, 'hold it there', before bending down himself and retrieving it for her.

Handing it to her he asks, "Are you OK? You look shaken up. He's stabilized you know. He looks like he'll be OK. These things can happen, he had a cardiac arrest, but we'll carry on here a while longer before we leave him to the nurse. Why don't you go and get yourself a coffee or something, hmm?"

It's still not much after 8.00pm in Stroud, but Sunny's feeling bone weary. Terry *can't* die. Not now, so much that's good is about to happen for him, and for Claire too. She's had a long day and will not leave the hospital, even if a team of wild horses were to be harnessed to her. But seeing the experts working around her 'dad', she decides to accede to the doctor's suggestion.

Minutes later, sitting in the hospital café, sipping a hot Americano with a dash of milk, she checks out her phone. Its screen is dark. She's worried that it may have been damaged when it dropped on to the hard floor in Terry's room in the ICU. She removes the back, takes out the battery, replaces it, close the back and presses the power button again. The phone comes to life and within a few seconds the screen shows her normal desktop. She locates Claire's number in her address book and presses the 'call' button on the screen. She doesn't get a ringing tone, nothing. What must Claire be thinking? Sunny knows that Claire must have heard the machine flat-lining and the sound of her phone hitting the floor. She probably heard Sunny's footsteps running out of the room too. What else did she hear? What's she thinking has happened?

'Oh God!' thinks Sunny, let her not think she's lost him.

It's late in Lindos. Claire is half-way out to the Tomb of Kleoboulos and shows no sign of stopping. Her right knee is bleeding from the fact that she's actually fallen down twice already from tripping over protruding stones in the ground, yet her mind isn't really registering anything. Her palms have grazes that make her smart from the soreness, yet she's allowing herself, her body, to simply react on its own. Alyson is a couple of hundred yards behind her now and can't really make her out very easily. At least there is some moonlight, so she's pretty sure she sees Claire's outline. Not much else is moving out here. There don't seem to be any goats in the vicinity tonight.

Claire's mind, though, is racing through her life and giving her irrational reasons why what's happened has happened. 'It's all my fault. It has to be. Here I am not knowing if I can believe in anything, a god or fate or anything like that, yet perhaps this is my punishment. My lack of conviction, belief, whatever, has brought the wrath of something, someone on to my shoulders. Everything I've ever had that I valued has been taken away from me. First Charles, then the baby and now, after years of not daring to attach myself to anyone again, I go and fall in love with Terry White and am stupid enough to think that everything will be fine and then this happens. It's my fault. I'm King Midas in reverse when it comes to people. Look what happened to Marianna and Eric too. I can't allow this any more. That poor man, if he hadn't fallen for me he'd probably still be clipping his roses, playing golf on the weekend, squash with his friends. Now look, and it's my fault. I must be cursed.'

And so the downward spiral of Claire's irrationality continues. She's falling victim to something that she always said was illogical, that of looking for meaning in things that have happened purely due to the randomness of existence. Humans who don't have any professed faith in anything much at all still seem to cling to the need to attach significance to happenstance. Perhaps that is what operates as the comfort blanket for the masses, this basic idea that somewhere behind it all something pulls the strings. Were this to be true of course, whatever or whoever is doing so would be inherently wicked, to be the cause of so much suffering. It's really a nod in the direction of the ancient Greek religion with its pantheon of gods up on Mount Olympus, all playing with humans like toddlers with toy soldiers. Yet still Claire's mind drives her along in this cyclone of self hate, self-blame.

Sunny sips her coffee and decides that she must try and call Alyson. Perhaps then she'll be able to talk to Claire. She taps the appropriate part of the phone's screen and is relieved to hear the ringing tone. Once again, in the dim moonlight on a Greek coastal path, the sound of Chris Martin singing:

"The lights go out and I can't be saved
Tides that I tried to swim against
Have brought me down upon my knees..."

...echoes across the rough vegetation, some of which has already scagged Alyson's calves. Alyson reaches into the side pocket of her shorts in haste, tugs at her phone and, as it exits the pocket she loses her grip. Just before it tumbles to the dusty, stony earth she manages to re-catch it and hastily taps the answer button. Holding it up to her ear she stops walking and answers.

"Sunny? Hi, what's happening?" Alyson suddenly realizes that, back on the hotel balcony, she hadn't heard Sunny's end of the brief call that Claire had made to ask how Terry was doing. All she knows is that the news must have been bad for Claire to react like she did. In her haste to follow Claire, she hadn't even thought of picking up Claire's phone, which, as she remembered had split apart when it had hit the hard balcony floor when Claire had suddenly declared that she was going out to walk. She had been so desperate to find her sandals when Claire had made for the door.

"Alyson! How glad I am to talk to you. How's Claire? Has she said anything? Can I talk to her, I can't get a reply on her phone."

"Sunny, she dropped the phone and walked out of the hotel room. It's very late out here, but she's marched off into the night. I am following her though, but her phone's on the floor on the balcony of our room. What's going on? Is Terry all right? I'm confused."

"He's OK now. He had a cardiac arrest or something. His heart stopped Alyson. I'd fallen asleep momentarily and Claire calling woke me up. The doctors were marvelous. I thought we'd lost him, the machine just went into a long monotonous tone and I panicked. They got him going again though Alyson, he's OK. The doctor told me 'these things happen' or something like that, but he said that Terry is OK. I don't know quite what that means, but he's alive, Alyson, you've got to be sure Claire knows."

"Don't worry Sunny. I'll catch her and I'll tell her. You just stay put with him and I'll call you in the morning. Thanks love."

They close the call. Sunny heaves a very long sigh of relief and senses that someone's standing beside her. Looking up she sees that it's the doctor who'd retrieved her phone.

"Can I join you for a moment?" He asks. Despite all that's going on and how ill Terry is, she can't help feeling a flutter as she looks into a pair of impossibly blue eyes. She's caught unawares and nods, fumbling with her bag to put her phone away.

"Tristan, and you'll be Miss Sunshine Geesin, right?"

Sunny makes a huge attempt at controlling herself, "Yes, right. Terry's my foster father, but he brought me up from when I was only four, so as far as I'm concerned he's my dad. How is he?"

"Look, it's no good saying everything's fine because that would be patently untrue. He is in the ICU after all. But, to be honest, I think you needn't worry. Cardiac arrests can happen for a number of reasons and not all of them relate to the heart's physical condition, OK? It's not the same thing as a heart attack for starters. A heart attack occurs as a result of coronary heart disease. In Terry's case he's had a condition for a few years that he probably wouldn't have known about. It may well never have bothered him, but in his case it gave him the heart attack that put him in here. Frankly, a couple of stents, inserted using a small tube through the groin and he'll probably be right as rain.

'No, the cardiac arrest sometimes happens due to what's called 'Long QT syndrome'. To be honest it gets complicated, but basically it has to do with a defibrillation that went wrong. We all get defibrillations during our lives. We often call it a flutter, know what I mean?"

Sunny knows exactly what he means. She almost feels her heart fluttering now as she gazes at this hunk of a man. She's ashamed to admit it to herself that at this precise moment, but what preoccupies her most is whether he's spoken for or not. "Umm, yes," she mumbles in reply.

"Right, well, in Terry's case it was something like this that threw his heartbeat out of sync for a moment, but it was long enough to keep the heart in spasm, so to speak. It may well never happen again. There are ways to regulate the heartbeat in patients who are at risk anyway, so that's why I'm saying please try not to worry too much. One week from now he'll probably be back home doing the weeding or something. By and large he's in good shape for a man of his age. That works in his favour."

"Thanks Doctor. You've helped a great deal." She heaves yet another sigh, this time of genuine relief. Then, as the doctor called Tristan rises, he adds,

"One more thing, Miss Geesin, Sunny. Are you free for a drink tomorrow evening?"

Back at the bedside a while later Sunny is relieved to see that uncle Gordon has returned. He'd had to go home for a while to see to his dog.

"Sunny, love, I'll stay with him now, OK? You go home my sweet. There's nothing more you can do and they tell me that he's out of danger. I'll ring you tomorrow some time. They say he'll be talking to me by mid-morning anyway, so you'll be able to have a little chat on the phone.

"Seriously, Sunny, you're all done in. I've got no one else at home, only Rex, and he's OK for a while now and my neighbour will look in and let him out into the garden in the morning." Gordon can see that she's unsure, "Go sleep at Terry's place, you won't want to drive all the way down to Bath now. You'd fall asleep at the wheel anyway. OK?"

Reluctantly Sunny sees that Gordon is talking sense, kisses him on the cheek and quietly leaves him to stand vigil at his brother's bedside. She's almost consumed with guilt too that she can't get doctor Tristan out of her mind. Not more than twenty minutes later she's letting herself into Terry's front door, where she goes straight upstairs, strips to her underclothes and slides under the duvet in the spare bed. Within minutes she's sleeping the sleep of emotional exhaustion.

In the dark of the night at the Tomb of Kleoboulos, across the bay from Lindos on the Greek island of Rhodes, Claire stands atop the tomb, staring down at the restless sea a couple of hundred feet below. She hears Alyson approaching and, without turning around, says, "I know you mean well Ally, but I told you I wanted to be on my own. Please leave me. Everyone I touch suffers; you don't want to be the next victim. Go Ally, go away, please."

"Claire, you've got it wrong. Terry's alive. He's OK. Sunny just called."

"Ally, I know you'll say anything to get me away from here. Like I said, you're a love and you mean well. But it's no good. I'm bad news for everyone."

"Claire, I'm telling you the truth. They saved him and he's stable. He's going to be all right. What do I tell him when he asks where you are? Come down here, sit down and we'll talk to old Kleo like old times. What do you say?"

Claire doesn't move. The breeze lifts her hair a little and it glistens as it moves, the moonlight allowing Alyson to even see the red colour of the henna dye. Alyson is wondering what she can say further to get Claire to see sense. Claire is thinking of turning around.

"You're sure? You're not just trying to stop me doing something, something..."

"Claire. I wouldn't lie to you. Sunny didn't give me all the details, but she did say to tell you he's OK. He's going to need you Claire. He's depending on you. You love him don't you?"

"Of course. Of course I do. But… You know Ally, you know. I seem to bring disaster to everyone around me. Maybe I ought to just leave him alone. You did that for Dean once didn't you? That way he'll be fine, he'll…"

"Claire, *stop it*, OK? You've got to stop punishing yourself. We all live in a world of chance. Everything that happens just happens. I'll tell you something else, there's no one whose life isn't touched by tragedy, not you, not me, not anyone. What we all need in times of trouble is for our loved ones to come through for us. Terry needs you to do that for him. I don't mean to be cruel, but this way of yours of heaping all the blame on to yourself, well, it could almost be viewed as a selfish attitude, thinking that you're the only one who suffers. It's like having an inflated view of one's own importance, really. You're just a regular human being, Claire, like the rest of us. Life has dealt you some rotten hands, but look at it from the other angle. You did have the privilege of a wonderful man in Charles, you do have such a privilege again now with Terry. You've got Sunny too, who's proud to think of you as the mum she never had and wants you in her life. You're still a beautiful woman at sixty. There are younger women who look like your mother! Dammit, I'll probably look older than you when I'm your age you silly bitch!!"

Alyson realizes that she's got through. She can see Claire beginning to laugh. Claire turns and walks away from the edge of the tomb and Alyson sees that she has a genuine smile of affection on her face, all the while with tears streaming down both cheeks too.

"Silly bitch yourself! Running all the way out here like that. Least you could have done is brought a bottle of Ouzo with you."

She climbs down to where Alyson is standing on the rough rocks around the side of the tomb and the two close friends embrace. They hold eachother tightly for several minutes before both let go and settle down with their backs to the tomb to stare out across the bay at the sleeping village across the water, its streetlights twinkling beneath a huge expanse of starry sky.

A week later Claire and Terry are sitting in Terry's kitchen. Julia's been on the phone and told Claire that all is fine at the gallery and that Amanda Brandonbury sends her love. In fact she's even sold a couple of the older oils that Claire had wanted to see the back of for a while, so there's been a nice little injection of cash into the gallery's coffers. The wedding will be postponed a while, but the girls at "Flight of Fancy" told Claire before she flew back that they can sort everything out. She can just leave it to them. Alyson's back home in South Wales catching up with a few hairdressing clients as her schedule had become a little backed up while they were in Rhodes. Gordon's been over every morning since Terry came out of hospital and both men are pleased to be drawing closer again after many years of spasmodic contact. In fact, Gordon's now bossing Terry about in order to get him to go walking with both he and his dog Rex. The doctors had told Terry that he needed to exercise regularly and not to be afraid to walk, even if squash is out of the picture for a while.

"You know, darling," Terry says, across the top of a mug of coffee as he raises it to his mouth and holds it an inch away while he speaks, "I can't believe what happened just over a week ago now. I feel so good. Life's weird."

"I know one thing," his fiancée replies, as he then sips from his mug, "You'll do anything to steal the limelight while I'm not around, you scoundrel. I'll just have to make sure that I don't leave your side again. You're going to be sick to death of me."

"I'm willing to take that risk," he replies and smiles as he reaches across the table to squeeze Claire's hand. The phone rings.

Terry says, "I'll get it," and does so. Claire studies his well-proportioned face and thinks how different he is from Charles. She marvels, as she watches him listening to the caller, at how things have blossomed between them. She thinks back to Alyson's strong words at the Tomb and, without forethought, finds herself uttering a kind of prayer to something or someone, in which she expresses her thanks for this moment, this situation, this relationship and this possible future for the two of them. She automatically comes to the realization that to be thankful is good for the soul. She silently blesses Alyson too for having come through as a real friend, much in the same manner as she'd told Claire we all need to do.

Terry is listening intently and, as he continues to do so, a smile creeps across his face. Claire rather likes the unshaven look. Makes him look rugged, even more like George Clooney, she muses.

Terry finally hangs up, saying thanks so much to the caller. He beams at Claire. "Well, darling, you're not going to believe what I've just heard." he pauses for effect.

"Why? What did you just hear? They've discovered a London bus on the moon, yea?"

"No, something much, much more pleasing. Something that'll release your muddled mind my darling from something you've agonized about for decades. Alan Evans has been talking."

"Talking? What about and to whom?"

"He's been undergoing a series of 'interviews' while in custody. The boys have been telling him that his only chance of seeing daylight again before he croaks is if he comes clean. There was enough on that tape to get him put away for a very long time, as you know. Tell me, how much do you know about the night Charles died Claire, love?"

"It's a long time ago. What I do remember is that they found him in the morning, a Saturday it was, and he'd fallen from the bridge. In the end it was an open verdict, but everyone unofficially seemed to think he'd killed himself. I was so neurotic back then, always burdening him with my fears, my doubts, my inadequacies. I think he'd got to the point where he felt that, even though he loved me, he was never going to be able to deal with me.

"Getting out of this life he knew he'd leave me well set up. Charles would never have done it if he'd thought that I'd be destitute. It's still a mystery, though, because I'd never have thought that he'd do such a thing. It wasn't 'him' if you know what I mean. But I can only blame myself and always have."

"Did you read the papers or see the local TV news at all at the time?"

"I was totally out of it, Terry. A third world war could have broken out and I wouldn't have known about it."

"Well, on the same night, a fella was knocked down and killed by a hit and run about twenty minutes walk from the bridge. The Force never connected the two incidents at the time; although it turned out that when the man was ID'd, it seems he had form. He was known to us as a contract felon. He was a freelancer who'd work for anyone who paid him enough and we suspected he'd been involved in some pretty heavy stuff; but, like Mr. Evans, he was covered in engine oil, always slipping out of our hands. So in the end it was laid to rest as an unconnected incident.

"But now, my dear, sweet, darling, NOW, our Mr. Evans is singing like a bird, it seems. That man who was knocked down was a certain Donny McBroom. On the night in question he'd gone to meet Charles Mason at the bridge to retrieve the account numbers so that Alan Evans could get his cash back. Nothing in writing, leave no trace. Thing is, he got himself killed in a million-to-one chance accident before he got the information to the man he was working for, Alan Evans. That was why Evans had no idea where Charles had salted the money away. Evans maintains that he only commissioned McBroom to get the info, never to kill your husband; but frankly, knowing Evans as we have for years, it's a safe bet that he'd suggested that the man who'd been minding the cash would be far less likely to ever spill any beans if he no longer lived and breathed."

Claire's face declares that she's having a moment of realization. Tinged with a sharp pain it may be, but it's offering her a completely different vista about how her beloved Charles came to fall from the bridge - and it wasn't because of her.

"So, you see, well I think you're ahead of me now, love, you've spent years wondering whether your dear Charles topped himself over your - as you call them - incessant neuroses, when the fact is, he was in all probability killed by a contract criminal. OK, so there won't be any way of going back and proving all this now, but it all fits together, you see?"

Claire Mason, after almost twenty-two years of beating herself up about the death of her first husband, can now finally see, breaking through the clouds of her mind's darkest recesses, a brief yet very welcome moment of sunshine.

"Terry," she says, "let's go out to lunch today. What do you say?"

"Sound like a very good idea. Then we'll get some work done on finishing off your new studio upstairs, agreed?'

"Agreed."

24. Sunny.

Sunny Geesin really enjoyed Lindos when she attended Claire's and Terry's wedding in Autumn 2012. In fact, she was so enchanted with the place that she and Tristan decided that they would also get married there in 2013.

So it was that in August 2013, Sunshine Geesin became Sunshine Guthrie, so her initials were still SG. Present at the ceremony were Julia Waters, Terry and Claire, Brian and Christine Worth, Dean and Alyson Waters, Amanda Brandonbury (whose husband was too busy to take time off to attend) and Terry's brother Gordon. Oh, and a few of Tristan's friends and family.

Not long afterward, Tristan changed jobs and came to work at the Royal United Hospital in Bath and his wife Sunny became pregnant with their first child, who was due to be born in summer 2014. It's apparently going to be a girl, so they've decided that she shall be called Claire.

Acknowledgments

I am extremely grateful to a number of people who rendered me great assistance during the writing of this book. I take great pleasure therefore in stating that which follows:

Firstly, I am indebted to Inspector Fionn Macdonald of the Avon and Somerset Constabulary for his invaluable help especially in the writing of the chapter in which the Police investigation of Charles Mason's death is discussed. His patience in answering my e-mails asking for clarification of Police procedure was exemplary and I couldn't have written that account without his help.

I also would like to thank Mr. David Anderson, the Bridge Master of the Clifton Suspension Bridge. I am eager to point out that nowadays the bridge is much more secure against anyone either falling or being thrown from it than it was in 1990. There are not only close circuit TV cameras in situ, but there is also a permanent bridge staff; plus there are now wires running horizontally along and above the level of the parapet on both walkways. These wires in no way inhibit the superb views which the pedestrian visitor may enjoy, but they do add to the safety of the experience. Hence, if you visit the bridge (and if you haven't yet done so, I'd urge you to do so some day) you need have no fear of falling from it. Since the Clifton Suspension Bridge is a wonderful testimony to the brilliance of Isambard Kingdom Brunel, it is truly a landmark of which the people of Bristol can be justifiably proud. I can honestly say, as a personal aside here, that in my humble opinion the bridge is one man-made structure that truly enhances the environment in which it has been placed, the marvellously dramatic Avon Gorge, running from the Cumberland Basin to the West of the city toward Avonmouth. I suggest that you Google it and peruse some of the images of the area and I hope that when you've done so you'll concur.

Next I need to thank Chris and Karen Watts, of Gallery Photography in Rhodes. Chris and Karen are wonderful photographers and I was truly stunned by the images that they came up with when they did the cover shoot for "A Brief Moment of Sunshine". They have a website, which I'm pleased to give you here:

http://www.gallery-photography.net/

They also have a Facebook page which you'll find here: *https://www.facebook.com/pages/Gallery-Photography/* as does this very book itself, the page of which contains a selection of the shots which were shortlisted for the front cover. It's here:

https://www.facebook.com/briefmomentofsunshine

I need too to thank Allison Wiffen, of ***Allison Wiffen Ceramics***, whose blog post ***'It's Bristol My Lover!"*** (http://www.awceramics.co.uk/blogs/blog55.htm) was the source of the photograph of Clifton Suspension Bridge, which I 'treated' in Photoshop and used on the back cover.

Finally, I very much need to thank my wife Yvonne-Maria and our close friend Brenda Dawson, of Pilona, Rhodes. Both women took part in brainstorming sessions as the story neared completion and both came up with new ideas that were eventually incorporated into the narrative and which I have to say in all humility, enhanced the story immeasurably.

Trivia

For those who may be interested, the majority of the main characters and a few of the marginal ones in the story were given Pink Floyd-related names. I stress that this was purely for fun. Names which have a Pink Floyd connection are listed in no particular order below.

Mason (Charles and Claire's surname)
Wright (Christine and Alyson's maiden name)
Waters (Julia and Dean's surname)
Barrett (Claire's maiden name)
Renwick, Wallis (Two of Alan Evans' henchmen)
Parry (Estate agent who sold Claire's house)
McBroom (Overcoat man)
White (Terry's surname. His nickname, which Alan Evans uses, gives the game away)
Guthrie (Tristan's surname)
Geesin (Sunny's surname)

If you are having trouble establishing the connection which some of the above names have with Pink Floyd, then you're probably not an anorak, as I am. Be grateful.

One other name used briefly in the narrative is *Jennifer Batten.* This has no connection with Pink Floyd that I'm aware of, but it is the name of a very talented female rock guitarist, who worked closely with Jeff Beck for a number of years. Jennifer Batten is the name of the WPC who visits Claire along with a male officer to inform her of Charles' death.

The rooms in which Charles and Claire stay on the island of Poros do exist and are exactly as described, but I have changed the name.

Any restaurants or bars named as existing in the village of Lindos, Rhodes, Greece are real, but I have no relationship with the staff or owners. I simply mention them because it suits the story.

The *"Rhodes Rock"* festival was indeed real and took place over a period of several years leading up to the summer of 2013. In 2014 it moved to Spain. Whether it returns to Rhodes in the future is not something I can predict. If you would like more information, this is the official website:

http://www.classicrocktours.co.uk

That's about it folks. Thank you for purchasing this book. If you borrowed it, cheapskate!

John Manuel
Rhodes January 2014

THE RAMBLINGS FROM RHODES ODDYSEY

1.
FETA COMPLI!

2.
MOUSSAKA TO MY EARS

A must for all Grecophiles, the ***Ramblings From Rhodes*** series of four travel memoirs traces the author's own story, from first meeting a half-Greek girl in the UK several decades ago, through visits with her family and holidays in her mother's country of origin to their eventually moving to Rhodes in 2005.

John Manuel writes in a witty, fast-moving style that has many readers falling about at some of the accounts in these sparklingly fresh Greek-themed books.

As the title of the series suggests, these are ramblings from all over Greece and her islands, with most chapters telling a short tale in themselves. There is a kind of chronology to the four volumes, but don't go looking too closely. Rather, these are books to be delved into much like that favourite chocolate assortment.

Read and savour each tale and be transported to the land of goats, olive oil, gods and golden sunny summer days.

THE RAMBLINGS FROM RHODES ODDYSEY

3.
TZATZIKI FOR YOU TO SAY

4.
A PLETHORA OF POSTS

"I recommend them to everyone who is off to Greece, and Rhodes in particular. Very funny, laugh out loud, and I am actually wanting to read them again on this year's holiday."

"Another great, feel-good book which I thoroughly enjoyed."

"I'll certainly be buying other books in the series."

"This author is a breath of fresh air. His work in uplifting and entertaining. I downloaded several of his books to read on holiday but have already read them. I'll just have to hope that he writes some more soon."

•

ALL BOOKS AVAILABLE FROM AMAZON WORLDWIDE IN BOTH PAPERBACK AND KINDLE FORMAT.

FOLLOW JOHN MANUEL'S ONGOING GREEK ADVENTURES ON HIS BLOG:
HTTP://RAMBLINGSFROMRHODES.BLOGSPOT.COM/

John Manuel was born in Bath, UK during the 1950's. He was educated at the City of Bath Boys' School and primarily excelled in the arts. He has always maintained a deep interest in music and writing, whilst having pursued a career as a graphic designer after having attended Gloucester College of Art and Design.

His wife's mother was born in Athens and his own love affair with the country of Greece eventually blossomed into his first published work, *"Feta Compli!"*. He wrote several articles for the now defunct "Greece" magazine and has also had a piece published in the in-flight magazine of EasyJet, the European budget airline.

He now lives with his wife in a quiet area toward the south of the Greek island of Rhodes and, since the death of his mother in July 2013, only occasionally visits the UK.

Both John and his wife are enthusiastic gardeners and walkers.